UNHITCHED

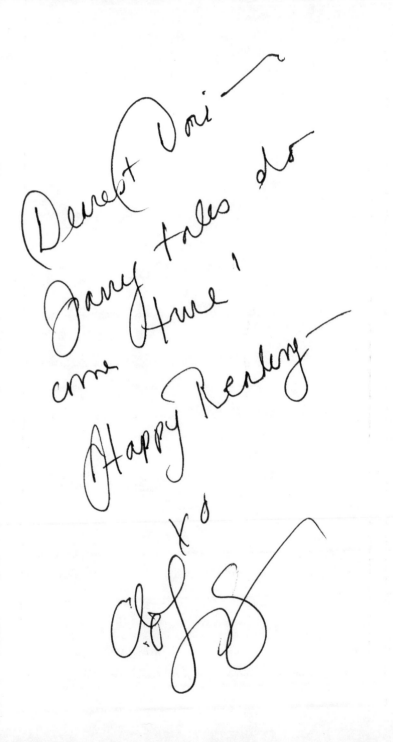

Dearest Vori ~

Fairy tales do

come true !

Happy Reading ~

xo

[signature]

E.L. SARNOFF

*Un*hitched

THE UNTOLD STORY OF THE EVIL QUEEN 2

NICHOLS CANYON PRESS
Los Angeles, CA USA

UNHITCHED: The Untold Story of the Evil Queen 2
By E.L. Sarnoff

ISBN-13: 978-0615724522
ISBN-10: 0615724523

Cover and Interior: Streetlight Graphics

Dedicated to my father
Who is always watching over me.

UNHITCHED

*Fairy tales are more than true; not because
they tell us that dragons exist, but because
they tell us that dragons can be beaten.*

—G.K. Chesterton

PROLOGUE

Somebody pinch me. It has to be a dream. The green blue water, the creamy white sand, the swaying palm trees. A palatial room in a palatial hotel. And My Prince beside me.

Only hours ago, Gallant and I were married by his father, King Midas. And now we are on our honeymoon at his father's newly constructed seaside paradise, Wonderland. Gallant insisted on a honeymoon. A chance to finally be by ourselves and get to know each other.

Slowly, he pulls down the bustier of my gown. My skin tingles with the touch of his fingers. I do not move a muscle, but inside I am a tremor of the earth.

I want him. More than anything, anyone. My skin grows so hot, so prickly that I want to climb out of it.

My gown falls to the floor. He rips off my petticoat and undergarments. I stand there naked before him. His piercing blue eyes glimmer with approval. He disrobes himself.

"Come to me, Jane." His voice is a soft, sexy command.

I behold his beautiful tawny body, each muscle sculpted as if by a master. My brain cannot decide whether it is frozen in shock or if it wants to leap into his arms.

I leap.

He catches me and sweeps me off my feet and into his arms. His lips crush into mine. His kiss is passionate and all consuming. I melt.

"Close, your eyes, my darling," he whispers into my ear.

Anything, My Prince. My love. My husband.

Closing my eyes, I imagine him transporting me to the gilded four-poster bed with its clouds of fluffy white down.

Cradled in his arms, I feel so secure. So happy.

A waft of warm air and the scent of jasmines make me realize that he has taken me outdoors. With my eyes still sealed, I picture the starry sky, the full moon, and palm fronds swaying. The gentle ebb and flow of ocean waves sounds in the near distance.

For five magical minutes, he carries me in silence. His silky, flaxen hair brushes against my fingertips. The balmy breeze blows against my skin as the gentle roar of the ocean gets closer.

A splash of water splatters my feet, making me certain My Prince has taken me into the sea. His pace slows down as the water grows deeper.

He gently puts me down. The warm water brushes up against my body, bathing and caressing me.

"Open your eyes, Jane."

I flutter them open. My Prince is before me, moonlit from the waist up. The rest of his beautiful body is bathed in the calm, black water that belongs to the night. I hold his gaze in mine. How handsome My Prince is!

Desire is burning in his hooded eyes. Holding me in his sculpted arms, he rolls his tongue down my neck, over the shimmering scars left behind by years of my mother's abuse, now so far behind me, and across the white flesh of my quivering breasts. He masterfully strokes his tongue all over my body, diving his head deep into the water not to miss any part.

He is an artist, and I am his canvas. His skilled hands gently stretch me. Another paintbrush. This one thick. Capable of deep, broad strokes. His warmth mingles with the warmth of the water. I move my body with his, rocking with the waves that caress me.

We moan with pleasure. He's not just an artist. He's a master. I explode inside—a fireworks display of color.

I know I will never swim away from him.

He whispers in my ear, "Jane, let's make a baby."

CHAPTER 1

Pain rips through me like a knife.

"Push," says the midwife, a heavyset woman with chestnut curls. "Push."

Tears cloud my vision and mingle with beads of sweat. I push harder and shriek in agony. The baby won't come out.

Another contraction. This one more excruciating than the one before. I roar with pain. I can't do this anymore.

"Push," the midwife says again.

I force myself to push one more time, clenching my hands so tightly my nails cut into my flesh. My scream is deafening.

Finally, a moist, fleshy mound slides out between my legs. It enters the world silently.

The midwife cups the tiny life form in her large, loving hands. She presses a thumb against the newborn's chest. Her lips part; her eyes grow wide.

"Give me my baby," I say hoarsely, my throat burning. Struggling to sit up, I take the infant from her and cradle it in my arms.

I gaze down at him. A boy! He's drenched in blood, my blood, but oh so beautiful. I study the tiny feet that had so often kicked me and marvel at their perfection. His eyes are glued shut, not ready to take in this world; his sweet little lips puckered. The poor little thing must be hungry, especially after his long, difficult journey.

I gently put his little head to my breast. The touch of his lips is as soft as the skin of a peach. *Suck, my little boy, suck.* Nothing. I must be doing something wrong.

I look up at the midwife, silently begging her to tell me what to do. Her eyes are watering. She can barely meet my gaze.

Wordlessly, she takes my baby from me. "I'm sorry," she says at last. "He has no heartbeat."

Her words slash through me, and numb my physical pain. I am so numb that tears are stuck in my eyes.

Cradling the lifeless child in her hands, the midwife hurries toward my chamber door. No! I can't let her take my baby from me!

I leap up from my bed, but exhaustion and pain hold me back. I collapse back onto the sheets. They're bathed in blood. My blood. So much blood. I grow nauseated.

And then it hits me. Like a spear to my heart. My baby is dead.

I cry like a siren in the night.

"What's wrong, my darling?" asks a familiar voice.

I snap open my tear-soaked eyes and bolt to an upright position.

A pair of powerful arms envelops me in the darkness.

"Did you have another one of your nightmares?" asks the voice.

Slowly, my terror gives way to the peacefulness of knowing that I am with My Prince in our bed.

Gallant draws me against him. His naked chest is warm and comforting against my torso, trembling and drenched in cold sweat.

I nod.

My Prince runs his fingers through my moist, matted hair. "What was it about this time?" he asks me tenderly.

"I don't remember," I lie. The same answer I always give him. I don't want him to know.

"Come, my darling, let's go back to sleep." Still quivering, I lower my body with his. He pulls me closer to him, so that my head is resting on his taut chest. The heat of his body courses through mine. He presses his lips against my temples.

"I love you, Jane."

"I love you too."

In no time, Gallant is back to sleep. Tucked safely in his manly arms, I feel my rapid heartbeat slowdown. But sleep eludes me.

There's no way I can tell Gallant about my recurring nightmare. He knows everything about my sordid past, including how a drunk, heartless king raped and impregnated me when I was only thirteen, and then abandoned me after his heir was stillborn. What he doesn't know is that I relive the loss of my child, this tragic and horrific life-changing memory, every night in my dreams.

How can I tell him? Gallant so badly wants to have a child with me. He's even made us consult with Lalaland's foremost fertility specialist, Dr. Jacob Grimm. The sign outside his office reads, *"Where Fairy Tales are Born."* But so far, after six months of treatments, running the gamut from magic elixirs to scheduled sexual encounters, no baby. As my best friend Winnie would say, "Maybe it's meant to be."

My eyes are wide open. Gallant snores softly. I turn my body slightly to caress his face. I've run my fingertips over his chiseled features countless times, but each time brings me wonderment and joy.

My heart clenches in my chest. How can I tell the man I love that I'm afraid to have his child?

CHAPTER 2

G allant and calla are already at the breakfast table when I get downstairs. I used to always be the first one there, but lately my insomnia has been causing me to get up late.

Taking a seat next to Calla, I help myself to some tea and warm blueberry muffins that have been lovingly prepared by our castle staff.

"Darling, I shall be home late again tonight, so please do not wait up for me," says Gallant, pouring himself a cup of tea.

My poor darling Gallant has been working so hard lately. The Midas Museum of Art is about to open, the inaugural exhibit being a retrospective of his paintings. For the first time, he will be able to share his extraordinary gift with the entire kingdom, rich and poor alike. The museum's opening is the most anticipated event of the year. In fact, there hasn't been so much excitement in Lalaland since our wedding.

For the past few months, Gallant has been spending most of his time in his studio, readying his paintings for the exhibition. I've hardly seen him. His long hours have begun to take their toll. Dark circles have made their way under his vibrant blue eyes, and a fine layer of golden stubble lines his chiseled face. A pang of guilt shoots through me. I feel bad that I keep waking him with my nightmares.

"Don't come home too late, my darling," I say, running my fingertips through his tousled golden hair. The truth is, I hate to go to sleep without him. As much as I feel guilty about interrupting his sleep with my nightmares, I can't bear the thought of not having him there beside me to comfort me.

Calla, already on to her second muffin, looks sheepishly at her father with her twinkly chocolate eyes. "What are you going to get Mommy for your anniversary?"

Dragonballs! Our second anniversary is coming up, right after Calla's ninth birthday. With all this baby stuff on my mind, I almost forgot. Calla, of course, would never forget. Our fairy-tale wedding was the happiest day in her life. She got a new mother. I got a new daughter.

Gallant cocks his left brow. "What do you think I should give her?"

"A baby!" shouts out Calla with glee.

I love the two of them more than life itself, but I hate this game.

"Boy or girl?" asks Gallant.

"Girl!" shouts Calla.

"Boy!" shouts Gallant, stepping on her answer.

He so wants another child. I already know the next question.

"Okay, My Little Princess, who is the baby going to look like?"

"Mommy," says Calla. "For sure, dark hair, green eyes. The prettiest skin ever."

"No, me!" chortles Gallant.

Despite myself, I imagine a wee Gallant. A tuft of silky golden hair, eyes the color of aquamarines, and pudgy, rosy cheeks that will one day give way to an unblemished layer of sculpted bronze.

Okay. Confession. As much as I've dreaded having a baby with Gallant, I secretly fantasize having one with him. I often picture myself walking a gorgeous (no question about it!) infant son in a pram, all eyes on us. Sometimes, I even fantasize baby names—Lancelot, perhaps? —and secretly wander into baby stores looking for cute outfits for my imaginary child.

Gallant's voice puts an end to my mental ramblings. "Darling, I shall take Calla to school before I go to my studio."

Calla gobbles her muffin, gives me a hug, and skips away, leaving her treasured doll, Lady Jane, behind on the table. "Hurry, Papa. I don't want to be late."

Gallant puts down his tea, then sweeps me into his arms. I gaze into his piercing blue eyes, noticing that his long hours have left more than dark circles. The whites of his eyes have become a canvas of spidery red lines. *Please don't let me wake him up tonight!* He so needs sleep.

Tilting up my chin, he plants a warm kiss on my lips and says, "I shall be in my studio all day and likely all night. Remember, don't wait up for me, darling."

After one more sip of his tea, he follows Calla out the back door that leads to our courtyard.

Clippity clop; clippity clop. The sound of the steed, carrying my beloved Prince and our daughter, fades into the distance.

Please don't come home too late, my darling. I already miss you and need you.

A mountain of crumpled up parchment lies by my feet in the small but charming main floor chamber I've claimed as my office. I stare blankly at the sheet that faces me on my desk. No matter how much I rack my brain, I can't write another word beyond "Once upon a time."

My first children's book, *Dewitched,* became a huge bestseller. Now, my publisher, Midas Books, wants another one as soon as possible. Make that yesterday. Actually, more like six months ago, but I've managed to hold them off, I suppose because King Midas is my father-in-law. Long live nepotism. My editor, Mr. Perrault, has no clue that I've had a nearly two-year long case of writer's block. The number of times I've written "Once upon a time" has cost me dozens of quills, and I bet the amount of parchment I've gone through could wrap around Lalaland. Shrink, my therapist, thinks my nightmares are contributing to my writer's block. She says they're making me tired and distracted. I've got to get over my fear of having a baby. They're paralyzing me. She's right.

If you asked me why I shouldn't have a baby, I could write a book. Yes, the fear of another horrific pregnancy and a stillborn child is one reason. There's no way I could handle it, physically or emotionally. The disappointment would be too much for me, and what a toll it would take on my sweet Calla, especially if this time I died. She lost a mother once. My stepdaughter, Snow White. I can't let it happen again.

But my fear runs far deeper. An ocean deep.

The possibility exists that my mother's evil blood runs through me. While after her death, Shrink left me with the hope that she could have born good and was a victim of an evil sorcerer's spell, I can never be sure. What if our baby is born evil? A monster like her? I shudder at the thought.

And then there's the possibility that I could be a terrible mother. While everyone tells me that I've been a terrific mother to Gallant's soon-to-be-nine-year-old daughter, Calla—and Gallant will be the first to tell you this—I still can't forget what a rotten mother, okay stepmother, I was to Snow White. In fact, I could take the prize of having been the world's worst mother. I even tried to kill the poor girl! While Shrink has worked hard with me to help me overcome my guilt, drilling it into me that I modeled my parenting after my evil narcissistic mother, a part of me still wonders if I can act that way again.

I tear off another sheet of paper, crumple it in my fist, and toss it into the pile on the floor. Damn my writer's block. Staring at yet another blank page, my mind wanders off yet again. What should I get Gallant for our anniversary? Finding the perfect present for the man who has everything isn't easy. The one thing I know he really wants is not happening. A son.

A gong sounds nine times. It's coming from the hand-carved grandfather clock in the adjacent great room, a wedding gift from my mother-in-law, The Queen of Hearts, who didn't want me to have the time management problems of her other daughter-in-law, Cinderella. She's married to Prince Charming, Gallant's identical twin brother.

She and Charming are like the most perfect couple. Perfectly groomed. Perfectly dressed. Perfectly behaved. They complete each other's sentences and laugh at each other's bad jokes. They even wear color-coordinated matching outfits and brag about being each other's stylist. Oh, did I mention they have perfect hair, skin, and teeth? And a perfectly decorated palace that's graced the cover of *Fairy-Tale Homes and Gardens* three times. Oh, yeah, and they never fight!

In other words, they're the most boring couple I've ever met. I put up with them because they're family. One day, Charming will rule the kingdom, and Cinderella will be Queen as Gallant abdicated the throne to pursue his passion for painting. I'm sure they'll be the perfect royal couple and produce the perfect heir... who is on his way.

Yes, Cinderella is having a baby. Of course, it's the perfect pregnancy. Seven months in and not a single day of morning sickness. When I was pregnant with my child, I was sick to my stomach every day and put on forty pounds. And then there was that horrific, tragic birth...

At last week's EPA meeting—that's Evil People Anonymous—a mandatory support group for former Faraway residents who have recovered from their addiction to evil like me, I confessed to having evil thoughts about my sister-in-law Cinderella. It was a stupid fantasy, but nonetheless evil.

"Imagine if those annoying little bluebirds that Cinderella sings to attacked her," I said in front of the entire group. HA! What an image! Miss Perfect Princess trapped in a storm of bird droppings! "For once, I'd like to see that perfect smile of hers disappear, and her perfectly coiffed blond hair get all messed up. And hear that sweet little voice croak," I added with a wicked smile.

There was dead silence in the room. Maybe I had gone a little too far. I couldn't help it. I was after all once The Evil Queen. And then Hook, a recovering alcoholic, leaped up.

"Yo, Ho, Ho," he chortled. "You're just jealous she's pregnant. Let *me* help you out, babe."

I cringed. Not because the once and always swine, who couldn't keep his hands off me at Faraway, hit on me, but because he was right. Damn it! I *am* jealous that Cinderella is having a baby.

I'll talk about it with Shrink. Yes, that's what I'll do. My bi-weekly appointment is in an hour. I'd better summon the coach. So much for my writing.

Grabbing a cloak to shield me from the chilly autumn air, I whisk through the French doors of my office. Passing through the dining hall, I stop to gaze at the magnificent portrait that Gallant painted of me with Calla in my arms before our marriage. That and his portrait of Snow White are the two paintings he's not including in his retrospective. They belong here in our house.

No matter how many times I've stared at this masterpiece, it always makes me tingle all over. My eyes pass over the words Gallant inscribed on it in the lower right corner. *"Forever in my heart."*

Forever. I suddenly have one of my brainstorms. I know what I will give Gallant for our second anniversary. The love letter I wrote to him on the eve of his almost wedding to my evil mother. The letter I signed, *Forever~Jane.* Forever, as in I will always love you. For the rest of my life. Until death do us part.

Whether we have a baby or not.

Why didn't I think of this before? As far as I know, he's never seen it, never mentioned it once. I sealed it with my tears and hid it in the top drawer of his desk. Could it still be there? What a perfect anniversary gift it'll make once I have it framed! Personal. Sentimental. Romantic. Forever.

I scurry to the great room, straight to Gallant's desk. My

hands tremble with excitement as I slide open the top drawer. Everything inside is meticulously stacked or stored in silver bins. Pens. Pencils. Sketch pads. Personalized stationary with the family crest, the Midas gold crown. And more. Gallant is such a neat freak.

Rifling through the drawer, careful not to make a mess, I experience the thrill of a thief. Like I'm stealing a treasure that doesn't belong to me—except theoretically, it could be argued that it does—and will get caught any minute. My heart pounds with anticipation. One of the stacks I come across is a bunch of Gallant's doodles. So charming! There's even a little full-color self-portrait. How handsome My Prince is!

The chitchat of servants resonates in my ears; it grows louder, meaning they're getting nearer. My heartbeat speeds up, and I hasten my search. The last thing I want is for the help to see me going through Gallant's desk. They might ruin my surprise.

In the rear of the drawer, I come across a stack of envelopes. Thumbing through them, I find correspondence with his father, King Midas… Letters to clients who have commissioned him to paint their portrait… Even several adorable homemade birthday cards from Calla, showing her own progression as an excellent artist. I'd love to read them all, but there's no time.

Finally, I find it. The ivory linen envelope—the one I used to seal my letter. It's addressed to Gallant. The penmanship is exquisite—bold and flowery—like mine. Except it's *not* mine!

The envelope isn't sealed. A little voice in my head tells me to put it back. I have no business going through Gallant's personal mail. Okay, I lied. The inner voice is screaming: WHAT THE HELL ARE YOU WAITING FOR? OPEN THE DAMN ENVELOPE! I practically tear it open. Inside is a perfectly folded sheet of parchment. I yank it out. My hands shaking, I unfold it and read:

Dearest Gallant~

It was so wonderful to see you yesterday. You mean so much to me. You always have. Thank you for being there for me.

Forever~ Aurora

Forever Aurora! The letter shakes in my hands as a burning sensation rips through my heart. I'm going to puke.

The fairy tale is over.

My Prince is having an affair!

CHAPTER 3

This is bad. Very bad," says Elz, after reading the letter. She adjusts her bejeweled spectacles. She has a pair in every color.

"It doesn't mean he's having an affair," says Winnie, brushing back her mane of flaming red hair.

Elz and Winnie are my two best friends. We met while doing rehab at Faraway. Elz, short for Elzmerelda, was one of Cinderella's evil stepsisters, and Winnie, short for Winifred, was the overweight witch who tried to eat her children, Hansel and Gretel. Like me, they've both come a long way.

We're having an emergency girlfriend meeting at Sparkles, our favorite hangout at The Trove. I'm stunned by Winnie's reaction. Almost hurt.

Always the eternal optimist, Winnie believes that everything in life happens for a reason. That it's meant to be.

Well, if Gallant's affair is meant to be, then it's over for us. Kaput! *Finis!* As they say in French.

"I'm going to get divorced!" I cry out. *"Unhitched!"*

Elz bawls. "But you and Gallant were so lovey-dovey together!" She takes off her spectacles and wipes her watering eyes.

"Stop it!" snaps Winnie. "Both of you are jumping to conclusions."

"What exactly should I do?" I yell at my know-it-all friend.

A server, dressed in a colorful jester suit, sets a platter of fanciful cupcakes on our table.

Winnie reaches for a chocolate frosted cupcake. "You need to investigate and find out what's really going on."

Here I am, shaking with the damning evidence in my hand… and she's eating cupcakes and telling me to investigate?

"Fine." I stab the word at her. What I should do is track down this Aurora slut and put an end to her sorry life.

Elz brightens. "I can help you with your investigation," she says in her singsong voice.

"You know Aurora?" I ask, my eyes wide with curiosity. Whoever the hell she is, she'd better watch out. They didn't use to call me The Evil Queen for nothing.

Elz puts her glasses back on and points a knowing index finger at me. "I bet she's the Aurora who owns Aurora's Secret."

That lingerie store for royal sluts where my wicked mother used to buy her sleazy corsets and undergarments?

"She's a self-made millionaire," Elz adds, clearly proud that she can be so helpful. "Although coming from royalty must have helped."

Of course. Gallant wants to be kept by a wealthy princess so that he doesn't have to depend on his parents to support his painting career.

"What does she look like?" I ask brashly.

"I've never met her, but I've heard she's beautiful."

Every muscle in my body tenses up. Jealousy gnaws at me like a rat at a slab of cheese.

"She's also known as Sleeping Beauty."

"Sleeps-Around Beauty is more like it." I can't help myself.

Winnie shoots me a dirty look. Elz, paying no attention to her, continues spewing information. Keep it coming. I want to know everything about her.

"I've heard she's very good in business."

"Probably in bed too."

Winnie shoots me another harsh look and slams her cupcake on the table. "Stop it! You need to get proof."

I'm growing impatient with Winnie. Almost furious. She's

my BFF. She's supposed to be compassionate and supportive. Helping me bring down this Sleeping-with-My-Prince Beauty.

"Well, I'm taking Jane's side," says Elz, chomping into a sparkly pink frosted cupcake. "I'm telling all my customers to boycott Aurora's Secret."

Winnie rolls her eyes and goes back to her cupcake. She licks the frosting and smiles with satisfaction.

Finally, I bite into one too. Usually, the first taste of the rich creamy frosting makes everything seem a lot better. Not today.

What good fortune that Shrink, my Faraway therapist, decided she wanted to spend more time with her twin sister, Tinkerbell, and opened a satellite office in Lalaland soon after I married Gallant. Despite being "cured" of my addiction to beauty, I still need her help. Why? Let me put it this way. I meditate. I burn candles. I drink tea. *And I still want to poison people.*

Like Aurora.

The timing for my weekly appointment couldn't have been better. Shrink will help me deal with my shocking discovery. She'll know what to do.

As usual, she's late. I squirm restlessly on the worn velvet chaise lounge she brought along from her office at Faraway. I've been on this chaise so many times you can see the outline of my body.

My emotions seesaw between extreme sadness and extreme anger. How could Gallant do this to me? When Shrink finally flies in like a streak of lightning, leaving a trail of fairy dust in her wake, I'm tipped on the side of anger.

"Jane, I would like to continue our discussion about having children," she begins, always one to get right to the heart of the matter.

I grit my teeth. And then I smirk. HA! I don't have to deal with the baby issue ever again. The pros and cons don't matter anymore. My "maternal ambivalence," as Shrink calls it, is a non-issue. My mind is made up. There's no way I'm conceiving a child with a man who's betrayed me and broken my heart.

"There is no discussion," I say curtly.

"Can you elaborate?" Her tiny winged-body hovers over my face. She gazes at me intensely.

"It's quite simple. Gallant is having an affair." The tears I've been holding back roll down my cheeks.

"And how do you know this?"

"I found a note. A love letter from another woman."

I dig into my purse and hand her Aurora's note. She slides the spectacles that are sitting atop her head over her face and scans it.

"Ah, Princess Aurora. Sleeping Beauty," she says, pushing the glasses back up.

"You know her?" My moist eyes grow wide.

"I treated her once for insomnia. After sleeping so much, she was afraid to go to sleep." Shrink hastily cups a tiny hand over her mouth. "Pretend you didn't hear that. It's privileged doctor-patient information."

Whatever! It just figures that Gallant would go after another beautiful princess with a sleeping disorder. First, Snow White. And now Aurora. Or maybe it's the other way around. It doesn't really matter. An affair is an affair.

"Gallant no longer loves me!" My own words come at me like a rush of flaming arrows. I start sobbing uncontrollably. God, how many tears have I shed on this chaise? Probably enough to make an ocean.

Shrink hands me a hankie from a large bin. I blow my nose loudly and take a deep breath. My sobbing subsides a little.

"How could he do this to me?" I sniffle. "I love him so much."

"You're jumping to conclusions," says Shrink, echoing Winnie's words.

I'm an emotional wreck. Is that all she can say? I know what I need to do and focus on getting out the words as fast as I can. Before another tsunami of tears hits me.

"I'm going to leave him!"

Shrink looks at me as if she didn't hear a word I said. I want to squish her between my hands and turn her into pixie pâté.

"Jane, that's a very premature decision. All you have is a hypothesis. You have to prove he's having an affair."

I hate it when she gets all scientific on me. "How do I do that?"

"You have to investigate and find more evidence."

I'm beginning to wonder if she and Winnie are in cahoots.

"Do you think I should ask Gallant about the letter?"

Shrink ponders. Her tiny wings flutter at the blinding speed of a hummingbird's. "My suggestion is that you don't do anything extreme," she says at last.

Is she suggesting that I might actually resort to evil? Like poison the bitch? My mind races. I could use a banana this time. I'll bite off one end and show her how yummy it is. Then she'll wrap her adulterous lips around the other end—the one I've dipped in poison—and bye-bye.

And there's this… I can suffocate her with one of those skanky corsets she sells. I'll pull the strings so tight, she'll turn blue in the face and take her last breath. Gallant won't be undoing them again! I smile wickedly. The possibilities are endless.

"What are you thinking?" asks Shrink, bringing me back into the moment.

The chime from the wall clock sounds. It signals that our time is up. Thankfully, I don't have to share my evil thoughts with her.

"Jane. I'll see you here at our next session."

She zooms out of her office, covering me in a cloud of fairy dust. As I peel myself off the chaise, her advice seeps into my brain. I hate to admit it. She and Winnie are right. I *do* need to prove that Gallant is having an affair.

I take a deep breath and am fortified. No more wasting time! I know exactly where to start.

CHAPTER 4

Lalaland princesses live for three things: 1. Marrying a prince; 2. Shopping; and 3. Knowing the latest gossip. Trust me, if you read about it in the *Fairytale Tattler*, it's true and already yesterday's news.

There's no better place for finding out the latest gossip—even before it hits the *Fairytale Tattler*—than the steam room at The Enchanted Spa. That's where my wicked mother leaked the news to me about her surprise wedding with Gallant. Which led me to writing that "Forever Jane" love letter and ultimately stopping their marriage. How different my life would have turned out had I not ventured into this steam room. Maybe for the better—with a faithful, loving partner. There I go again jumping to conclusions! *Stop it, Jane. Stop it!* I tell myself as I change into a fluffy white robe. I need to gather more evidence. If Gallant really is seeing Aurora, chances are I'll hear about it shortly.

When I step into the steamy spa room, my eyes are immediately drawn to the hazy outline of two chatty towel-clad women seated next to each other. They're skinny. Very skinny. Obviously, princesses. The steam obscures their faces, and I don't recognize their voices. Usually, I would sit far away from them and ignore them. Today, I plop down right next to them. I'm all ears.

Yes! They're gossiping! I learn about a catfight over a dress on sale at the Ballgown Emporium… a disturbed a little girl named Alice who's banned from playdates with their daughters… and the exorbitant asking price of Beauty and The Beast's palace—and it's only a fixer upper.

What crap! I'm already tired of hearing about it. Get me out of here! Just as I'm about to split, one of them says something that makes my heart jump.

"Did you hear about Aurora?"

What about Aurora? My ears are burning.

"She's splitting up with her husband, Prince Phillip."

"For another man?" gasps the other woman.

YES! MY MAN! I scream so loudly inside my head it hurts. I don't need to hear another word. I dash out of the steam room, almost killing myself on the slippery wet floor. It won't be long until the *Fairytale Tattler* gets hold of this story, and everyone in Lalaland knows that Gallant is having an affair. With that Sleeping Slut, Aurora.

The news of Aurora's split with her husband has shaken me to the core. My hands tremble as I button up my gown in one of the spa's private dressing rooms. There's one person who will never be unbuttoning it. Gallant.

As I throw my damp hair into a ponytail, I remember my standing side-by-side hair appointment with Winnie at My Fair Hair. My distress gives way to a momentary sense of satisfaction. I can't wait to rub my new evidence in her face.

Hoping I won't be too late, I dash through The Trove to the hair salon located at the other end of the mall. My nerves are more frazzled than my hair. When I tear through the entrance, the place is bustling with fairy-tale princesses.

Perfectly coiffed hair, I've learned is yet another one of their royal obsessions. Seriously, have you ever seen a princess who didn't have fabulous hair? I read in some magazine that there's a correlation between good hair and a good marriage. Good Hair = Getting married to a prince + Staying married to one. When I think about Gallant and Aurora again, I think about all the money and time I've wasted. Rage seeps through my veins. Keeping up my hair didn't save our marriage. I'm going to ask Gallant to pay me back every cent in the divorce settlement. And I might even sue that magazine.

My eyes dart around the salon for Winnie. Phew! Though almost done, she's still here. I run up to her. Her long wavy flame-red hair looks gorgeous. As she takes a glimpse of herself in a mirror, I tell her about the conversation I overheard at The Enchanted Spa.

"How's that for P-R-O-O-F that Gallant is cheating on me with Aurora?" I boast.

"You don't have a thing," says Winnie, admiring her hair.

"What do you mean?" I ask, incredulous.

"You didn't actually hear those two gossip girls mention Gallant's name. You're assuming something that may not necessarily be true." With a shake of her head, her mane of red hair cascades gloriously down her back. "You can't even be certain that Aurora left Phillip for another man."

I feel like a balloon that's been poked with a pin. Totally deflated. Winnie's right. I have no proof. I should have stayed in the steam room longer.

Winnie flings her long green cloak over her shoulders. It matches her sage-green eyes and makes her red hair stand out even more.

"You're leaving?" My voice borders on despair.

"I have a double birthday party this afternoon; there's a lot to do."

She gives me a peck on my cheek. As if that's supposed to make me feel better. "Promise me that you won't say anything to Gallant until you have proof."

"Fine." Grimacing, I watch my friend, Lalaland's most in-demand event planner, dash out the door. I'm convinced. She *is* conspiring with Shrink.

I'm in no mood to get my hair done. Though I really could use a good haircut. It's still growing out from that dreadful bob I got a couple of years ago at Faraway that left me practically bald. My hair stylist Goldilocks says it will take years for my hair to get long again.

I brighten. Goldilocks knows everything about everyone. While she's not the brightest star in the universe—I mean, she almost got eaten by a bunch of bears for stupidly eating their porridge—she's a great listener and has a big heart. Every Lalaland princess confides in her. There's something about her—a *je ne sais quoi*—that makes you want to tell her everything. Maybe because she's so non-judgmental. I'm sure she knows the dirt on Gallant and Aurora. In fact, Aurora probably told her herself. Egad! There I go again, jumping to conclusions.

I sprightly march up to the hair fairy receptionist to check in for my appointment.

"Sorry, you're too late," she says, with a flutter of her wings. "Goldilocks had to leave for her next appointment. The princess bride booked her a year ago for hair and makeup."

A fairy-tale wedding. The memory of mine, soon to be ancient history, brings a rush of tears to my eyes. Oh, how in love Gallant was with me on that unforgettable, magical day! We exchanged gold bands that were inscribed with the word "forever." I'm beginning to believe that word doesn't belong in the dictionary.

The receptionist gives me a sympathetic look before hovering over her appointment list. She runs a teeny finger down the schedule, then stops and smiles. "Gothel has a cancellation and can take you."

Gothel? Gothel was my roommate at Faraway for less than twenty-four hours. She arrived just when I was getting out. Let's put it this way: it wasn't the beginning of a beautiful friendship. Her farewell words to me were: "Fuck you." Despite attending EPA meeting together, she still hasn't warmed up to me.

What little I do know about her is that she was committed to Faraway for cutting off the floor-to-ceiling braids of some princess named Rapunzel. Since when was haircutting a crime? If it was, those two hair fairies at Faraway, who butchered my hair and Gothel's, should have gotten life. There must be something else I don't know.

For her post rehab stint, Gothel was sent to Lalaland to apprentice as a hairdresser. I suppose Shrink figured she would be good at cutting hair since she chopped off Rapunzel's.

Well, it turns out that Shrink was right as usual. Gothel proved to have extraordinary talent with hair shears and grew a huge clientele of fairy-tale royalty. When she gave Cinderella layers, it caused a kingdom-wide sensation. Every princess and her sister wanted her hair that way.

Now, she's a haircutting legend. It takes months to get an appointment with her. I've tried for over a year. But no luck. She's always booked up, I'm told. But if you ask me, I don't think she likes me. Maybe because Hook has always had a thing for me.

So why now? I'm suspicious. Even a little scared. Her tempestuous on-and-off relationship with Hook is always in the tabloids. After the last EPA meeting, she ran after him, screaming madly with her hair shears pointed his way.

Suddenly, I get it. Of course! *She* knows that Gallant is seeing Aurora. I'll be a free woman in no time. And she's threatened that Hook will go after me again. The picture is crystal clear. She wants me out of the way! So, she's going to stab me with her sharp scissors! I'm going to be a dead woman... and Gallant is going to be married to Sleeping Beauty!

Ouch! Someone yanks my hair and jerks me out of my train of thought. I wheel around. It's Gothel!

I eye her with trepidation. She's dressed in tight black leather britches and spiky-heeled pirate boots that make her long, toned legs look endless. A matching, tightly laced corset reveals her ample breasts and sinewy arms. Truthfully,

I've never seen arm muscles bulge like hers. On one bicep, there's a large tattoo—a skull and crossbones. On the other, an anchor with Hook's name inscribed below. Around her boyishly narrow hips, she sports a thick studded leather belt with pockets that hold her cutting tools. Or should I say murder weapons. Her jet-black hair is short and razor-blade spiky. And her nose is pierced. You get the picture. She's scary. Very scary.

She gives me the once over with her fierce violet eyes. I don't move a muscle.

"You need help, babe!" she says in a deep, husky voice that could easily be mistaken for a man's.

What does she mean by that? Shoving me into a chair, she whips out her large, shiny shears and starts chopping my hair. SNIP! SNIP! SNIP! The sound gives me the shivers, and I squeeze my eyes shut. I don't want to look. Any moment I expect to feel a sharp blade digging deep into my back and warm blood—mine! —pouring down my spine. And then the sound of the scissors ceases. I bravely open my eyes, catching sight of myself in a mirror. Wow! She is sheer (shear?) genius! My raven-black hair looks amazing! Falling like a cape around my shoulders, it perfectly frames my faces, bringing out my high cheekbones and almond-shaped green eyes.

Gothel admires her handiwork. "If you think I work magic with shears, just wait until you see what I can do with a sword."

She hands me a card and moves on to her next client. I read it:

LADY GOTHEL: DRAGONSLAYER
No job is too big or too small.

I wonder why she has handed this to me. Does Dragon Lady slay man-eaters too? I'm afraid to ask.

My new haircut has given me back my self-confidence and a fresh perspective. I can't find any evidence that Gallant is having an affair. Maybe he's not. Shame on me for thinking that he was. His beautiful face with its dazzling smile fills my head. A sudden burning urge to make love to him comes over me.

My insides are throbbing. Just the thought of making love with My Prince can have that effect. He's incredible. An artist. Believe me, he could write a book on *The Art of Making Love*. And illustrate it too.

With thoughts of his tongue masterfully stroking my body, I fly into our palace and collide head on with him. His eyes are narrow; his lips pressed into a grim line. My heart, hammering with desire moments ago, hammers with apprehension. The expression on his face is not one that says: Let me take you in my arms.

"Where have you been?" Each word is a sharp staccato.

What happened to "darling"? I'm totally taken aback by his snippy tone. Doesn't he even notice my haircut?

"You were supposed to be back here an hour ago," he growls. "Dr. Grimm put us on a tight schedule."

I grimace. I totally forgot to check my ovulation calendar. My preoccupation with Aurora has thrown off my memory and sense of time.

"I rushed back here from my studio to make love to you." Clenching his paint-splattered fists, he's growing more furious by the minute. "I have wasted precious time waiting for you when I could have used the time to paint. The museum gala is less than two weeks away."

I know his painting retrospective has been stressful. He's been working around the clock, and he's exhausted. But he's never taken it out on me. In fact, he's never snapped at me before.

"I'm sorry," I say meekly, hoping that an apology will lead him to sweep me off my feet.

"Forget it. It's too late."

Forget it? His words sting me like an angry bee. He doesn't even care about having a child with me.

"I'm going upstairs," I say frostily. "I'll be there if you want me."

Dressed in my sexiest black lace negligee (a present from Gallant), I lie sprawled on our palatial bed, counting down the seconds for My Prince to burst into the room and ravage me. Okay, he may be miffed. But he's never been able to resist me. *Ever!*

A faint gong emanates from the grandfather clock. An hour passes. And then another. No Gallant.

My emotions have shifted from desire and anticipation to anger and despair. As the gong strikes yet another hour, reality strikes me. I was right. I should have trusted by gut. He no longer wants me. He's found someone else. Aurora.

Tears burn my cheeks. I should be glad that I missed an opportunity to try to conceive with the cheating bastard. But the pathetic truth… I'm not.

I cry myself to sleep.

CHAPTER 5

Gallant never came to bed last night. I know because when I woke up screaming and soaked from the nightmare, he wasn't there. I couldn't fall back to sleep and watched the sun rise. He'll probably tell me that he had to pull an all-nighter in his studio to make up for lost time. But I know better. He was out gallivanting with his new Sleeping Beauty. As I trudge downstairs to face another day, I'm depressed. And frustrated. If only I could prove it.

To make matters worse, Gallant is not at breakfast. He's never missed this meal. My heart sinks deeper. The cheating bastard spent the night with her.

"Mommy, what's wrong?" my perceptive Calla asks over a plate of buttery scrambled eggs.

"Nothing." *Everything!* I can't, however, tell my sweet little girl that Daddy is screwing Mommy royally, and we're going to get a divorce. The time has to be right.

Calla rambles on about her most recent class project. I pretend-listen, my mind in a dark, distant place. After sending her off to school with one of our servants, I sip my tea and mull over my future and course of action. Though in my heart I know the bitter truth, I still need proof. With luck, my investigation will go better today—that is, if I can muster up the energy to pursue it. Yesterday, anger powered me; today, sadness has zapped everything out of me. I stare at Calla's treasured doll, Lady Jane, wishing she could tell me what to do.

One of our cooks teeters into the breakfast room. "Miss Jane, there is someone at the front door to see you."

That's odd. I wasn't expecting anyone. Leaving my tea behind, I follow the cook to the entrance of our palace.

Standing erectly outside is a squat little man with an oversized egg for a head. He's carrying a large briefcase and wearing a sleazy, ill-fitting suit and garish polka-dot bowtie.

"Morning, mam. I'm Humpty Dumpty, and I'm here to ask you a few questions. Can I come in?"

There's something unctuous about him that gets under my skin. Against my better judgment, I usher egghead into the castle and escort him to our newly decorated great room. Plopping onto one of the Fairy Tale Regency velvet couches, he makes himself at home.

"Nice place you have here," he says, surveying his surroundings. "Mind if I smoke a cigar?"

Before I can protest, he pulls out a cigar from his jacket pocket, lights it up, and takes a puff. I swear if he gets one ash on my new couch, I'm going to crack open his head and turn his brains into an omelet.

"I have some papers I need to serve you," he says, drawing on his cigar.

I freeze. Holy crap! He's a divorce attorney. Gallant is one step ahead of me. He can't wait to make Sleeping Beauty's bed his own. Permanently.

He unlocks his briefcase and pulls out a sheet of parchment and a stylus. "Before we get going, you'll need to sign this release form."

A release form? Before I even read it, I see the words in my head: *I, Jane Yvel, officially release Prince Gallant, firstborn son of King Midas and The Queen of Hearts, from our marriage and all future marital responsibilities to me, allowing him the freedom to choose a new wife whenever he so desires.* Nausea rises to my chest. The cigar smoke is not helping. I'm going to be sick.

My lips quiver. "Where do I sign?" *Why am I making it*

so easy for him?

"On the dotted line."

Shaking, I glance down at the sheet of parchment. Scrawled across the top are the words, "*Fairytale Tattler* Release Form."

Wait! This egghead isn't a divorce attorney. He's a shyster reporter for the *Fairytale Tattler*. He's already gotten wind of Gallant's affair with Aurora and is here to corroborate the facts. Holy crap! Tomorrow everyone in Lalaland will read the headline: *"Royal Marriage Doomed! Prince Gallant Finds Himself a New Sleeping Beauty!"* My mind immediately jumps to Calla. It'll be the talk at school. My poor sweet little girl. This is so not how I wanted to break the news to her.

The reporter puffs his cigar and continues. "We thought, in light of your upcoming second anniversary, we would treat our readers to a scoop about your marriage with Prince Gallant."

Wait! Is he trying to trick me? I wouldn't put it past one of these sleazeball tabloid reporters.

"The staff was delighted that you agreed to this interview."

I suddenly remember that several months ago I agreed to let the *Fairytale Tattler* do a profile on me if they allowed me to pre-approve the questions. I relax a little but don't look forward to the memories this interview will dredge up. Or the feelings.

Humpty Dumpty pulls out a notebook from his briefcase and begins.

> **HD:** What is the secret to your marriage?
> **ME:** Honesty. *Lies.*
> **HD:** Will the two of you be going anywhere special to celebrate your anniversary?
> **ME:** We'll just be staying home. *I'll be house hunting.*
> **HD**: Will anyone be joining you to celebrate?
> **ME:** Not really. *The Sleeping Slut will be doing a happy dance with Gallant.*

HD: Do you have something special you're giving him on your anniversary?

ME: A special letter. *Farewell forever.*

HD: Do you have any idea what Gallant will be giving you?

ME: Absolutely none; it's a surprise. *Heartbreak and tears.*

HD: Two last questions. What made you fall in love with Prince Gallant?

ME: I can't remember. *His piercing blue eyes, dazzling smile, courage, kindness, forgiveness, passion, the tender touch of his fingers, that first kiss... oh, that first kiss that awoke every part of my being...*

HD: The fire in many marriages dies out. Are you still madly in love with Gallant?

ME: Yes. *Yes, damn it, I am.*

The last two questions have totally unraveled me. Damn Gallant. Yes, damn him! I hate this man. I love this man. How could he betray me? Tears well up in my eyes. As Humpty puts his notebook and stylus back into his briefcase, I splutter, "What are you calling your article?"

Humpty puffs his cigar and rudely shoves the release form under my nose. "It's written on the second page. Read it for yourself."

I flip to the page. *"Jane and Gallant: The Perfect Fairy-Tale Marriage."* The words churn in my stomach as I sign on the dotted line. Humpty snatches the form and waddles to the front door, leaving a trail of ashes on our brand new white rug. "G'day, mam."

I feel like I've just signed my life away. Sadness sweeps over me as I battle waves of nausea. How could Gallant leave me for another? What did I do wrong? (I called his mother a fat cow once, but not to her face.) Maybe I'm not pretty enough? (The former *Fairest of All* does have a few more lines and has recently put on a pound or two.) He doesn't like my cooking? (It is bad.) I'm not fun to be around? (I do get moody from my writer's block.) I'm not a good enough mother to Calla? (Okay, I did miss this month's PTA meeting.) He still holds my attempt to kill his first wife, Snow White, against me? (I dealt with that in therapy.) I'm infertile? (But I'm trying to conceive despite my insecurities.)

Stop it, Jane. Stop it! Moping is not going to help me prove that Gallant is having an affair with Sleeping Beauty. And it's not going to make her go away. I need to cheer myself up.

Only one thing will cheer me up. Shopping. Not because I'm a shopaholic who gets a sick pleasure out of buying way too many things. Not at all. I'm going to shop 'til I drop at The Trove and send the bill to Gallant. Let him eat it, the cheating asshole. I smile wickedly. I'm back to being evil.

The Ballroom Emporium is crazy busy as usual, and the doors have been opened for only ten minutes. It's astonishing how fairy-tale princesses always need a new ball gown. Even if there's no ball to go to. What most of them *really* need is to get a life to get their mind off shopping.

Wouldn't you know the first person I run into is my sister-in-law, Cinderella. She's as perfect as ever. You'd never know she was seven months pregnant under her stunning empire-style gown. The chiffon dress floats like a cloud and is in a shade of blue that perfectly matches her sparkling eyes.

"Can't wait to see you tonight," chirps Cinderella, cheerfully meandering through the racks of magnificent gowns.

Dragonballs. I totally forgot. Gallant mentioned last week that he had invited Cinderella and Charming to dinner. I wish he had consulted with me first. I would have said we're busy. Or come up with some other excuse like we're starting a holistic cleansing fast or doing spring cleaning even though it's fall. *Or getting a divorce*. Anything to get out of having dinner with the royal duds.

"Eight o'clock sharp," I reply with a forced half-smile. I could have said midnight or noon tomorrow. Time has no meaning for Cinderella. She shows up when she shows up.

"Wonderful! Which of these two dresses do you like better?" She holds up two almost identical silky blue gowns. I pick the first one, not that it really matters.

Her eyes dart back and forth from one to the other.

She sighs. "Oh, Jane, I just can't make up my mind."

She waltzes out of the store with both of them. Size 4. Even with the baby bump.

"Dahling, I sooo love your hair," comes an all-too-familiar voice from the distance. It's Emperor Armando, the proprietor of the Ballgown Emporium and Lalaland's hottest fashion designer. He knows me well. He just happens to me my fairy godmother and created the magnificent ivory wedding gown I wore when Gallant and I exchanged our forever vows.

Forever Aurora. I can't the words out of my head. They make me want to run home and take a sharp scissors to Armando's bridal gown. Or throw it into the fireplace. And hear it go snap, crackle, and pop.

Wearing his signature caftan gown, this one with a blazing pattern of orange and gold threads, the big burly Emperor sashays up to me and plants a big kiss on each cheek.

"Dahling, you look miserable. What's going on?" he asks.

I silently debate whether to open up to him about Aurora. With his insightfulness and brutal honesty, he could be helpful, but in the end, I decide not to bare my heart. I sigh instead. If only he could make Aurora magically disappear. Unfortunately, his fairy godmother powers are limited to makeovers.

"I need something new," I tell him before he can give me a lecture on the aging effects of frowning.

"Wait 'til you see my new collection. It's to die for. Everyone's clamoring for a piece to wear to Gallant's museum gala."

The mere mention of his name makes my temperature rise. While I stew, Armando takes off. He returns with a dozen stunning gowns folded over his arms. Exactly what I like. Tight-waisted, full-skirted, and lots of layers. But wait. They're all Size 8.

"I wear Size 6."

"Dahling, trust me, with all that rich food you've been eating, go with the 8's."

I catch a glimpse of myself in one of the mirrors that line the walls of the store. Damn it! He's right. I have put on a few.

Hastily, without trying the gowns on, I tell Armando that I'll take them all. Gallant's having an affair, and I'm getting fat. It doesn't get worse than that. He's going to pay for what he's done. And this is just the beginning.

———❦———

Next stop: The Glass Slipper. I order a pair of every shoe Elz has in stock even if she doesn't have it in my size. "Send the bill to Gallant," I tell my shoe store mogul friend. I can't wait to see the expression on his face when he opens it up.

"How's it going?" Elz asks sympathetically.

"Terribly. I don't have one solid piece of evidence to prove that Gallant is sleeping with Aurora."

"Just show him the letter."

"I can't do that. It would show him I'm a lowbrow thief."

"Right." Elz thumbs her lips as she thinks. "You know, Rump always opens up to me when he's had a lot to drink."

Say no more, my friend. I'm already uncorking a bottle of wine in my head. I'll get him drunk tonight, and he'll tell me everything.

My shopping expedition has definitely done the trick. I'm cheered up; I've just gone through a boatload of Gallant's money, and I've got a plan of action. Okay. Just one last thing to do before I go home. Make a stop at Aurora's Secret.

Maybe she'll be there. I'll get to see what Sleeping Shrewdy looks like. As I step out of The Glass Slipper, I get cold feet. I'm not ready to face the competition.

———

Readying for our dinner party, I silently curse Charming and Cinderella. Damn it! I wish they weren't coming over. They're just going to get in the way. Especially Cinderella. She never stops chattering about herself. I'll never have a chance to interrogate Gallant.

Alone in my dressing room, I slip on one of my new gowns—a pouf of black and white Chantilly lace—and struggle with the fastenings along the side. I can barely close them; the dress—Size 8—is miserably tight. Under all the layers, I can't even feel my hipbones. It's as if they've melted away. Dragonballs! I'll need to diet, something I've never done in my entire life, if I'm ever going to land myself another husband.

Stop it! Hold your tummy in and just get through the night, I tell myself as I catch a glimpse of my not-so-thin self in the mirror. Mr. Infidelity won't even notice. I mean Gallant. I need to remember. Innocent until proven guilty.

When I get downstairs, Gallant is pacing the length of the great room. He must have just gotten home. He's disheveled. His blousy shirt hangs out of his britches, both covered with remnants of paint, and his tumbled locks of hair look like he's just gotten out of bed. Just not mine. *Stop it, Jane; don't go there.*

Gallant wheels around when he hears my footsteps. He gazes at me, not giving me even the faintest smile. He says nothing about my new dress.

"We should have canceled dinner," is all he says. He sounds irritated.

As usual, Cinderella is late. Very late. She has a major time management issue. I'm sure leaving the ball past midnight, which caused her coach to turn back into a pumpkin, was not the beginning. My mother-in-law, The Queen of Hearts, has begged her to get help. She just laughs it off. "One should always be fashionably late," she says.

I sense an opportunity. "Why don't we share some wine while we wait for your brother and Cinderella?"

"Perhaps later. I am going to work on my speech for the museum opening." He crosses the room, heading toward his desk. "Let me know when they arrive."

He takes a seat at his favorite work place and slides open the top drawer. My heart skips a beat. Shit! I still have Aurora's letter in my bag. What if he notices it's missing? It'll change everything. He might even turn on me if he thinks I stole it. Which I did!

I hold my breath as Gallant scours the drawer. His brows furrow; my heart flutters. Has he discovered it's gone? I exhale loudly when he pulls out a sheet of parchment and puts a stylus to it. Mental note to self: Put the letter back. No, on second thought, once he confesses everything, I may want to stuff it down his throat. Now, if I could only get him smashed.

A tug on my dress startles me. It's Calla. Lady Jane is dangling from one hand. Her other is clasped around something that I can't make out.

"Mommy, I'm hungry!"

I glance at the grandfather clock. It's almost nine o'clock. Cinderella's already an hour late. Poor Calla! She was so looking forward to having dinner with her aunt and uncle and partaking in our adult evening. The precocious little girl just loves adult chitchat and gossip. I've even caught her sneaking peeks at the *Fairytale Tattler*.

"Come, let's eat, my sweet girl." I wrap an arm around her thin shoulders and shuffle her toward the kitchen.

The kitchen smells delicious. A fragrant blend of fresh breads, stews, and tarts wafts through the air.

Our cooks, most of whom have families of their own, are scurrying about, trying to keep the lavish meal they have prepared warm.

"Go home to your families," I tell the weary-looking workers. The truth is they could be here all night waiting for Cinderella and Charming to show up.

With smiles of relief, they gather up their belongings and file out the back door. I bid them a good night. They are all so hard working, kind, and loyal.

I quickly throw together a little bit of everything—succulent braised ribs, velvety potato purée, golden buttery beans plus a chunk of warm crusty bread—on a plate and serve it to Calla at the large butcher-block table in the center of the kitchen. Lady Jane sits propped up on a stool beside her. Lately, this is where the two of us—actually make that three, if you count Lady Jane—have been eating since Gallant's been coming home so late. *Or* not at all. While I sulk, Calla scarfs down her meal. She is still holding that mysterious object in her right hand.

"What's in your hand?" I finally ask her.

She unclamps her slender fingers.

Aagh! It's a frog. He jumps onto the table.

"This is Henry," beams Calla. "I found him at school today."

Henry ribbits as though acknowledging his introduction. His big, black bulging eyes gaze at me. I stare back at him, speechless.

"I'm in love with him."

Ribbit.

"O-kay." I don't know what else to say.

"One day, I'm going to kiss him, and he's going to turn into a handsome prince."

"Have you kissed him yet?"

"Yes." Calla puckers her lips. "But nothing happened."

"He's probably not ready for a relationship," I say consolingly.

"That's what I thought," nods Calla. "You know, men are so immature." Her beyond-her-years words of wisdom make me want to laugh—something I haven't done in the last twenty-four hours.

In a heartbeat, Henry hops off the table and takes off at lightning speed. By the time Calla and I leap up from the table, he's nowhere in sight.

"Henry! Where are you?" cries Calla.

We both get down on our hands and knees and search frantically for the missing frog. The kitchen is vast—cluttered with cooking utensils, food bins, and storage containers. He could be anywhere. Hiding in a pot. Or a barrel of oats. Or even in the garbage. I just hope he hasn't gone for a steam bath in the bubbling cauldron or a sauna in the smoldering hearth.

After a frantic half-hour of crawling in every direction, we take a well-deserved break. We've turned the kitchen upside down. And no Henry.

Calla bursts into tears. "My prince doesn't love me anymore!"

Her words slash through me like a sword. *And mine doesn't either.*

I give myself a mental kick. *Jane, you have no right to go there until you find out from Gallant what's really going on. Stop jumping to conclusions!*

I grab a clean napkin and gently dab Calla's tears. She can't stop crying. I think she's just overtired, but her sobs tug at my heart.

"Come, my sweet girl. Let's get you into bed."

"But what about Henry?" she sniffles.

I kiss her forehead. "You know men; they like to wander. But absence makes the heart grow fonder."

Calla looks up at me with tear-soaked chocolate eyes, perplexed. "What do you mean?"

I wink. "He'll be back in your arms tomorrow."

"You mean cage." Calla lets out a giggle and gives me a hug.

No, I meant arms, I think wishfully.

—◆—

After tucking Calla into bed, I tiptoe downstairs and find Gallant still working on his speech. Crumpled sheets of parchment are piled up on the floor. I guess it's not going well. He must have writer's block. Good. Serves him right.

The grandfather clock gongs. It's now ten o'clock. Cinderella and Charming are still not here. It's not unusual for her to show up close to midnight. It's now or never. I've got to use her tardiness—or should I say rudeness—to my advantage. This is my chance to interrogate Gallant. To find out what's really going on between him and Aurora. My heart pounds. Am I prepared to face the truth?

"Darling, let me get you some red wine," I say calmly and seductively though my pulse is racing. "You need to unwind." God! I'm good.

"Fine." He crumples up another sheet of parchment and tosses it to the floor. "This speech is going nowhere."

Perfect. I hurry to our bar, find a carafe of red wine, and pour him a goblet full. And one for me. With my nerves growing edgier by the minute, I need it more than he does.

"This is nice," he says, after taking a sip.

I let him savor the wine and take a few sips of mine. I gaze at his face. His gorgeous face with its strong, chiseled features and layer of golden stubble that makes him even sexier. My skin prickles, and a fire kindles in my core. Why does he still do this to me? *Focus, Jane. Focus. Stay on task.*

He drains his wine. I quickly refill the goblet.

His leans back in his chair and kicks up his long muscular legs on his desk. He's loosening up. And so have I. I've finally worked up the courage to ask him about the letter. *Take it slowly. Very slowly.*

"So, darling... by any chance, do you know someone named... Aurora?"

That dazzling smile spreads across his face, rendering me, damn him, breathless. "I adore her. She's an amazing woman."

I choke on my wine. He knows her! Adores her!! Beds her!!! *No, Jane, stop it! Don't jump to conclusions. Keep your cool. Prove it!*

I take a deep breath and steady my voice. "So how do you know her?" Good. I didn't sound too suspicious. Or desperate.

"We've been meeting."

I almost spit out a mouthful of wine. I force myself to swallow.

"Where?" My stomach is sinking with dread.

"At her new place."

Oh my God! That proves she did split up with Prince Phillip. And now, she's doing it with Gallant at her new bachelorette pad. Rage rushes through my bloodstream. My lips part. The words are about to fly out. *Did you sleep with her?* Just at that moment, Cinderella and Charming breeze in through the front door. Three fashionably hours late. Their timing couldn't be worse.

We help ourselves to the now cold dinner that's laid out buffet-style in the kitchen and bring our plates back to the dining room. There's little on my plate. I've totally lost my appetite. My stomach feels like a punching bag, and a painful lump in my throat makes it impossible for me to swallow. I was not at all prepared for Gallant's confession. Not one bit.

I can hardly look at him. On his fourth goblet of wine, he's seated opposite me, talking nonsense to Charming who's pretty smashed himself. It's hard to tell them apart, now that Charming has let his hair grow longer. They're arguing about whose toy soldier collection is bigger. Please! Just kill me now.

Still registering the shock of Gallant's confession, I am so not in the mood for Cinderella's chitchat. She hasn't stopped babbling since she arrived. I can't focus on a thing she's saying. All I can think about is Aurora. How could

Gallant have…

"Jane, I want you to take a look at these." Cinderella reaches into her dainty beaded purse that perfectly matches her pearly blue gown and shawl.

Oh no, here we go again. Paint chips for the baby's room. The child isn't even due for two months, and she's already decorated the nursery five times. And, did I mention that it's not even built yet?

In addition to her time management problem, my annoying sister-in-law has a hard time making decisions. I think one issue just feeds the other. The Seven Dwarfs, the kingdom's top construction company, labored 24-7 rebuilding her palace after her evil stepsister Sasperilla, now serving a life-term behind bars, set it on fire. She played eeny-meeny-miny-moe with every stone and then couldn't decide if she liked brick better than stone. She's been obsessed with the new nursery wing. You can't imagine how many times the Dwarfs have had to knock it down and rebuild it from scratch because she's not 100% positive that it's right. Poor Grumpster had a nervous breakdown and is on disability leave. I don't know how Charming puts up with her. But like I said, they seem perfectly suited for one and other. Unlike Gallant and me.

"Well, Jane, which one should I go for?" Cinderella displays three shades of yellow that I truthfully can't tell apart. I'm not big on yellow in the first place. And honestly, how does she expect me to deal with pathetic paint chips when I've got a much, much bigger chip on my shoulder.

Randomly, I point to the middle one.

"Do you really think so?" She studies the three paint chips. "Hmm. Maybe I should paint the nursery lavender."

A typical response. Why did she bother to ask for my opinion in the first place? I wish this evening would just end. I need to be put out of my misery.

Cinderella continues to play with the paint swatches, contorting her face as if she's making a life or death decision. "Jane, maybe you can get Armando to work his bippity-boppity-boo magic on the nursery."

Ever since my fairy godmother Armando redecorated our palace in Fairytale Regency (and since opened his latest emporium, Armando Home, to great success), it's been the talk of the kingdom. It was time to say good-bye to Snow White's so-yesterday flowery décor and to create an environment that showed off some of Gallant's masterpieces that now hang on our walls.

Like the one facing me of me holding Calla in my arms. I gaze at it, and a stabbing pain shoots through my heart. Gallant painted it when he was madly in love with me. The memory of beholding this painting for the first time, thinking that Gallant was dead and that I'd never see him again, fills my head. My heartache was deeper than a bottomless pit. I glance over to the man I soon after married. The beautiful man who swept me off my feet and filled my life with light. Playing a game of thumb wars with his brother, he's totally oblivious to me. Of course. My Prince is in love with someone else. "Forever in my heart" no longer has meaning to him. I fight back the tears that are forming in my eyes.

A blood-curdling scream hurls me back to the moment. Cinderella's mouth is agape. Her eyes, round as blue marbles, gaze down at the table.

Holy crap! Henry, The Frog Prince, has jumped onto her dinner plate. But it's not Henry that's freaked her out.

"My water just broke," she shrieks.

Great! She's late for everything. Who would have ever thought that giving birth would be the one thing for which she'd be early?

She breaks into panicked sobs. "The nursery isn't ready!"

Charming staggers over to her and takes her into his arms. He hiccups.

"You must stay calm, my love," he manages. Beads of sweat are clustering on his forehead, and his skin is turning a ghastly green. He's either going to pass out or throw up.

Gallant leaps up. "Quick, send for Dr. Grimm!" he shouts,

slurring every word.

Doesn't the drunken bastard know that our help has left or retired for the evening? My mind races; thank god, I'm still thinking straight. Our coach is parked by the stables almost a mile away, and it'll take too long gear it up. It makes sense to use Cinderella's which is parked right outside our front door. Charming's in no condition to drive… and neither is Gallant. There's only one person who can—*Moi!*

———❦———

The wind whistles as Cinderella's pumpkin-shaped coach races through the moonlit countryside. Having only once before driven a vehicle like this, I should be worrying about losing my life. Instead, all I can think about is losing My Prince. Gallant's confession totally consumes me. How could he cheat on me? How could he betray me like that? My shock and sadness once again morph into rage and hatred. I don't know whom to hate more. My deceitful, infidel husband? The Sleeping Slut? Or myself? For trusting the man I married. And being so stupid.

My stomach lurches as the coach flies across potholes. With lightning-fast reflexes, I duck a dangling tree branch. A close one. *Focus, Jane. Focus.* Stop thinking about that lowlife whore! Cinderella's life is at stake and so is her baby's!

I slap the reins to make the two horses pick up their speed. My pulse gallops. The wind kicks up, sending a shiver through my body. My cloak flaps loudly as my hair whips across my face, making it difficult to see ahead of me. Thank goodness, I know the way to Dr. Grimm's house, having been there for fertility treatments so many times over the last six months. I won't be needing those anymore.

At last, I arrive at Grimm's storybook cottage. There's not another one like it in all of Lalaland. Constructed of stone and stucco, it is an eye-catching feast of diamond-paned windows, stained glass, chimney pots, turrets, and a whimsical wavy slate roof. I park the coach outside the wrought iron gate and jump out. I unlatch the gate and pass through the fragrant garden. Cute little baby animal statuaries, illuminated by the moonlight, line the pathway.

Bypassing the hanging doorbell, I knock loudly on the thick wooden door. Almost immediately, a little white-bearded man appears. He's clad in a long white nightshirt and matching nightcap and holding a candle. It's Dr. Grimm.

"Jane, what can I do for you at this wee hour? You should be home making a baby with your dear husband."

His comment makes my stomach churn. I take a deep breath.

"It's Cinderella! She's having her baby!"

"Wonderful! Another fairy tale is about to be born!" chuckles the good doctor.

This is no laughing matter. But there is no time to chastise him. Nor to address his comment about making love with Gallant. That's never going to happen again!

Dr. Grimm dashes back inside and quickly reappears with his medicine bag in hand. Yes, another fairy tale is about to be born, and I'm driving the delivery coach.

An earth-shattering scream emanating from inside the castle awaits us. Followed by another and another, each one more piercing than the one before. I recognize them. They're the screams of a woman in labor, I know. I've been there.

Dr. Grimm races inside, carrying his medicine bag, with me right behind him. My stomach tightens. I am not looking forward to this. Not at all!

Cinderella is now lying on the dining room floor, shrieking. Charming, drenched with sweat and as white as a ghost, is holding her hand, trying to comfort her. Gallant, by his brother's side, faces me, his expression, a combination of fear and relief. I avoid his gaze and rush over to Cinderella, crouching down beside her. A sick thought permeates my brain. HA! Miss Perfect Princess doesn't look so perfect. In fact, she looks frightful. Her hair is as disheveled as a wind-blown haystack, and her contorted face is bathed in sweat and tears.

Dr. Grimm remains as calm as a cucumber.

"Put me out of my misery!" moans Cinderella. "I want to die!"

"Don't say that!" I dab the sweat on her forehead with the skirt of my gown. "You're having a baby! You have everything to live for!"

The memory of my tragic miscarriage flickers in my head. Shuddering inwardly, I try hard to suppress it.

Another contraction. Cinderella winces. "Jane, I'm scared," she whimpers.

Despite my loathing of her and all that's happened to me this day, I feel her pain, her fear. Please let her get through this! And the baby too!

"Cinderella, my dear, focus on something calming and breathe," says Grimm, his voice soothing.

Cinderella stares at him with her wretched eyes as if he's said something in a foreign language. She shrieks again and squeezes my hand. So tightly that I, too, want to scream out in pain.

What can she look at? Clearly, not her husband Charming who still looks like he's about to pass out. Or Gallant who's not in much better shape. When this is all over, I'm going to confront him. There's no way I'm going to pretend that I don't know what's going on. Another sharp cry from Cinderella brings me back into the moment. The contractions are coming faster and faster, each one more agonizing than the one before. Dr. Grimm is right; she needs something calming. In the corner of my eye, I see the tranquil painting of Calla in my arms. Yes, that's it!

"Cinderella, look up at the painting!" I urge. "Look how beautiful it is and how much I love Calla!" Sadness ransacks my heart once again when I think about how much Gallant's love for me inspired this masterpiece once upon a time.

Dazed, Cinderella rolls her eyes up at the painting. A faint smile crosses her face. "Jane, I think the baby is coming!" she whispers.

"Push!" says Dr. Grimm, getting giddy with happiness. His command brings back painful memories I want to forget but can't.

Between short, rapid breaths, Cinderella grunts, obviously giving a push.

Grimm tells her to push again. Then miraculously, in his hand, he's holding a tiny head. No bigger than a grapefruit, it is covered with a thick layer of gooey blood. Charming instantly passes out, falling to floor with a loud thud. Looking rather queasy himself, Gallant rushes to his brother's side. I hate the sight of blood and try hard not to faint myself.

"One more push, my dear," says Grimm with a bright smile.

GRUNT! And then a loud wail. Unmistakably, the wail of an infant new to this world. The wail I never got a chance to hear. Grinning broadly, Grimm cups the tiny, blood-soaked infant in his hands as melancholy falls over me.

"Congratulations! It's a girl," exclaims a proud Grimm.

"A girl?" repeats Cinderella weakly. She gazes at the baby and bursts into tears.

Tears of joy, I think.

Wrong.

"She's an ugly duckling!" she wails.

To be dead honest, the baby *is* ugly as sin. Her crimson face is all scrunched up; her smooched nose spreads cheek to cheek, and under all the blood, her scrawny little body is covered with a layer of duckling-like yellow fuzz.

"No, she's not," I force myself to say. "She's as beautiful as a swan."

"Swan!" echoes Charming who has regained consciousness and is beaming. "What a perfect name for her. Princess Swan!"

Cinderella gazes at her husband wearily with an

expression that says "whatever."

Personally, I'm glad Charming has chosen a name. If it were up to I-can't-make-up-my-mind Cinderella, the poor child would never have one. Actually, Swan isn't a bad name for the child; she's got the longest, skinniest neck I've ever seen. It makes her head look oversized and totally disproportionate to her tiny body.

"Jane, I need a warm damp cloth," says Dr. Grimm, without taking his eyes off the tiny life form in his hands.

I hurry to the kitchen and return with a soft hand towel that I've moistened with water and warmed in the hearth.

Grimm takes it from me and gently washes off the blood that's begun to cake on the newborn's fuzzy skin. The pink, wrinkly, squirmy infant that slowly emerges mesmerizes me.

The doctor smiles, clearly proud of his handiwork. "Now, we need something to wrap her in."

My eyes dart around the room, landing on Cinderella's pale blue cashmere shawl that's folded over the back of her chair. Perfect.

Taking it from me, Grimm swaddles Swan in the soft wrap.

She continues to wail. Her scrunched up face turns redder. It resembles a big soggy overripe tomato that may burst if you touch it.

"She's hungry," smiles Dr. Grimm. "Jane, place the baby on Cinderella's breast."

He wants *me* to do this? He's got to be joking. It's been so long since I've held a newborn. And this one is so tiny. Hesitantly, I take the baby from him, carefully supporting her fragile, silky head. My entire body prickles as a fusion of unexpected emotions surges inside me. Joy. Envy. Fear. Sadness. I catch Gallant's eyes on me, never leaving me for a second. I ignore him as I nervously place the baby on Cinderella's right breast.

Cinderella makes a face of disgust. "Turn around," she snaps at Charming and Gallant.

Cinderella reluctantly slides down the shoulder of her gown. The baby sucks voraciously. Cinderella's expression morphs from disgust to horror. And then she yelps.

"Ow! She bit me!" Maybe they should have named her Princess Piranha.

Gallant smiles at me dreamily. "Jane, you looked so natural holding the baby."

Is he kidding? I was freaking out. Afraid that I would drop it. Afraid that it would die in my arms. Like my infant son.

But Gallant's right. It *did* feel so good. Almost magical. Sadly, a baby is something we're never going to share. How cruel of the betrayer to taunt me with motherhood!

Dr. Grimm grabs his bag and bids us goodnight. Gallant offers for Cinderella, Charming, and Swan to spend the night. Tomorrow, Calla will wake up to her new baby cousin.

I inhale deeply. I'm just glad this nightmarish night is over. Just as I think that it can't get worse, Gallant grabs me and pulls me to the floor.

"Jane, let's make a baby." My heart does a flip-flop. The wine has made him lustful. He wants to make love to me! Right here on the floor. My brain battles the tingly sensation rising inside me. I can't let him do this to me! I can't!

Throwing himself onto me, Gallant pulls up my gown. He yanks off my pantaloons and spreads my legs. I feel his hard warmth inside me. His lips consume mine, and despite myself, I find myself meeting his every thrust. Moaning with pleasure. Building to that climactic release. Oh God. Why can't I resist?

After a loud satisfied groan, he pulls away and rolls off me. My insides throbbing, I run upstairs, taking two steps at a time. I stagger into one of our guest chambers. There's no way I'm sharing a bed with the adulterer tonight. And I'm too drained to confront him.

Without bothering to undress, I collapse onto the bed. My head spins, swarming with emotion. Cinderella's baby… My infertility… My cheating husband… Henry the Frog… My lustful husband. Tears burn my eyes.

Damn it! I wanted him.

CHAPTER 6

M ommy! Mommy! Wake up!" I pry open my eyes. It's Calla. She's jumping up and down. "Come look at all the people outside. They've come to bless Baby Swan."

She takes my hand and leads me to the window. Groggily, I pull open the velvet drapes, adjust my eyes to the jolt of sunlight, and gaze down on an endless stream of well-wishers. There are royals and non-royals alike, including your everyday Lalaland freaks like ogres, giants, gnomes, and dwarfs. Many have presents in their hands to bestow upon the royal newborn.

"Mommy, I love my new baby cousin! She's so cute!" Calla presses her nose against the glass pane.

"And guess what! I found Henry! Right next to my pillow!" She gives me a hug. "I'm keeping him in his cage from now on."

At least, she has *her* prince under control. Gallant's lustful assault flashes into my head. The truth is, it kept me up almost all night. I couldn't stop thinking about it. And wanting him to come into my bed.

Calla looks up at me with her inquisitive brown eyes. "Why didn't you and Papa sleep together last night?"

Her innocent question is a dagger to my gut. I want to crawl back into bed and never see Gallant's face again. Calla skips out of the room, sparing me from answering.

When I get downstairs, utter chaos surrounds me. I barely recognize my own house. Big red heart-shaped balloons welcoming Swan are everywhere. An army of servants is frantically moving furniture and bringing out heaping platters of food from the kitchen. Except they're not mine. They work for my in-laws, King Midas and The Queen of Hearts.

"Move it!" roars The Queen. "Or off with your head!"

She pounds a red, heart-tipped staff into the floor. Trust me, she hasn't changed much. Even after attending Faraway for her anger management issue, she's as hotheaded as they come.

The weary-looking workers scuttle about the room like mice. The Queen grins like a Cheshire cat.

An elegant cradle, probably a gift of the royal family, occupies the center of the room. King Midas, in his royal finest, crouches over it, goo-goo eyeing his new grandchild. Calla, Midas's precious *bambina*, is beside him, shaking a silver rattle.

I make my way to the kitchen and can smell deliciousness wafting in the air. To my surprise, Winnie's there. Zigzagging from corner to corner, she's overseeing a team of cooks who are busily preparing breads, tarts, puddings, and other scrumptious baked goods. She orders several servants to bring more platters to the great room. She's totally oblivious to me.

Weaving my way through the workers, I sidle up to her. "Winnie, what are you doing here?"

"Your mother-in-law's people woke me up at some ungodly hour to organize a coming out party for Cinderella's baby." She adjusts some red roses in a vase on a counter. "You try blowing up three hundred balloons and baking a heart-shaped red velvet cake that will feed an entire kingdom before dawn."

"Why didn't you just tell her no?"

A smirk flickers on her lips. "Do the words—'Off with your head'—mean anything to you?"

She's right. Her Royal Bossiness has a no-tolerance policy for anyone who defies her. I'm glad, however, that Winnie's here. A fountain of wisdom, she can help me sort my conflicted feelings toward Gallant.

"I desperately need to talk to you. Last night, Gallant—"

She cuts me off. "Later. I need to check on the cake." She brushes her hair off her face and dashes over to the hearth.

Nice friend. I'll remember this. Next time she wants to talk about something important to me, I'm going to tell her to take a hike. A long one to Neverland.

Stealing a scone, I stalk back to the great room. Charming is perched under the arched entrance, brightly greeting well-wishers that stream into the castle. Cinderella, standing beside him, is in the same gown she wore at dinner last night. Except now it's two sizes too big on her thinner than ever frame. Her blue eyes are sunken, her shoulders hunched, and her hair a mess. She acknowledges each visitor with a faint nod. The expression on her face reads: I don't want to be here. This is clearly not the chirpy perfect princess that everyone in the kingdom worships. Except me.

The well-wishers deposit their gifts for Swan on a large table, then circle around the cradle where Midas shakes their hands. Many peek their head inside, hastily covering their gaping mouths upon setting their eyes on the homely infant.

My eyes roam around the room. Many of my fellow Faraway inmates are here as well as the Seven Dwarfs. So is that crass egghead reporter for the *Fairytale Tattler.* He's snooping around and taking notes. I worry about tomorrow's headline: *"Cinderella Gives Birth to Ugly Duckling!"*

My wandering eyes land on the sweeping staircase. My stomach muscles tense up. Gallant! His bloodshot eyes meet mine briefly, and then avert them. He strides right past me and heads over to his brother and Cinderella.

Not even a good-morning kiss. Or even a hello! A horrifying thought crosses my mind. Of course! He's on the lookout for Aurora, the Sleeping Slut. I bet she's here under the guise of showering the newborn princess with a trousseau of trashy lingerie. What a perfect opportunity to see each other! They can sneak away. Maybe even have a quickie in his painting studio while no one's looking. Bile rises to the back of my throat.

A thunderous announcement from The Queen voice brings my ruminations to an abrupt halt. Just in time before I throw up.

"Bring me the baby! It's time for the pee test."

Why does she have to test the baby's pee? Is there something seriously wrong with Baby Swan other than her unfortunate homelessness? A look of horror spreads across Cinderella's face as Charming lifts the tiny, blanketed infant out of the cradle and strides across the room to his mother. The imperfect princess trails lethargically behind him.

A tall white-gloved butler steps forward, holding a silver tray with an elegant porcelain plate. In the middle of the plate, there's a single green *pea*. I'm confused when he removes the pea and places it on the floor. I'm even more confused when an army of elves marches in—each, carrying a tiny, thick mattress and a plush feather bed. I count them—twenty little men in all. One by one, the elves stack the mattresses and feather beds, one upon another, on top of the pea. When the heap gets too high and out of reach, two more elves file in, each holding the end of a wooden ladder. They lean the ladder against the stack of mattresses and feather beds, allowing the remaining elves to climb up and add to the pile. When all is done, the stack of mattresses and featherbeds almost reaches the ceiling.

I steal a glance at Gallant. The impassive expression on his face makes my stomach churn. Is Aurora among the onlookers? Has he made eye contact with her? Damn! I wish I knew what she looked like.

I refocus my attention on the white-gloved pea-bearer, who carefully takes Baby Swan from Charming. Cuddling her in the crook of one arm, he ascends the ladder and places her on top of the twenty-foot high pile of mattresses. The baby wails on the top of her lungs. Everyone's eyes are pointed up at her.

"A baby's skin is very delicate," says The Queen in her booming voice. "We'll have the results of the test in five minutes."

Swan continues to wail. Louder and louder. Her scrunched up face turns beet-red. She clenches her little fists as if she wants to fight back. The poor little thing! I hope she doesn't fall off. Cinderella looks dazed and confused. I have no idea what's going inside her head. She seems so detached from the baby. As if she's in another world.

The Queen lumbers over to me. "Well, dear, how does it feel to be an aunt?"

"Great," I lie. I won't be one for long. My blood is curdling with the knowledge of Gallant's affair. My eyes survey the room. So many beautiful princesses. Which one is she?

The Queen glances at Cinderella and huffs. "That girl has no consideration of anyone's time but her own. She could have at least given me some advance notice that the baby was coming early." She continues to rant. "You cannot believe what I've had to go through. Do you think it's easy to find a fairy godmother spur of the moment? They were all booked. Every one of them! It's a good thing I was able to pull a favor. I had to beg Fairweather, Flossie, and Fanta to come out of retirement and get their big butts over here. It's the least they could do for all the money The King and I donate to Faraway."

She gazes down at her red heart-shaped watch. "They were supposed to be here already," she pouts. The Queen has no tolerance for lateness. That is why she and perpetually late Cinderella have never really gotten along.

"Time's up!" roars The Queen. "Bring me the baby."

The butler climbs back up the ladder and brings Swan to her. The baby is still wailing, her face contorted and scarlet red. The Queen removes the infant's blanket and gown, draping them over the butler's arm, and cradles the diaper-clad baby in her ample arms. She peeks inside the diaper. Her lips purse in disgust—I think Swan has pooped—and then she grins. She yanks off the diaper and proudly holds the baby up high so that everyone can see her little wrinkled butt. Smack in the middle of one of her tiny cheeks is a purple bruise the size of pea.

"Our little Swan is indeed a princess!" roars the jubilant Queen. "She felt the pea through all those mattresses and feather beds. Only a *real* princess would do that. From this day on, she will be officially known as Princess Swan!"

Cheers and applause. King Midas leads a toast for his new granddaughter, Princess Swan. Cinderella, who has retreated to a corner, listlessly raises her cup. The poor girl seems so lost and forgotten. I actually feel sorry for her. Maybe she needs someone to talk to.

A loud thud, accompanied by the sound of a few broken things, stops me dead in my tracks and startles everyone. The Badass Fairies, Fairweather, Flossie, and Fanta, have landed. Or should I say crash-landed.

One by one, they stagger to their feet, adjusting their bent wings.

"It's about time," grunts The Queen.

"The trip was challenging," says a flushed Fairweather, unable to mask her embarrassment.

"We haven't flown this far in ages," says Flossie, as if giving an excuse.

"We had to stop for a bite to eat," says Fanta, her voice matter-of-fact. Fairweather gives her a "shut-up" nudge with her elbow. Fanta cringes.

The three Badass Fairies haven't changed a bit—except their butts are even bigger. They're still wearing their frumpy frocks and matching bonnets, completing each other's sentences, and about to bicker.

"Excuses, excuses." The Queen rolls her eyes with disdain. "Let's just get on with the blessings."

Taking turns, the Badass Fairies waddle over to Princess Swan, wave their magic wands over her, and bestow her with a blessing. Fingers crossed one of them blesses her with Beauty. She sure could use some help in that department.

"Princess Swan, I bestow upon you the gift of eternal thinness," says Fairweather.

What a waste of a blessing! While I'm sure every Fairytale princess yearns for this lifetime-guaranteed gift, this poor scrawn-of-a-child needs some meat on her bones.

"I bestow upon you the singing voice of an angel," says Fanta.

Good one! I wish someone had done that for me.

"And I bestow upon you the gift of eternal beauty," says Fanta.

Phew! I was getting worried.

"Let's par-tay!" bellows King Midas.

Winnie, once again, has done her magic. The feast that follows is spectacular—a savory symphony of fresh baked breads, pastries, tarts, and salads. Villagers mingle amongst royalty. The gifts they have brought for Princess Swan are abundant—ranging from a basket of freshly baked muffins from a little village girl in a red hooded cloak to a coach full of toys from Pinocchio, my dear Faraway friend who inherited his father's toy business and turned it into an empire. His constant companion, Peter Pan, has offered Princess Swan a coupon good for one free trip to Neverland when she turns ten.

The Queen, still cuddling Swan in her bountiful arms, mingles with her guests and is the center of attention. "Isn't she drop-dead gorgeous?" she thunders. My mother-in law is extremely myopic but too vain to wear glasses. She's oblivious to Swan's ugly duckling looks. No one has the nerve to tell her the truth. They want to keep their heads on their shoulders.

In the crowd, I spot Elz at the banquet table, standing next to a much more relaxed Winnie. I make my way over to them.

"I'm now officially Auntie Elz," gloats Elz in her singsong voice. She's bestowed upon Swan a closet-full of fabulous shoes that every Lalaland princess would die for. Except they won't fit her until she's twenty.

"The baby's adorable," gushes Elz. She's not wearing her glasses. She's in for a big surprise.

"Cinderella looks like she's drowned in a moat," comments Winnie.

"She probably just needs a hug," says Elz. She waltzes over to her.

They have grown quite close. Cinderella, the perfect, kind-hearted princess she is, readily forgave her stepsister for her not-so-nice behavior when they were growing up. She knew Elz's wicked mother had manipulated her. Thanks to Cinderella's support and generous investment, Elz was able to turn The Glass Slipper into a multi-million dollar empire with shoe stores all over Lalaland.

I hover over the banquet table with the svelter than ever Winnie, who carefully measures how much food she puts onto her plate. At last, a chance to talk to her.

Keeping an eye out for Aurora, I hastily fill in her about last night. No, not about Cinderella's mama drama. About Gallant's confession.

Winnie shrugs. "Just because Gallant knows Aurora and went to her house doesn't mean he's sleeping with her."

I want to shake her. What will it take to convince her that Gallant is having an affair?

"Keep your eyes peeled for the homewrecker," I whisper in her ear.

"Jane, that's absurd. What makes you think she's here?"

"With all these people, it's a perfect opportunity for her to see Gallant. No one will notice when they secretly saunter off."

She dismissively rolls her eyes. There's no point to telling her about my sexual escapade with Gallant. Or my torn feelings that teeter between regret and desire.

Her attention is diverted. "Guess who's coming our way."

Oh no! Gallant and the man-eater. My stomach gets all

knotty. And my heart skips a beat. I'm not ready to take her on.

"Yo, Ho, Ho," It's Hook, dressed in his pirate-finest. Tight britches, shiny black boots, and a blousy linen shirt that's opened wide enough to reveal the forest of hair on his taut chest. For once, I'm relieved to see him.

"So, Jane, are you ready for a little baby of your own?" he asks, eying me up and down.

My relief is short-lived. I want to yank off that hook of his and hang him by his balls with it. "You'll be the last to know," I say through clenched teeth.

His lips twitch, and he straightens up. Gothel, in her mile high leather boots, struts over to us and jerks him away. Her fierce violet eyes clash with mine. I can read her face perfectly. It says, "Watch it, sister, or you're dead." She's even scarier than I thought.

"What was that all about?" asks Winnie.

"No idea," I reply, not wanting to get into details. I'm just glad to be rid of Hook. And the dragonslayer. My eyes flicker around the room. I'm sure Aurora's beautiful. The problem is that there are dozens of gorgeous princesses strutting around. The gift of beauty must be a fairy godmother standard.

"Winnie, Aurora's got Gallant on her brain. You're a mind reader. Which one is she?"

Winnie rolls her eyes again. "Jane, you're being ridiculous. I have no idea. I've never even met her." She takes a small helping of the fanciful cake she's baked and wanders over to Hook and Gothel. Traitor! Just wait till she asks me for an itty-bitty favor.

Okay, I'm on my own.

I eliminate all the redheads; Gallant isn't the redhead type. My evil mother was a blonde, albeit a fake one. And she doesn't really count because she had him under a spell. She's got to be a brunette; make that a raven-haired beauty; I'm sure. Snow White had ebony hair, and so do I.

My eyes finally land on several extremely attractive dark-haired princesses. They are chatting away with a stunning blonde, wearing a sparkly tiara that must have cost a small fortune. *Which one is that bitch Aurora?* I'm waiting for a sign. My eyes widen when one of the stunning brunettes, with curls down to her waist, breaks away from the pack. My gaze follows her across the room. With long, graceful steps, she weaves through the crowd. Holy shit! *She's going after Gallant!* Catching up to him, she wraps her arms around him like she owns him. Gallant's face lights up like a lantern. My heart slams against my chest. I'm more than 100% confident. It's her! For sure! The man-eater! *Jane, chill. Don't overreact.* I take deep yoga breaths, but when Gallant plants a big kiss on her cheek, I start panting like a dog. I'm so heated up I can smell smoke.

"Get your hands off *My* Prince, missy!" I scream inside my head. Time to charge. I elbow my way through the packed room.

Someone grips my arm. So tightly, I can't take another step.

"My dear, you look like you've gained a little weight."'

I whirl around. It's Fairweather. Flossie and Fanta flank her.

"And seem a little stressed out," adds Flossie.

"You must get back into yoga," tisks Fanta.

Dragonballs! This is so not the time for Badass Fairy chitchat. I struggle to break free of Fairweather's forceful grip. But can't. All that yoga has given her the strength and stamina of a behemoth. I swivel my head toward Gallant and Aurora! Where are they? Frantically, I search the crowd. They're gone!

"You know, we didn't really want to come today," says Fairweather.

"It's been such a long time since we've used our fairy magic!" chimes Flossie.

"The last time we used it on Princess Aurora was such a horrible experience!" exclaims Fanta.

Princess Aurora? They know Aurora? A hazy recollection comes back to me. Of course, they were Sleeping Beauty's fairy godmothers before they retired and became life coaches at Faraway. They must know *everything* about her!

"Oh, have you seen Aurora here today?" I ask as calmly as I can.

"We saw her earlier," beams Flossie. "My gift of beauty really paid off."

Gulp!

"As beautiful as ever," chimes Fairweather.

Gulp!

"A knockout!" exclaims Fanta.

Gulp! My blood is sizzling. *And, by chance, does she have waist-length chestnut hair and move with the grace of a gazelle?* My throat thickens. Before I can get the words out, the three Badass Fairies plow through crowd, heading toward the open French doors.

"Wait!" I shout out, chasing after them.

"We must get back to Faraway," says Fairweather.

"We can't be late for our newest inmate," says Flossie. "A very nasty fellow—Bluebeard. Our first wife murderer!"

"And at our age, we need to give ourselves plenty of flying time," says Fanta. Flossie and Fairweather shoot her a dirty look.

"You must come visit," says Fairweather as she adjusts her fairy wings and attempts, like her sisters, to bounce into the air. It takes them several embarrassing tries.

"I'll do that," I reply. In fact, I'll be there tomorrow. I want—and need—to know everything there is to know about Aurora. I'm going to take her down! Even it means being Faraway's first mistress murderer.

I elbow my way back through the crowd. My stomach muscles clench as my eyes search in every direction. Still no sign of Gallant and Aurora.

Dazed and distracted, I bump head on into The Queen of Hearts. Humpty Dumpty, with his notepad and stylus in hand, is peering around her gown, all ears.

"So, my dear, when are *you* going to give us a

grandchild?" she asks, stuffing her mouth with a heapful of the red velvet cake.

I'm so taken aback by her question that I stumble and knock her plate out of her hand. It lands on Humpty's head, cracking it down the middle. Yellow goo oozes out as his eyes roll back into his head.

I'm tempted to give the dazed egghead a scoop. First things first. *Not before Gallant and I get a divorce!*

CHAPTER 7

T he Badass Fairies had better be good for something, I think, as Faraway rises in the distance. The journey has been long and stressful, my stomach in knots every mile of the way. I've been unable to read the book I brought along. Or use the time to work on my next children's book. I've been too distracted. Only one thing has been on my mind. Aurora.

As my coach travels down the yellow brick road that leads to the gatehouse, an arsenal of memories explodes in my head. I remember the first time I saw Faraway, thinking I was being sent to a spa. Whoof! Was I wrong. It turned out to be a rundown rehab facility for people like me who were addicted to evil. Yes, I was here for a makeover. Just not the kind I was expecting.

Memory after memory flashes through my head. The hair fairies who deloused my waist-length hair by chopping it all off... My first encounter with Elzmerelda and her evil scary-skinny sister Sasperilla... Bread making with Winnie... Our yoga classes with Fairweather... My painful therapy sessions with Shrink... And my humiliating group sessions with Dr. Grimm, where, one by one, my fellow inmates and I came to grips with our addictions and the demons of our pasts. And as the coach crosses over the moat, I shudder at the memory of my near-fatal escape. It's been a little over two years, but it feels like only yesterday.

"Jane, welcome back!" says the gatehouse guard. It's Gulliver. The same goofy giant that I tricked into thinking I was Fanta when I tried to escape. "What brings you here?"

"I'm here to see the Bad—I, mean Good Fairies." At least, he didn't think I was checking back into this place.

He unlocks the gate with a large metal key without asking another question. My heart beats like a ticking clock as the coach pulls up to the front entrance. The memories of this place have messed with my head. I'm consumed with dread and belonging. I am The Evil Queen again. That vain, jealous woman who tried to kill Snow White. "Get a grip, Jane. Remember why you came back here," I find myself saying aloud. Easier said than done. It takes all I have to hold on to who I am.

A pixie greets me. "Ah, you must be Jane. The Good Fairies said you might be visiting." Despite her wee size, she manages to swing open the heavy front door and escorts me inside.

My eyes grow wide. Faraway is way less rundown than I remember it. In fact, it's rather luxurious. The stone walls are freshly painted in bright colors (not that drab yellow), and posh furniture and rugs are scattered throughout. There's even a gold-leaf mirror hanging over a gilded credenza. Life is so unfair! Why couldn't it be like this for me? I would have killed to look at myself in a mirror and hear it say, "You, My Queen, are the fairest of all."

A familiar voice jolts me back to the present.

"Hello, Jane. What brings you here?" It's Dr. Grimm, who happens to be the slightly older brother of my renowned Lalaland fertility specialist. Faraway may look a hell of a lot better, but Grimm doesn't. He's still wearing the same somber, ill-fitting frock coat. And as unkempt and morose as ever. So the opposite of his spiffy, jovial brother. It's interesting how two people so close in age and raised in the same household can turn out so differently.

"I'm here to see the Good Fairies," I tell him without mentioning the purpose of my little surprise visit.

"I'll let them know you're here," he says in his usual

glum, monotone voice. "By the way, how's Gallant doing?"

I'm taken aback by his question. How come he didn't ask me how I'm doing? I'm the former inmate, the one with issues. The mere mention of Gallant's name makes every muscle in my body tense up.

"Oh, he's just fine and dandy," I say, unable to hold back the sarcasm.

Grimm nods approvingly. "Good to hear," he says with a hint of surprise.

Why shouldn't Gallant be? He's got it all. A wonderful family... a brilliant career... *and* a beautiful rich mistress.

Grimm slumps off, and I'm back to fuming. Gallant's probably with the Sleeping Slut right now. Tilting back her head... pressing his lush lips against hers... peeling her gown off her lithe body. Burning bile rushes to the back of my throat as the Badass Fairies waddle toward me, one behind the other.

"Jane, we weren't expecting to see you so soon," says Fairweather.

"Did you come for our party?" asks Flossie.

"What party?" I ask with surprise. This joint *really* has changed. We never had parties when I was here except when someone was being released. Make-believe birthday parties to celebrate an inmate's recovery. A rebirthing so to speak. Mine was one of the happiest days of my life.

"We're celebrating the completion of our extreme home makeover," chimes Fanta.

"Isn't it wonderful?" exclaims Flossie, her voice giddy. "It's thanks to all the money raised by the Midas Foundation."

Yes, King Midas was once an inmate at Faraway. He came here for his evil addiction to gold and the power of wealth. While undergoing treatment, he met his second wife, The Queen of Hearts, who was being treated for her major anger management issue. They've since devoted their lives to fundraising and improving Faraway. Frankly, it's about time they gave this place a makeover. It sure needed it.

Flossie continues. "The King and Queen will be

here shortly to cut the blue ribbon. I hear they're coming with Gallant."

My blood runs cold. Midas and The Queen of Hearts are on their way here? And Gallant too? I need to interrogate the three fairies quickly and get the hell out of here. I don't want any members of the royal family to see me here, especially Gallant.

"Come, dear. Let us show you the new and improved Enchanted Garden," says Fairweather before I can get out a word. "It's all decked out for the party."

Flossie and Fanta each take me by an arm and escort me outdoors. Fairweather waddles close behind us. They're wasting precious time. I need to know everything about Aurora before Gallant and his parents arrive. Panic grips me. How should I begin? I don't want them to be suspicious. *Think, Jane, think!*

Okay. I've got it. Sometimes I'm just an unexpected creative genius.

"I'm writing a new children's book," I say, walking down the long corridor that leads to the garden. "It's about Sleeping Beauty."

The three fairies' pudgy faces brighten.

"We could tell you everything about her," says Flossie.

Everything? Just the word I wanted to hear. I suppress a wide smile.

"Once upon a time—"

Fairweather immediately cuts her off and rolls her eyes. "Flossie, we don't have all day for an epic story. Jane can read all about it in *Grimm's Fairy Tales.*"

I want to stuff Fairweather's mouth with an apple. She's so damn rude and bossy. And she's defeating the purpose of my trip.

"Jane, since we have so little time, why don't you ask us each a question."

Why can't we at least play "twenty questions"? I need info. Lots of it.

"Me first," says Flossie, raising her chubby hand like an eager schoolgirl.

Dragonballs. Just three questions. But I have a zillion! I need to narrow them down and choose wisely. *Think, Jane. Think!* Okay. Question #1. "What does the wh—I mean Aurora look like?"

Flossie chimes in first. "Well, let's put it this way. They didn't call her Sleeping Beauty for nothing. I was the one who gave her the gift of beauty. She has the face of an angel and a mane of hair that is beyond compare."

I shudder inwardly. Just like the princess Gallant ran off with!

"Jane, do you have a question for me?" asks Fanta eagerly.

Question #2. "Did she ever have a relationship with Gallant?" Boy, that wasn't subtle.

Fanta grins broadly. My heart thuds. I'm not sure I want to hear the answer.

"Ah, yes."

Yes? The word penetrates me like a bullet. I'm shell-shocked.

"When we disguised ourselves as peasants and kept Aurora hidden in the woods to protect her from her curse, Gallant used to send her secret notes all the time. Such beautiful words he wrote. So caring and loving. Aurora always wrote him back."

My heart sinks to my stomach. *They were childhood sweethearts? They wrote each other love notes?*

"Such a sweet, smart boy, that Gallant was. He used to address them to Briar Rose so that Malevolence wouldn't get wind of where we were hiding her."

"Who's Malevolence?" I stammer. Crap! I meant to ask: *"Did she always sign them 'Forever, Aurora'"?* Damn it! I just blew my third and final question.

A dark cloud descends on the three big-butt fairies. Their lips press together into hard, grim lines. Silence. Finally, Fairweather answers.

"Malevolence is a distant relative. A dark, sinister fairy also known as The Mistress of Evil. She was not invited to Aurora's christening but showed up anyway."

"She was angry, very angry," chimes in Flossie.

"And she bestowed upon Aurora the curse of death," adds Fanta.

Fairweather shoots her sisters a dirty look. "Shut up, you two. I'm telling the story. More specifically, she proclaimed that Aurora would prick her finger on a spindle and die. The terrible day came on her sixteenth birthday. We were busy making preparations for her Sweet 16."

Fairweather pauses for a moment and sighs. "It was our fault. We should have been more on our guard."

Flossie and Fanta bow their heads in shame.

Fairweather takes a deep breath and continues. "Thank goodness, we were able to save her by using our magic powers and putting our beautiful princess into a deep sleep."

"We were a little rusty," giggles Flossie. "We accidentally ended up putting the entire kingdom to sleep."

"But we covered it up by saying our little faux pas was on purpose," smiles Fanta.

Fairweather's mouth drops open. "Shame on you two! How could you give away one of our best kept secrets?"

Flossie shrugs apologetically while Fanta cowers with fear. Fairweather continues to give them her stink eye. I'm growing impatient. Enough about Malevolence. I want them to get back to Gallant and Aurora. Fairweather continues.

"The spell worked like this: Aurora—and everyone else—would awaken after she was kissed by her true love."

Her true love? My ears are burning. *And...*

"Lo and behold, Prince Phillip came along, kissed her, and broke the spell."

"Wait!" I cry out. "What happened to Gallant?" Uh oh! That's my fourth question! I've exceeded my limit. I'll never find out!

"He battled the dragon," replies Fairweather. Phew! No

one's counting anymore.

"What dragon?" I'm confused. Very confused.

"Sorry, I forgot to mention that Malevolence had the power to transform into a monstrous fire-breathing black dragon."

So, Mr. Smooth Operator, Phillip, got to the Sleeping Slut first and literally fed Gallant to the coals. No wonder Gallant wasted no time wakening Snow White with a kiss. He didn't want to be burned again, no pun intended.

In my spinning head, I begin to piece it all together. Aurora's probably always had a thing for Gallant, her first love. And now for whatever reason she and Phillip are in splitsville, and she's making the moves on him. And he's falling in love with her all over again. I want to vomit!

Something startles me and stops me in my thoughts. A rabbit scampers over my feet. We're in the Enchanted Garden, where the extreme makeover party is going to take place. I've been so wrapped up with this Sleeping Beauty story that I've lost track of my surroundings. The sunlight contrasts sharply with the darkness filling my heart.

"Jane, what do you think about our new and improved Enchanted Garden?" asks Flossie. She sounds sickeningly cheerful.

"It looks great," I mumble, still in shock from what I've learned from the Badass Fairies. Truthfully, it looks the same as it did before, with its overgrown patches of fruits, vegetables, and herbs. The Queen of Hearts, the cheapskate that she is, probably skimped here.

Ahead of us, a handful of bizarre looking people are picking fruit and setting picnic tables. One of them has wings of bright orange hair sprouting from under his tall, crazy hat. Another has a blue beard that extends to his knees. Of course, Bluebeard. Inmates. A maniacal fire burns in their eyes. They make me feel more unsettled than I already am. In fact, frightened as I'm reminded that I used to be one of them. I've had enough.

"Let us introduce you to some of our new inmates,"

says Fanta.

"They're an extremely challenging group," adds Fairweather.

Obviously. Not one of them is dancing or singing "lalala."

"You'll be such an inspiration to them," chimes in Flossie.

I need to get out of here. I don't have any time to be anyone's rehab goddess. Nor do I want to be. It's too late. Fanta and Flossie grab me by the arms and pull me over to a tall, wiry man wearing a tattered topcoat. He's playing an eerie tune on a musical instrument. A flute, I think. There's madness in his eyes. The hypnotic melody makes my skin crawl.

"Jane, say hello to the Pied Piper."

The man leans into me until the instrument is right under my nose. His carnal eyes burn a hole in me. The hair on the back of my neck rises. *Get away from me, you creep!* I jump back.

"Don't worry, Jane, He won't hurt you," says Fanta. "He prefers little children."

Flossie, on tiptoes, whispers in my ear. "He's a pedophile. The first we've had here."

An image of Calla flashes into my head. My sweet little girl. Thank goodness, she's safely at home. I hope The Queen's not bringing her along to the party.

The fairies drag me over to another inmate. The one with the tall hat. He's pouring tea.

"Jane, this is the Mad Hatter."

He removes his hat and bows down to me. "'Twas brillig, and the slithy toves did gyre and gimble in the wabe; all mimsy were the borogoves, and the mome raths outgrabe."

I don't need to hear a word more. He's definitely mad! There's even a teapot on top of his crazy hat.

As the Badass Fairies tow me away, he shouts out, "What a lovely head you have. Can I hat you?"

I shudder. This place is whacked. Even more whacked than I remember.

"He's here for animal cruelty," Fanta tells me.

"He once even tried to stuff a poor dormouse into a teapot," adds Flossie.

"The Queen almost had his head but The King convinced her to send him here instead," says Fairweather.

I don't want to know more. About him or any of these nutjobs. I just want to get out of here. To my dismay, the Badass Fairies usher me over to a frail, fine-boned woman with long, straggly gray hair, who is picking wild flowers. At one time, she may have been extremely beautiful. Even now, beauty transcends her haggardness. She lifts her head, and her eyes, purple with a rim of gold around the irises, connect with mine with disturbing intensity. There's something frighteningly familiar about her.

"Who is she?" I ask.

"We don't know," replies Fairweather. "She was found wandering, close to death, in the Forbidden Forest. She hasn't spoken a word since her arrival."

The women's full lips curl into a faint smile before parting. "Jane." She says my name softly, almost like a prayer. It reverberates inside my head, sending a shiver up my spine.

How does she know my name? Did one of the Badass Fairies tell her about me?

Without taking her eyes off me, she stretches her withered, bony hand toward my face and brushes her fingers against my cheeks.

Her touch, tender but disturbing, sends a shockwave through me. I jump back. Get me out of here! Get me far away from Faraway and all these loonies. They're making me insane. I don't belong here anymore!

"I've got to go," I say, panic in my voice.

"But, Jane, you'll miss our tea party," says Flossie.

"The Royal Family will be here any minute," adds Fanta.

The Queen! Midas! That cheating asshole Gallant! I can't let them see me here!

Calling upon every muscle in my body, I break loose of Flossie and Fanta's tight grip and run madly back toward the entrance…

Smack into Fairweather. How did she get here? Magic, I suppose. She blockades me with her buxom body and looks straight into my eyes.

"Jane, there is something we didn't tell you that you must put in your story."

Oh, God. She's going to tell me that Aurora and Gallant had a little romp in the woods.

"Everyone thought Gallant killed Malevolence. But he didn't. She survived."

Okay. I can handle that.

"Eventually, your father, The Huntsman, caught her and brought her to Faraway. But she managed to escape."

What? I thought no one ever escaped Faraway. That's what Shrink told me. The liar!

"She fooled us all by morphing into a fire-breathing dragon once again."

Information overload. "Why do I need to know this?"

"Because, Jane, she's out there. Hiding somewhere in the Forbidden Forest that separates Faraway from the rest of Lalaland. Sometimes, I see her flying over us at night when there's a full moon."

I flashback to the night I tried to escape from Faraway. Pretending to be Fanta, I was wearing her magic wings and flying high in the sky. Just when I thought I had the flying thing down, a dragon came after me in hot pursuit. Roaring. Full of rage. Shooting its fiery breath at me. The flames singed my wings, and I fell from the sky. I would have died had I not landed on a tree branch.

A shudder runs through me. It must have been Malevolence.

"Be careful, Jane. She's Lalaland's most wanted criminal, and she's out for revenge." Fairweather releases me.

My body quakes.

Mission accomplished. Back in my coach, I head back to Lalaland, peering out the window. The darkening autumn sky mirrors my mood. My visit to Faraway has left me drained and disheartened. The Badass Fairies told me what I needed to hear. Not what I wanted to hear. Gallant and Aurora were childhood sweethearts. They've always had a thing for each other. A thing called love. A mixture of hatred, jealousy, and sadness courses through me.

The tears that I've been holding back trickle down my cheeks. The evidence is piling up like dirt. I'd better keep track of it all. Why not start now on the long, depressing ride home? From my purse, I take out my favorite stylus and the sheet of parchment I brought along (in case I got an inspiration for my next children's book) and start writing everything down.

MY GROWING LIST OF EVIDENCE
(WORK IN PROGRESS)

1. Aurora's love letter.

2. Steamy steam room gossip—Aurora's split from Philip. (Gallant himself substantiated it.)

3. Gallant's late night disappearances.

4. Gallant—thinks I'm fat (okay, it's more like he hasn't said I look thin lately.)

5. Gallant—seeing Aurora but pretending they have a business relationship. ("We've been meeting.")

6. Gothel's jealous behavior; she's worried that I'll soon be single again and available for Hook.

7. Gallant—his audacity to invite Aurora to Princess Swan's coming out party. Embraced her and stealthily slipped away with her!

8. Badass Fairies' story—Gallant and Aurora were childhood sweethearts!

9. Fact: Aurora married the wrong prince and wants Gallant back.

10. TBD (I'll come up with something.)

I read over my list. There's a shitload of incriminating stuff. The list actually makes me feel a little better. I'm glad I wrote it down. I definitely have enough evidence to prove that Gallant is having an affair with Aurora. Wait until I show this list to those naysayers—Winnie and Shrink. I can't wait to see the look on their faces.

And then I'll stick it to Gallant! I try to imagine the look on his face. I can't. Instead, my heart drops to my stomach. As much as I've relished gathering evidence about his affair, the truth is, I dread confronting him with it. I'm afraid of his reaction. He could deny it, laugh in my face, or even ask for me a divorce on the spot. The bitter reality of two words— The End—makes me feel sicker than I already am. I'm just so not prepared to lose the man who once loved me. *Admit it, Jane. The man I still...*

A blinding flash of light stops me in my thoughts. I shield my eyes with both hands. As quickly it flashed, it's gone. An unsettling thought zaps my mind. What if I'm being followed by that evil fire-breathing dragon-fairy, Malevolence? For the rest of the trip home, I'm on edge, wishing Gothel the Dragonslayer were around. Trust me, I don't want to be roasted by a fire-breathing dragon and end up as dinner. Wouldn't that be convenient? I'll be dragon dung while Gallant and Aurora live happily ever.

The frightful scenario gives way to one of my brainstorms. I know. I'll track down Malevolence and make a deal that she can't refuse. I'll dig into Gallant's trust fund and buy her a castle of her own if she devours Aurora with her fiery breath.

I play out the fantasy in my head. It's all so perfect. Malevolence goes for it right away. Hey, she always wanted Aurora dead, and now I've made it worth her while. *Snap, crackle, and pop.* The sound of the slut becoming toasty breakfast cereal is music in my ears. But when I get to the part where Malevolence is about to blast Aurora with her fiery breath, everything goes south. A handsome prince shows up on his white stallion and carries off the damn princess just in the nick of time. Dragonballs! It's Gallant. My evil plan has just crashed and burned. It'll never work.

I silently curse the past. If only Gallant hadn't saved her from being toast the first time.

CHAPTER 8

I get back to Lalaland In the early evening only to remember that I have my weekly EPA meeting. It's held every Thursday night at 7:00 p.m. in a covert cave that's located somewhere below The Trove.

Our mantra—"Just say NO to evil!"—has really paid off. Over the course of attending these meeting for the past two years, most of us have had fewer and fewer evil tendencies. Or at least, less evil ones. Even my confession last week that I'd like to see birds poop all over Cinderella wasn't that evil. I'd say it was more on the mean side.

But this week, I've regressed. Terribly! That Sleeping-with-My-Husband hussy has rattled me. The insane, flesh-eating jealousy that's plagued me most of my adult life has come back with a vengeance. I've been consumed with evil thoughts. I've wanted to turn Shrink into pixie juice for not being supportive. I've wanted to punch out Winnie for challenging every piece of evidence I have. I've wanted to wipe out Gallant's inheritance. And I've wanted to kill Aurora! To be dead honest, I don't think I can say "no" to evil much longer.

Ten minutes late, I stealthily slip into the cavernous, candle-lit room, careful not to bring attention to myself. Gothel notices me immediately; her eyes send me daggers. Seated next to Hook, she leans in close to him and seductively drapes her long legs over his lap so that her boots are resting on the empty chair to the right of him. Okay. I get it, Dragon

Lady. There are plenty of other chairs. I settle into one in the back row. The group is already in progress.

As usual, my father, The Huntsman, Lalaland's go-to person for law and order, is at the podium, presiding over the session. "Who would like to share next?" he asks.

Hook untangles himself from Gothel's long legs and stands up. "I would." He swaggers up to the podium where he hangs his head low. "I stopped by Puss 'n Boots and ordered myself a bottle of rum."

He pauses. Gothel's violet eyes morph into swords.

"I smashed the bottle."

Applause and cheers. Except from eye-stabbing Gothel.

"Thank you, Hook, for sharing," says my father.

Hook returns to his seat. Gothel elbows him hard. He winces.

"Who else would like to share?" asks my father.

Not me. Winnie, seated in the second row, surveys the room. Her eyes land on me. I give her an icy stare. Read my face. It says: "I'm not talking to you."

Winnie returns the stare. The temperature in the room has suddenly dropped ten degrees.

"Anyone?" asks The Huntsman again.

Elz and Rump, seated next to Winnie, stand up together. They're holding hands.

"We have something we want to share," says Elz, her singsong voice quivering.

What possible evil inclinations could they have? They're the sweetest couple in the world. There's not an evil bone left in their bodies.

Still holding hands, this odd couple, she, a six-foot pillar, and he, a four-foot troll, heads up to the podium.

A former stutterer, Rump hammers out the words as fast as he can, never taking his eyes off a beaming Elz. "We're having a baby!"

A baby? They're having a baby?? But I thought Elz and Rump didn't want to have children. That they wanted to focus on their careers. And that Rump especially didn't want to have children, given the guilt he's had to deal with for having once tried to extort a baby—a forgiving queen's first-born child.

"Way to go, Matey!" shouts Hook, leaping to his feet. "Yo, Ho, Ho, let's hear it for them!"

The entire group joins Hook in a standing ovation, breaking into cheers and applause. Except me.

I'm in a state of shock. I'm numb when I should be happy—in fact, thrilled—for my dear friend. *Elz and Rump are having a baby.* They didn't even try. No magic potions. Birthing stones. Candles or chants. It just happened. I re-register the news. *Elz and Rump are having a baby.* I feel nothing. Except jealousy. Insane jealousy that's eating me up alive.

My father adjourns the meeting. Everyone swarms Elz and Rump to congratulate them. Except me who's frozen in my chair. As Winnie hugs Elz, she shoots me a scathing look. I guess I'd better congratulate them too. I slump over to the joyous couple.

"That's great, Elz," I say glumly. I can't even fake a smile.

Elz gives me a big kiss. "Thanks, Jane. I hope it happens for you and Gallant soon."

Her words sting me like salt in a wound. I fight back tears. How could she say that to me when she knows what's been going on? I inhale deeply, and on the exhale, I tell myself that she didn't mean what she said. She just wasn't thinking. That's all.

"Jane, can't you be one ounce happy for her?" I turn around, and there's Winnie in my face.

"It's just like you to be totally wrapped up with yourself. And to think that your problems take precedence over anything else in this world." Her hazel eyes flare. "You know what… I think I liked The Evil Queen better than The Drama Queen."

Her words lance through me. She storms off before I can say a word.

I feel like crap. This whole day has been this way. One

slap in the face after another. A fat tear rolls down my cheek. I just want to go home and hide under the covers. A strong arm wraps around my shoulders, and I pivot on my heel. A tall, burly bearded man with twinkly green eyes that are exactly like mine faces me. It's my father. The Huntsman.

I totally breakdown. A avalanche of tears pours from my eyes, and I heave unabashedly. He hugs me, and I bury my face in his broad chest. It's the first time I've ever cried in my father's arms.

My father takes me to Puss 'n Boots, a favorite tavern among Lalaland commoners and unsavory misfits like one-eyed ogres, deformed dwarfs, and grotesque giants. And Hook. We find a table in the corner, away from all the rowdy locals gathered at the bar. My father removes his pelted hunter's hat with its single blood-red feather and orders a couple of beers. After all that's happened today, a refreshing ale is just what I need.

As we await our drinks, my eyes dash back and forth to the front door. Despite his confession tonight, I expect Hook to show up any minute. Regulars still talk about his jousting match with Gallant. Both drunk out of their minds, they dueled for my hand and almost killed each other. A what-if pops into my head. If Hook had dueled Gallant to the end, I wouldn't be sitting here right now, depressed, confused, and contemplating a crime of passion. Putting an end to my wretched life.

"Jane, I am worried about you," says my once estranged father. The look on his face is warm, loving, and compassionate. "You don't seem to be yourself."

A one-eyed ogre delivers our beers. Taking a sip of the cold, frothy beverage, I debate whether or not to tell my father about Gallant. We've become close. So close. He's worked hard at making up for lost time. And so have I. Bottom line…

the man whom I once despised most in my life is now the other man I love most in my life. It hasn't been your everyday father-daughter relationship, but it's been the best.

I take yet another swig of beer and then chug the rest. Finally, I unwind.

"Father, there's someone close to me whose husband is having an affair. I think I gave her some bad advice."

"Winnie? She seemed upset with you at our meeting."

Good. He's making it easy for me.

"I really can't say who." I'm not telling him it's me.

"What did you tell her?"

"I told her she needed to prove it, and she did." I sigh. "Now she's all upset and doesn't know what to do."

My father lowers his mug to the distressed oak table. We share a stretch of silence.

At last, he breaks the ice. "Many years ago, I knew a beautiful woman who was madly in love with a handsome, hard-working man whom she trusted and respected. One night, the man drank too much and made a terrible mistake. He slept with a barmaid, but the love of his life caught him and never forgave him. She banned him from her bed forever."

"What happened?" I ask, my eyes wide.

"The woman gave birth—to a beautiful little girl—and forbade her lover from ever seeing her or the child."

My heart leaps to my throat. It doesn't take a genius. My father, The Huntsman, is talking about himself. And my mother—Nelle! Despite our newfound closeness, this is a subject we've avoided. A painful one that neither of us has wanted to touch. All I've ever known is that my father abandoned us. No details. But now, I know why. The *real* truth. He had no choice. My mother forced him out of our lives. But, what does this story have to do with my problem?

My father's eyes water. "Jane, I am sorry that I let you believe that your mother was wicked. She was wounded and did what she thought was right. She never recovered."

I reach my hands across the table and clasp his stout

fingers in mine. They're cold and trembling.

"Did you still love her?" My voice waivers.

"My dear Jane, I have always loved her. I made one terrible mistake, but she could not see it that way. She thought because I slept with another woman I no longer loved her. But that was not the case."

"Why didn't you tell her the truth?"

"She never gave me the chance." My father hangs his head low.

A long silence follows. We are both at a loss for words.

"Father, what should I tell my friend?" I say, finally ending the silence.

"Tell your friend to have an open mind. That perhaps her husband strayed, but his heart has remained true to her."

My father squeezes my hands. "And tell her to keep an open heart."

And forgive him? I keep the thought to myself.

"Yes, my child. And to forgive him." He has read my mind.

"Two more beers over here!" shouts my father with a sudden burst of jubilance. Our conversation has freed of him of the demons he's battled all these years.

And talking to my father has given me an entirely new perspective on Gallant's affair. Maybe Gallant's affair with Aurora *is* just a one-time fling. A silly divergence he'll regret. He'll get over it, apologize to me, and I'll forgive him. And it'll be back to happily ever after.

My father and I toast each other when the beers arrive. I'm blessed to have such a wise and loving father. As I chug down the cold beverage, a warm feeling washes over me. For the first time all day, I have a glimmer of hope.

That Gallant still loves me.

And that maybe my mother was not born evil after all.

CHAPTER 9

For the first time in months, I sleep soundly. Not even my recurring nightmare disturbs me. At the crack of dawn, I wake up, refreshed and renewed with hope. Yes, Gallant still loves me. I can't wait for him to confess his little transgression and beg for my forgiveness. But I'm not going to make it that easy. He's going to have to get down on his knees, and he'd better have a gift for me. Yes, something sparkling and expensive. Very expensive.

It's amazing how much better the world seems when you can be forgiving. My face lights up when Gallant strides into the kitchen. He, too, looks rested. And clean-shaven. And oh so heart-stoppingly handsome. Maybe while he was at Faraway, the Badass Fairies mentioned my visit and knocked some sense into him.

He helps himself to the tea I've brewed and says, "Good morning, my love."

He called me *my love!* That's it; he's done with Aurora. It's only a matter of time until the confession. And we kiss and make up.

"Darling, is there anything you want to tell me?" I say, prodding him.

He gazes at me with his piercing blue eyes that still make me melt. I'm ready to hear the truth and forgive him.

He takes a sip of tea. "Jane, don't forget that we have an appointment with Dr. Grimm at noon."

I'm a little taken aback by his response but glad he's

reminded me; I almost forgot. I brighten. Of course, another sign he loves me. He's still determined to have a child with me!

"Is there *anything* else?" I say, pushing harder.

"I'll be in my studio most of the day." He finishes his tea and dashes off. Without kissing me good-bye.

My heart sinks. Maybe, he's still working on his confession speech and wants to give it to me tonight over a romantic dinner. And there's also that perfect I-love-you bauble he needs to buy.

Moving to the window, I keep my eyes on the man I married as he gallops off on his beautiful white steed. His loose flaxen hair blows in the wind. How handsome he is! And smart and creative. He's such a good father too. And what a lover! How lucky I am that he's mine! And that Aurora is out of the picture!

———◆———

Dr. Grimm's waiting room is exactly what you would expect to find inside a storybook cottage. It's a whimsical hodgepodge of colorful furniture—a cozy couch and a couple of rocking chairs, plus a silly cuckoo clock on one wall and a brightly painted mural of baby lambs jumping over a rainbow, one after another. "*Where Fairy Tales are Born*" is brightly written above the scene in a large, flowery font.

I'm disappointed that Gallant isn't already here. The truth is, I'm early. I couldn't wait to get here. All morning, I fantasized snuggling next to him, holding hands, and exchanging our favorite baby names between little kisses. Regret fills me. I should have played it closer to the clock— even have been late—to angst him out a little. To make him think that I wasn't that into having his baby or that maybe my eyes had wandered. He should pay for his affair with Aurora!

Sighing, I plunk down onto the couch and look for something to read. On the coffee table, there are three choices. One is a copy of my children's book, *Dewitched*, which I personally autographed for Dr. Grimm. Next to it is a copy of *Grimm's Fairy Tales: Vol. 2,* a recently published sequel to the bestseller Dr. Grimm co-wrote with his brother, Wilhelm, my group therapist at Faraway. And, lastly, a copy of today's *Fairytale Tattler*.

I've been eager to read the new Grimm book. I open it and gasp. *CHAPTER ONE: Sleeping Beauty.* My mind races. Did the Brothers Grimm write about Gallant and Aurora's little childhood romance?

"Jane, close the book," a little voice inside my head whispers. "Don't read it!" I ignore it.

> *Once upon a time, there lived a king and queen who could not bear any children. They tried everything, but nothing seemed to work. Finally, after much time, The queen became pregnant and gave birth to a beautiful daughter. They named her Aurora.*

Aurora! I toss the book back on the table as if it's poison. Enough! I've got to get her name out of my head. Needing a distraction, I pick up the *Tattler* and leaf through it. My stomach twists with apprehension. What if there's a story about Gallant and Aurora? I can already see the headline: *"Snow White's Prince Finds a New Sleeping Beauty."* I tear through the pages. Not a word about Aurora and Phillip splitting. And not a word about Aurora and Gallant! HA! Those two gossip queens in the steam room were dead wrong! I take a deep breath and calm myself down. There's no way that Gallant is having an affair with what's her name! At least not anymore.

Feeling much better, I make a deal with myself to stop projecting things that aren't necessarily true. And to stop distrusting Gallant. I can't wait to see *my* Prince. I just wish he'd get here already.

A woman the size of a cow totters into the waiting room and plops into the large rocking chair across from me. She picks up my children's book and begins to read it. I'm flattered and can't help smiling. Yet, another soon-to-be mother who will be reading *my* story to her little one. She gets to the last page and flings it back on the table.

"What did you think?" I ask, debating whether I should tell her I wrote it.

She shakes her head and makes a disgusted face. "An appalling story!"

"What do you mean?" I say, shocked. That hurt!

"The Evil Queen didn't deserved to live happily ever after." Her voice grows more contemptuous. "Evil shouldn't be rewarded in our society. It sends a bad message to our children."

What! She's missed the entire point of my fable. Life can be rewritten, and everyone has a chance at happily ever after. I want to scream out and tell her that hundreds of women have written me letters, thanking me for giving them hope. And for at last putting a kibosh on that evil stepmother myth. I want to give this bitch a piece of my mind. My mouth opens wide on the verge of a tirade, but only one word comes out. "Whatever." It's not worth the effort to defend my book. She's probably too stupid and pigheaded to get it. I've also made up my mind. I'm not telling her I'm the author.

The woman folds her pudgy hands on top of her ballooning belly and gives me the once over. I'm hating her more by the minute. "So, what are you doing here?" Her tone is snarky. "You don't look pregnant."

I clench my fists. "I'm trying to have a baby."

She smiles at me smugly. "I'm having multiples."

No wonder she's the size of a cow! Okay, I admit, I'm a little jealous, but I'd kill myself if I ever got that fat.

"They're very active." She rubs her humongous belly. "I can feel one kicking right now."

"That's nice," I say coolly. I just want to punch her.

"Dr. Grimm thinks I'm having twelve dancing princesses."

The wall clock spares me from having to say another

word to this peasant. "CUCKOO!" says the little birdie twelve times. It's noon. Time for our appointment. Where the hell is Gallant?

Dr. Grimm teeters into the waiting room. He's wearing a long white coat and a tall cone-shaped white cap that sits just above his rimless spectacles. His white flyaway hair sticks out on the sides, and his white beard falls to his chest. To be honest, he looks more like a sorcerer than a doctor.

"My dear Jane, let's see how we're doing in the baby department," he says warmly.

"Shouldn't we wait for Gallant?" I ask tentatively.

Dr. Grimm wraps an arm around my shoulders and escorts me into his office. "No need, my dear. He messengered over a note saying he couldn't make it."

What! He's not coming? I thought having a baby was the most important thing in the world to him. He's even the one who forced me to see Dr. Grimm to help us along. He's never missed an appointment! Ever!

"Did Gallant say what he was doing?" I ask nervously.

"He said he had an emergency meeting."

My breath catches in my throat, and every muscle in my body tightens. "*We've been meeting.*" Gallant's words from the other night ring in my head.

I was wrong. Dead wrong. Gallant's affair with Aurora is far from over. He can't resist her! He's still sleeping with the beauty!

⎯⎯⎯⎯◆⎯⎯⎯⎯

Dr. Grimm's small office looks like it *does* belong to a sorcerer. Or an evil mad scientist. There are large flasks of candle-warmed bubbling potions, test tubes dangling from wires, and frighteningly complicated arrays of dials, controls, and strange gurgling apparatus. On one wall is a library of books dealing with magic spells, chants, diets, and other bizarre fertility aids. On another is a shelf filled with neatly labeled bottles. Like evening primrose, birthing stones, and sparkling crystals. Magic fertility enhancers.

What the hell am I doing here? I ask myself as I sit hunched over on Dr. Grimm's examining table. There's no rhyme or reason to be here while Gallant is off gallivanting with his mistress of evil. How could I be so foolish to think that he only loves me? A fat scorching tear rolls down my cheek. Dr. Grimm catches sight of it before I can wipe it away.

"My dear, you must be experiencing a maternal meltdown," says Dr. Grimm sympathetically. "Where are we on our cycle?"

Our cycle. I hate when he says that. It's *my* cycle. *My* body. *My* life. And I'm not having *my* baby with Gallant. Ever!

"I don't know," I splutter. The truth is, ever since my awful miscarriage, my cycle has been totally irregular. It's been even more erratic with my fertility treatments. A month with no period. Followed by some spotting. And then no period again—sometimes for several months. I think the stress of having a baby with Gallant has taken a toll on my body. I'm glad it's finally coming to an end.

"Well, then, we'll have to put you on a regiment of tribulous, mugwort, and black cohosh. It will enhance your fertility and help you get over your mood swings," he says cheerfully.

He mixes up a vial of the awful sounding herbs. He then fills up a bag with glistening multi-color stones. "My very special Magic Birthing Stones. I want you and Gallant to take a love bath with them every night."

A love bath? I don't think so. I grab the bag and the vial and stuff them into my purse. As soon as I'm out of here, I'll scatter their contents in his front yard. Maybe they'll help some unfortunate infertile critters reproduce.

"My dear, I've had wonderful success with those stones. Princess Aurora would have never been born without them."

Aurora! Why did she have to ever be born! I silently curse Dr. Grimm. I hate this sweet man for ruining my life!

Rage races through my bloodstream. It takes all I've got not to pummel him with the stones. Or stuff them down his throat. I need to get out of here. FAST!

"Now, dear, just follow my instructions, and we'll have a wee Gallant or mini-Jane before no time. I'll see you back here a week from tomorrow."

Next Saturday. The day before the opening of The Midas Museum of Art. My blood runs cold.

The cheerful doctor escorts me to the door and reminds me once again to take his *"Are You Ready for a Baby"* quiz. Is he kidding? It's been sitting in my desk drawer for months. The first thing I'm going to do when I get home is tear it up and watch the shreds burn to ashes in the fireplace. I can't wait to get out of here. And I'm never coming back.

When I lumber into the waiting room, the big fat pregnant woman is still there. She glares at me with a scornful air of superiority. *That's it!*

"Cow!" I scream at her. Her mouth drops open in horror.

A familiar voice steals my attention.

"Jane!" It's Elz, loping through the front door. Trust me, she's never been a beauty, but today she's glowing. She rushes over to me and gives me a big hug.

"My first check-up!" she beams.

My last. I muster up the courage to wish her good luck.

I hurry out the door. As soon as I'm outside, I toss the vial of herbs and bag of stones as far away as I can. There's never going to be a wee Gallant or a mini-me. *Never!*

CHAPTER 10

My fertility quiz bonfire will have to wait until after my appointment with Shrink, the second one this week. I feel sick. Weak. Nauseated. And worst of all, stupid. As my coach heads to her office, I ask myself over and over again: How could I have thought, even for one second, that Gallant was over Aurora? That their relationship was a mere fling? I love my father, but he was wrong. Dead wrong.

I'm on the verge of crying, but do something constructive to stifle the tears. I pull out my *"Growing List of Evidence"* from my purse and add—*#10: Gallant—Missed important Dr. Grimm appointment/Has lost interest in baby making.* I read over my list once again, and my gloom gradually lifts. I can't wait to show it to Shrink. HA! She wanted proof; here it is. It'll make her speechless. For a change.

As I stumble into to Shrink's office, I collide head-on with the last person I ever thought I'd run into here. Cinderella. She's covered with fairy dust. Why the hell is Miss Perfect Princess seeing Shrink?

"Hi, Jane," she murmurs. To tell the truth, she still looks like crap. Her normally perfectly coiffed blond hair is disheveled. Her face is pale and gaunt. Her blue eyes, sunken and surrounded by dark circles, have lost their glimmer. And she's swimming in her expensive gown. I mean, she was thin before she had the baby—and even throughout her pregnancy—but now she's scary-skinny. Scrawny. Size 0.

"What are you doing here?" I ask.

"Please don't tell anyone. Especially Charming," she stammers. She makes a desperate attempt to fix her straggly hair and ill-fitting gown. And then tears stream down her sallow cheeks.

"We should talk," I tell her. "Meet me at Sparkles in a half hour."

I actually won't be there for at least an hour, but knowing how late Cinderella always is it's wise to give her some lead-time.

———

"Why is Cinderella seeing you?" I begin my session with Shrink.

"Jane, I can't tell you that," says Shrink. "Doctor-patient privilege."

Whatever. I'll find out soon enough. And besides, I'd better focus on myself, especially since I've just wasted the first five minutes of my session.

"So, Jane," starts Shrink, "how's it going with you and Gallant?"

I hand her my "*Growing List of Evidence*" with a proud smirk.

"Interesting," she says, reading it over. Is that all she can say after all the hard work I've put into finding evidence? I thought she would be proud of me. I've proven my hypothesis. It's a fact now. Gallant *is* having an affair with Aurora.

"Have you confronted Gallant with your suspicions?"

I don't like her choice of the word "suspicions." What I've got is hard-core evidence. Even a confession from Gallant himself (#5 on the list) and now, his missed appointment with Dr. Grimm because of "an emergency meeting." Some emergency; he just couldn't keep his pants on.

Reluctantly, I shake my head.

"So, when are you planning to confront him?"

Shrink is making me uneasy, almost sick to my stomach.

"I'm waiting to catch him in the act," I finally say.

"Why are you afraid to confront him?"

Damn Shrink. She knows me too well. I take a deep, painful breath.

"Jane, I'm waiting for an answer." Shrink zigzags around the room impatiently.

"What would you do?" I ask, shirking the question.

"I'd confront him as quickly as possible. And move on with my life."

I fiddle with my gold marriage band, the one identical to Gallant's that has "forever" inscribed in it. A giant wave of nausea falls over me. I need to get a toilet. Fast! But it's too late. I blow chunks all over Shrink's office. She manages to flit away just in time.

"I'm sorry," I stammer between tears. "I think I'm coming down with something."

The chime rings.

"Time's up for today, Jane. I'll see you at our next session."

Shaking, I get up from the chaise and head for the door. My failed marriage is making me sick. Gallant is my disease.

❧

I wish I could cancel my meeting with Cinderella. I'm in no mood to listen to her ramble on about her problems. Nor am I in any condition to give her advice that she'll probably reject anyway.

I still feel like crap. The bumpy coach ride to The Trove does little to help my nausea. I'm growing weaker, dizzier, and more hopeless with every pothole we traverse. Why can't I accept the fact that Gallant is over me, confront him, and just move on? I just want to go home and bury myself under my covers.

To make matters worse, I'll probably have to wait an hour, if not more, for my sister-in-law to show up. Forget it! If she's more than fifteen minutes late, I'm going to ditch her.

I'll tell her truth the next time I see her. That I waited but fell ill. She needs to pay the price of always being so late. It might as well start now.

Surprise. When I get to Sparkles, Cinderella is already seated inside at a corner table. I can't believe Miss Fashionably Late is actually on time. Early in fact. Perhaps having Princess Swan early was a turning point.

The place is buzzing with Lalaland princesses, taking a break from shopping. Many keep subtly turning their heads toward Cinderella. I'm sure they're gossiping about how bad she looks and enjoying every minute of it.

Her forlorn face brightens slightly when she sees me. I suppose spending a little time with her is the least I can do. We order a pot of tea and two sparkly chocolate cupcakes. The tea makes me feel better. Cinderella doesn't touch a thing.

"What's going on?" I ask.

"I think I'm having some kind of breakdown." Her voice is glum, her eyes watery.

"What do you mean?"

"Ever since the baby came, I've not been myself. I feel sad all the time and worthless." She bursts into tears. "Oh Jane, I'm not meant to be a mother!"

"Of course, you are," I console her. "It just takes practice." HA! As if I know what I'm talking about.

"I'm a terrible mother," she whimpers.

"But everyone loves you, Cinderella. Even mice worship you."

"That's only because I feed them." She blows her nose with a napkin. "The other day, I slammed a window on a little baby bird. I killed it!"

She *is* having a problem.

"All Swan does is pea, poop, and cry. I don't know how to comfort her. I think she hates me," sobs Cinderella.

"Babies aren't capable of hate," I say, sounding like I wrote the go-to book on babies.

"She doesn't want me." Cinderella is inconsolable.

"Of course, she does," I reply. "All babies want

their mothers."

I'm sure I, too, as a baby wanted my mother despite the fact that she never wanted me. A pang of sadness shoots through me. I sigh silently.

"It's good you're seeing Shrink. What does she think?"

"She says I'm having a mild case of post-baby blues. It's not uncommon for women to fall into a depression after giving birth."

I flashback to the birth of my stillborn son. How deeply depressed I was after his birth. But that was different. I had suffered the loss of a child and a husband's rejection. Cinderella has it all. A healthy, beautiful—okay, not so beautiful—baby and a loving husband.

"Have you talked to Charming about the way you feel?"

"He hasn't been around much. Now that he's taking over ruling the kingdom from Midas one day, he's started intensive training. He comes home late, kisses the baby, and goes to sleep." She bursts into tears again, crying even harder. I wish she would stop. People are looking at us.

"Charming is in love with Swan. But I don't think he loves me anymore," she wails.

Well, I certainly know how that feels. At least, Charming's not a two-timing cheat. Life for Cinderella is just not as perfect as it was.

"I think you and Charming need some alone-time together. To reconnect." I bite into one of the cupcakes. "I'll take care of the baby."

Cinderella brushes away her tears and brightens. "Yes, a fairy-tale getaway! That's a great idea, Jane. Where do you think we should go?" She starts spewing an endless stream of destinations, each one fabulous in its own way.

She can't decide which one to go to. Some things never change. And I'm beginning to regret my generous offer. What possessed me to do that?

"Jane, thank you for being here for me." She gets up and hugs me. "Sometimes, I wish I had a mother to talk to. A mother who could have been a role model for me."

Poor Cinderella. Like me, she was a child of abuse. Her wicked stepmother treated her like a lowlife servant, working her to the bone and making her sleep in dark, damp attic. How interesting it is that she lived a life of goodness while I chose evil. Maybe, it's because my mother was a monster; she even tried to kill me. Still, the emotional scars are there. For the first time since I've known her, I feel a bond.

"Well, I'd better get back to the baby," says Cinderella, her voice fifty shades brighter.

I bid her farewell and scoff down my cupcake and Cinderella's, something I quickly regret given my current weight problem. I'll walk home and burn off the calories. And contemplate my next move with Gallant.

As I'm about to leave, a regrettably familiar man, holding a pad and pencil, races up to me. It's that slimy egghead reporter, Humpty Dumpty. He's wearing big bandage over the crack I made in his head.

"Is it true that happily-ever-after is over for Cinderella?" he asks.

"NO!" I scream indignantly.

But it is for me!

My heart practically stops. The brunette beauty that I saw with Gallant at Princess Swan's party breezes into Sparkles and takes a seat at a table for two. Aurora! Humpty dashes over to her table and plunks himself down onto the empty seat. The egghead asks her a question—I can't make it out. A warm, beautiful smile spreads across the Sleeping Slut's face, and she starts chatting. Humpty scribbles notes feverishly. Though I can't hear what she's saying, I swear she's just mouthed Gallant's name.

I fling a plate at Aurora, but it misses. SPLAT! It smacks Humpty's in the forehead, cracking it wide open. Dazed, the shell of a man slaps a hand to the jagged crack to stop the putrid yellow goo that's oozing out. I swear next time I'm going to scramble his brains. Fearful of another round of nausea, I sprint out of Sparkles. It's only a matter of time until Gallant's affair with Aurora is front-page news.

CHAPTER 11

The clickety-clack sound of galloping horses and loud whinnies awaken me. Downstairs, the grandfather clock gongs twelve times. Sunlight pours into my room. Holy crap! It must be noon; I've overslept once again. Oddly, my stillborn baby nightmare never interrupted my sleep. I must be moving forward in some way, yet sadness envelops me.

I have no idea if Gallant came home last night. One thing for sure, he didn't kiss me and awaken me from *my* deep sleep. A painful knot forms inside my stomach. What if he spent the night with that other Sleeping Beauty? Did he meet up with her at Sparkles and carry her away on his horse? The thought sickens me. I fight the nausea brimming inside me.

Rising from my bed, I stumble to the window and gaze outside. I'd recognize that pumpkin-shaped coach anywhere. It's Cinderella. Miss Fashionably Late and Indecisive is already taking me up on my offer? I'm so not mentally or physically prepared to take care of Princess Swan.

When I get downstairs, Cinderella is already there, holding Swan in a basket in one hand, and an oversized pink suitcase in the other.

"I just couldn't make up my mind where to go with Charming," she says cheerfully. "So we're going on a road trip. I can't wait!"

Dressed in a stunning blue velvet cloak, Cinderella is considerably more chipper since I saw her last. And gorgeous. A nauseating pang of envy courses through me as I admire her perfectly upswept golden hair and the sparkle in her blue eyes. Lucky her! Her Prince is taking her away. On a romantic getaway.

With a twirl, she hands the baby off to me.

"Caring for her will be a breeze. All you have to do is change her diapers and sing her nursery rhymes."

What! I've never changed a baby's diaper in my life. And I don't know any nursery rhymes. Not even one. Trust me, they were not in my wicked mother's repertoire. And it's no secret, I've got the worst singing voice in all of Lalaland. It even scares off warthogs. I can't imagine what it will do to an innocent baby.

I glance down at the tiny, squirming infant. I have to admit that Swan's gotten a lot cuter. Her skin is now vanilla silk, and her head no longer looks as if it will topple off her long, slender neck. Clad in a delicate pink silk gown, she has filled out a lot and begun to grow into her features. Fanta's blessing of beauty must have already kicked in. The little ugly duckling has swan potential after all.

"Jane, why don't you hold her?" Setting the basket down on the floor, Cinderella carefully lifts the baby out of it and places her in my arms. My skin prickles and my heartbeat speeds up. I'm simultaneously awed and frightened by this tiny miracle of life.

I gently rock the baby in my arms. So far so good. Then, without warning, Swan's puckered mouth opens wide, and she begins to wail. Louder and louder. Turning an awful shade of crimson, her face scrunches up while her tiny arms and legs flail wildly. Tears soak her little body and gown. I clutch her tighter, afraid she'll wiggle out of my arms. Cripes! What have I gotten myself into?

"She's probably hungry," says Cinderella.

Wait! There's a way out of this! I can't feed her! She needs her mother's breast!

"Don't worry," chirps Cinderella. She unlatches the suitcase. Inside are dozens of baby bottles filled with an icky, yellowish, milky substance. "I pumped my milk into these," she says proudly. "You wouldn't believe how time consuming it was!"

Spare me the details.

"Give her one whenever she is hungry. And don't forget to burp her after each feeding."

Burp her? Huh? How do I do that? A distraction at the front door cuts my thoughts short. Heaving, Cinderella's driver lugs a humongous wardrobe across the threshold. I've actually never seen such a large wardrobe. It can barely squeeze through the doorway. What on earth can be inside?

"Where should I put this?" asks the driver, barely able to catch his breath.

Cinderella scratches her head and ponders. "Hmm... I don't know. Let's see, we can move it into the great room, but then again maybe it would be better to bring it upstairs... "

I cut her off before her indecision will kill the poor driver. I tell him to leave it right in the hallway. The panting driver breathes a sigh of relief.

"What is this?" I ask, not really wanting to know.

"All of Swan's favorite clothes and toys," says Cinderella brightly after the driver slumps out the front door. "I just couldn't decide what to bring, so I packed her entire wardrobe and toy chest."

"Great," I say, gritting my teeth. The baby is still wailing and squirming in my arms.

"Do you think you'll be okay?" asks Cinderella.

"No worries." *Am I kidding?* Panic is already gripping me.

Cinderella gives the wailing baby a light kiss on her forehead. "Be a good girl for Auntie Jane." The baby wails even louder. Maybe the baby really doesn't like her.

"We'll be back on Sunday night by 6:00 p.m.," croons Cinderella, waltzing toward the front door. Singing "lalala," she disappears. Through the window, I watch her pumpkin-shaped coach fade into the distance. Baby Swan continues to cry at the top of her lungs. Every muscle inside me clenches.

Don't be late Cinderella. Just don't be late. I gaze down at the tear-soaked baby. *Or your baby's going to turn into pumpkin pie.*

Grrr. Why did I ever volunteer to take care of Swan? She's a handful. Much more than I bargained for. So much more!

Feeding her is a nightmare. When I give her a bottle, she spits it out. Then she becomes a little wise-ass and refuses to open her mouth. I have to manually part her lips and shove the bottle in. She tries to spit it out again. But I don't let her. Holding the bottle firmly in her mouth, I make her suck it dry. HA! Score one for me. But then the little sucker spits it up all over herself and me. Ewww! I guess I didn't burp her in time.

Changing her into a clean outfit isn't fun either. I grab one of the hundreds of little look-alike pink dresses Cinderella packed and place her on the middle of my bed. She doesn't stop squirming or wailing as I wiggle off her stained, drenched gown and struggle to put on another. I had no idea how hard it is to get a squirmy baby's tiny arms and head into those tiny openings. As soon as I can claim victory, a squalid odor, something beyond horrid, rushes into my nostrils. Crap! She's pooped.

Time for a diaper change. Putting one on her is no picnic either. She won't stop squirming. And I have no clue what corners to pin together. Her flailing makes me prick my fingers. Droplets of blood are everywhere. *Give me a break, Swan!* Finally, once I have it securely on her, she kicks it off. I grunt in frustration. She obviously doesn't like her new diaper. Repeat performance and finally success.

Okay, now time it's for a little nap, Princess Swan. I need a break. Desperately. I lower her into her basket and cover her with one of the three dozen cashmere shawls (one in every color) Cinderella packed. "Okay, Swan, go to sleep." She looks up at me with her big blue eyes as if I've spoken in a foreign language. "Make night-night." Maybe she understands that. As I tiptoe out of the great room (sprinting is what I should be doing!), a shrill cry stops me in my tracks. *Whaaaaaaa!* Swan's wailing again.

Damn! She obviously doesn't want to take a nap. I guess she's not tired, even after all that sucking and wailing. I know. I need to wear her out. Play some games with her. That'll do it.

Let's see. What kid games do I know? Hide and Seek. Chess. Gin Rummy. Oh, yeah, and Dress-Up. Dragonballs! Swan is too young to play any of these games. What am I going to do? Suddenly, I remember, my favorite game as I child. Make-believe.

Hovering over her basket, I make-believe that I'm a dog. "WOOF! WOOF!" Then I'm a lamb. "BAAAH! BAAAH!" And then I'm a pig. "SNORT! SNORT!"

Swan's watery eyes stay riveted on me. Her sobs turn into sniffles, and her tears subside. With her teeny weeny fingers, she clutches the mirrored locket that I always wear around my neck—a treasured gift from Shrink—and does something amazing that I've never seen her do before. She smiles. My heart melts.

The rest of the afternoon goes surprisingly smoothly. Swan takes to her bottles nicely. I have the burping thing under control, and I've become a diaper-changing maven. She even takes a long nap, letting me take one too, on the couch right next to her. We awaken at the same time. When she sees me, she coos. We're bonding. Maybe I've got a knack for babies after all.

As the clock strikes three, Calla comes racing into the great room, back from her standing Saturday playdate with Winnie's daughter, Gretel. I'm seated on the couch, feeding Swan yet another bottle. This baby has some appetite. No wonder she's grown so much since her birth.

Calla's face lights up. "What's baby Swan doing here?" There's excitement in her voice.

I tell her that I'm taking care of her so that Aunt Cindy can go on a little vacation with Uncle Charming.

"Can I feed her?" Calla asks, her big brown eyes begging me to say yes. "Please. Pretty please!" She plops down on the couch next to me.

After a moment of hesitation, I gently place the baby in Calla's lap and hand her the bottle. Cradling the baby in her arms, my sweet little girl feeds Swan as if she's done it every day of her life. The baby voraciously sucks the bottle. Calla beams with joy. How much she would love a little sister or brother! As I take in this tender scene, a bittersweet smile crosses my face. A tingling sensation accompanies the unexpected maternal feeling surging inside me. YES! I'm finally ready to take Dr. Grimm's *"Are You Ready for a Baby?"* quiz. Trusting Calla with Swan, I dash to my desk where it has been stuffed in the bottom drawer for months.

I find the quiz quickly and don't even bother sitting down. With my stylus in hand, I read each question aloud, answering it with one single gaspy word.

1. *Do you long to feel the warmth of a baby nursing against your breast? YES!*

2. *Do you crave to inhale the warm toasty scent of a baby's head? YES!*

3. *Do you yearn to run your fingertips over a baby's silky skin and tickle its sweet little toes? YES!*

4. *Do you dream about hearing the sound of little pitter patter feet? YES!*

5. *Do you long to change stinky diapers for the next three years of your life? YES!*

I can't believe I even answered "YES" to that last tricky

question. *YES! I'm ready! I want to have a baby!* Joy swells in my heat. And then tears spring to my eyes. I have to stop fooling myself. There is only one man whom I want to father my child. *Gallant.* The man I still love.

My heart clenches in my chest as tears cascade down my face. He's no longer mine; he belongs to another. Having a baby with him is a forgotten dream. I roll my gold wedding band with my thumb. I should just take it off. Throw it in the hearth. I start to wiggle it off, but it's stuck.

Hold on! There's a reason it's not coming off. He's still not hers. For the moment, at least officially, he's *mine!* Yes, *My* Prince. *"Don't let him go. Your Prince comes along only once in a lifetime."* Those were once Elz's words of wisdom. They echo in my head. *"Don't let him go."*

Brainstorm! I'm going to win him back. When Gallant comes home and sees me with Princess Swan and Calla—such a blissful picture of love and domesticity—he'll want to sweep me in his arms, carry me to our bed, and make a baby immediately. *Our baby!* He'll drop Aurora like a hotcake. And I'll forgive him for his errant ways. My heart pounds. I can hardly wait for him to return home!

Now, I'm sorry I tossed Dr. Grimm herbs and birthing stones. A hot, romantic bath with Gallant, washing each other in the magic water, would have been the perfect prelude to a session of explosive let's-have-a-baby lovemaking. But if Elz could get pregnant without all these aides, so can I. It can't be that hard, now that I'm over my maternal ambivalence.

Determined and full of desire, I head back to the great room where I find Calla, still on the couch, playing a game with baby Swan's tiny toes. She tugs on each toe, coming to Swan's teeny pinky toe.

"… and this little piggy went crying all the way home."

The baby gurgles in delight.

"What are you doing?" I ask upon moving to the couch.

"Playing *This Little Piggy.*"

Baby games. I'll need to learn more of them. I ask Calla

if she knows any others. My sweet little girl is more than happy to oblige. In the course of a half hour, I learn a dozen or so Mother Goose nursery rhymes. *Jack and Jill… The Itsy Bitsy Spider… Hickory Dickory Dock…* just to name a few. They're all so fun to say aloud, especially the ones you can act out with your hands and fingers. Princess Swan can't get enough of them, and Calla breaks out in laughter every time I mess up the words or try my hand at making up an original one like *"Henry the Frog who sat on a log… "* My sweet little girl is going to make such a great mother's helper and such a great big sister. My heart swells again with happiness, something I've not felt for a long time.

Calla continues to be the perfect mother's helper, feeding, bathing, and helping me get Swan ready for beddy-bye. After tucking Calla into bed and reading her a good-night story, I gather Swan, sound asleep in her basket, and venture for the first time in days to the chamber I share with Gallant. I gently place the basket on the carpeted floor beside the bed and crawl under the silky sheets. Gallant's intoxicating scent blankets me, making me even more eager for his return. And assault.

Sleep betrays me. The anticipation of Gallant combined with Swan's periodic awakenings—wailing for a diaper change or feeding—prevent me from falling asleep. I toss and turn as my heart grows heavy under the covers. Each time, the grandfather clock downstairs gongs the hour, my heart sinks a little more. No Gallant. My hope gives way to despair and a face full of burning tears.

I finally drift off only to immediately be awakened by Swan's hungry cry. Sunlight filters through the drawn damask drapes. It's dawn.

I pry my eyes open one at a time. With a weary, heavy heart, I stagger out of bed and retrieve one of the bottles I brought upstairs. I gather the wailing infant in my arms. A fat tear falls onto her little face as she happily drains her bottle.

It's Sunday. Having no school, Calla is thrilled to be able to spend the whole day with Swan. She feeds the baby another bottle and changes her into one of the many outfits Cinderella has packed. I try hard to not show my dismay and let it get in the way of her joy. *Why didn't Gallant come home?*

By early afternoon, Calla is eager to get outdoors. "Let's go to Papa's studio and surprise him," she says.

Maybe Gallant pulled another all-nighter. *Maybe.*

Holding Swan bundled up in her basket in one hand and Calla's hand in the other, I stroll down the pebbled, flower-lined path that leads to Gallant's painting studio in the rear of our property. The crisp fall air does little to invigorate me. My emotions teeter between anticipation and dread.

As we near the thatched-roof shed that houses Gallant's studio, Calla breaks away from me and runs over to it. She peeks inside one of the windows and then skips back.

"Papa's not there."

What does she mean? Picking up my pace, I head toward the studio, wanting to have a look for myself. The door is unlocked, and I step inside. Calla's right. He's not here. I survey the space. There's not an open tube of paint or wet canvas in sight. Gloom descends on me. He probably hasn't stepped foot inside here for days.

"I bet Papa's at The Trove buying me a birthday present," exclaims Calla upon joining me.

Calla's ninth birthday is just a few days away. I totally forgot. I've been too wrapped up with Gallant's affair. And even now, my mind is elsewhere. Where can Gallant *really* be?

Only one thought fills my head as we head back to the castle. Aurora. How could I have let myself believe that I could make him still want and love me? I hang my head low. It's a walk of shame.

Thank goodness, Calla is able to get me through the rest of the day. Inside I'm numb. It takes all my effort to do even the littlest task. She feeds Swan her final bottle of the day and helps put her down for the night.

Rocking the baby in her basket, she sings a sweet lullaby—probably one Snow White once sang to her—and the baby falls asleep. Her sweet soprano voice has a calming effect on me. At least for the moment.

"Mommy, what are you going to get me for my birthday?" asks my sweet little girl as I tuck her into her princess bed with Lady Jane. Henry the Frog, safely in his little gilded cage on the nightstand, ribbits.

"It's a surprise," I stammer. The truth is I haven't bought her a thing. Guilt eats away at me.

"What about a new brother or sister?"

Her question rips me apart. All my hopes have evaporated into smoke. Holding back tears, I give her a good-night kiss.

"Mommy, one more thing. Do you think Henry will turn into a prince if I kiss him on my birthday?"

"Maybe." I kiss her one more time.

I can't bring myself to tell her he could turn into a prick.

Alone in the kitchen, I lose it. I consume everything in sight. Even a raw apple, something I never eat. Where the hell is Gallant? Why hasn't he contacted me? Oh my God! *The cat ran away with the fiddle.* What if he's taken off for good with his mistress of evil?

As the grandfather clock strikes nine, the sound of a carriage pulling up to the castle comes from outside. It must be Cinderella and Charming. Of course, they're late. Three hours late.

I meet the royal couple at the front door; they're holding hands. Cinderella is rested and positively radiant. Charming's blue eyes are twinkling, but I can't look him in the face because he reminds me too much of Gallant.

"We had an amazing time!" beams Cinderella. "We ended up going to the Wonderland."

"You'll never guess who we ran into," adds Charming.

Cinderella finishes his sentence. "Gallant and Aurora!"

My heart almost stops. Gallant and Aurora!? Gallant took that Sleeping Beauty tramp to the romantic coastal paradise where he and I spent our honeymoon? Where we made love for the first time. Passionate, endless, magical love. Burning bile rushes to my throat. I'm going to be sick.

"How did Swan do?" asks Cinderella, heading over to the basket by the couch.

"She was a perfect angel," I can barely get the words out; I'm in a state of shock.

As soon as Cinderella and Charming leave with baby Swan, I puke.

With Calla fast asleep and Swan back with her parents, the house is as quiet as a dormouse. Despite my ongoing waves of nausea, I'm too worked up to go to sleep. There's no doubt about it. There never has been. Gallant is having an affair with Sleeping Beauty. *Think, Jane, think.* What should I say to him when he gets home? A gut wrenching pain assaults me. That is, *if* the ugly, cheating bastard ever comes home.

In the candlelit kitchen, I pour myself a goblet of wine. I guzzle it down. I pour another and then another. The wine takes effect quickly. It soothes my ailing soul and makes me drowsy. I'm about to nod off at the kitchen table when the sound of loud, distinctive footsteps startles me. My drunken heart leaps to my throat. It's Gallant!

His tall, muscular body leans against the entryway, his beautiful face flickering in the candlelight.

My hooded eyes fire flaming arrows his way. "Where have you been?"

"I've been working all weekend on a portrait. It's someone important to me."

Someone important to you? You mean that bitch, whore, man-eater—Aurora?

"I'm exhausted. I'm going upstairs."

Of course, he's exhausted. He's been fucking his brains out.

Before I can throw the wine goblet at him, he disappears.

I was wrong. My husband is not an ugly cheating bastard. He's an ugly, *lying*, cheating bastard!

With tears scorching down my face, I stagger to my office. I crumple the *"Are You Ready for a Baby"* quiz in my fist, hurl it into the hearth, and watch it burn.

CHAPTER 12

I wake up in the morning in my private quarters to a pounding headache and regret.

Damn it! I should have confronted Gallant last night. But I never got the chance. When I stormed upstairs in my drunken rage, he was already conked out on our bed. I tried shaking him and yelling his name, but nothing made him budge. Her distinctive floral scent—identical to that of her love letter—was all over him. Couldn't he have had the decency to bathe before coming home? Another wave of nausea came over me, and I had to flee before I threw up all over him.

Maybe it was meant to be as Winnie would say. I was in no state to confront him last night. Too confused and emotional. And too inebriated. It could have gotten ugly and violent.

Though drained, rage is still whipping through my bloodstream. I want a confession! The truth! Wasting no time, I jump out of bed and march down the hallway to our chamber. Or should I say former chamber. I swing open the heavy mahogany door.

"Okay, Gallant. Out with it. What were you doing with Aurora in Wonderland?" My fists clench so tightly my nails dig into my palms. Standing in the doorway, I wait for a response. Not a word. Rage pushes me to yank off the duvet. I've been talking to an empty bed. Gallant is gone.

I race downstairs, my blood pounding. I feel like a pit bull in attack mode. I want to dig my teeth into him and rip out his heart. I frantically search for him, dashing from room to room. He's nowhere to be found.

"Have you seen Prince Gallant?" I snap at one of the servants.

"His Highness left early in the morning for a meeting," says the servant, frightened by my behavior. With a shaking hand, she hands me a note. I recognize the stationary and handwriting immediately—and the nauseating scent. Aurora's!

My Dearest Gallant~

What a wonderful weekend! I can't wait to see you today. Meet me at Sparkles at noon.

Love and kisses~ Aurora

MY Dearest Gallant? Love and kisses? Another secret romantic rendezvous? My heart pounds so hard against my chest it may actually leap out. I tear the note to shreds, only to regret that I've destroyed yet another piece of evidence. That's it. Sleeping Beauty, you're going down.

⚬⚬⚬

Another emergency girlfriend meeting at Sparkles. Except it's only Elz. She tells me that Winnie couldn't make it. "She's meeting with The Queen to go over details for the opening of the museum." I cringe. Gallant's gala!

I share Cinderella's encounter with Gallant and Aurora. And then the note.

"Wow! Wonderland sounds amazing! Do you think Gallant can get Rump and me a discount?" She stuffs a cupcake into her mouth. "We could take a pre-baby holiday."

Sheesh! I'm losing a husband, and she's trying to score discounts? I'm in a state of total panic. In less than fifteen minutes, Gallant and Aurora will be sitting here goo-goo eyed and feeding each other cupcakes. And licking the frosting off each other's fingers. I wish Winnie were here to give me advice. On second thought, she'd probably say that I'm freaking out for no reason. That there's still no proof Gallant is having an affair with Aurora.

You know what, I've had it with Elz and especially Winnie. What is wrong with them? They're my girlfriends. My best friends. They're supposed to be helping me bring Gallant down. Winnie's actually supporting Gallant by planning his retrospective at the museum. A true friend would have figured a graceful way to decline. Or, at least, consulted me on what poison to feed the man-eater should she attend.

"Maybe you should just hang out here until noon," singsongs Elz. "You can catch them in the act!"

Another one of Elz's absurdly naïve ideas. I want to shake her, baby or no baby. Of course, Gallant's not going to let on that he's having an affair with Aurora right in front of me. He may be an asshole, but he's not stupid.

A pudgy server, who's close to bursting out of his skin-hugging jester uniform, brings us another round of cupcakes. The bells on his silly three-pointed hat jingle as he lowers the platter to the table. *Jingle. Jingle. Jingle.* Brainstorm! Elz's suggestion was a good one after all. I grab the waiter by an arm.

"Here are five gold pieces for the cupcakes. And fifty for your costume."

As the server eagerly pockets the coins, Elz gazes at me with bewilderment.

"My treat." I smile wickedly.

⊸•⊷

Damn it! I can barely get into this ridiculous costume. I know I've put on some pounds, but not this many. I'd better cut out all these cupcakes before I turn into a fat cow.

In the corner of Sparkles' hectic kitchen where batches of

cupcakes are being baked, I finally manage to wiggle into the tight, stretchy one-piece jester suit. I adjust the jingling fool's hat on my head, tucking my hair inside it, and snap open my mirror locket for a quick peek at myself. Dragonballs! Even in this absurd get-up, I still look like myself. Gallant will recognize me in a heartbeat. My pulse is racing. Time is running out. One for promptness, he'll be here any minute.

Okay, Jane, think! Remember, you're a master of disguise. Yes, a master! When I was at Faraway, I disguised myself as Fanta. No one recognized me, and I managed to escape. Well, almost. And then there were those old hag disguises I used when I tried to kill Snow White. They were brilliant! Although in the end, they failed me too. A tinge of sadness sneaks up on me. Poor Snow White! I bet Gallant cheated on her too! Bastard!

"Hey, you, over there! Get to work!" yells the manager, a short dumpy man with rolls of chins. He obviously eats too many cupcakes. "Bring this tray of cupcakes to table thirteen. They're complaining that their waiter's disappeared."

I can't go out there! What if Gallant and Aurora are there? The rude manager thrusts the tray at me and shoves me toward the exit, past a huge wad of dough and vat full of chocolate chips. *Jingle! Jingle! Jingle!* Another brainstorm! On the way out, I stealthily grab a clump of the dough and slap it on my nose. And then I grab a handful of chocolate chips, lick them, and stick them all over my face. Perfect moles! I'm a creative genius. I'm unrecognizable.

Being a server is ridiculously hard work. Racing back and forth to the kitchen. Carrying heavy trays. Cleaning up messy leftovers. And it's totally demeaning. I never knew how truly rude royals can be. And cheap! The princess at the last table I waited on had me get her six different cupcakes until she tasted the one she liked, and she didn't even leave me a tip!

All this grueling work had better pay off. It's noon. Where is Gallant? My heart skips a beat when he at last strides in. He sits down at a table. For two! *Okay, Jane. Take a deep breath. Get your act together.*

Quaking inside, I head over to his table. "Can I get you something?" I ask in the deepest, manliest voice I can muster.

"I am waiting for someone."

"Oh, your wife?"

"Hardly," he chuckles.

No kidding. Every bone in my body is jointed with evil. I want to take a knife and cut out his heart. And put it in the center of a cupcake. And then bite into it.

My fantasy is cut short by the sweeping entrance of a tall, elegantly dressed woman with a lean, athletic build. The mesmerizing blonde who was at Swan's coming out party. All eyes are on her, including mine. Her golden tresses cascade past her waist; her flawless skin is the color of honey, and her deep-set eyes are two sparkling blue gems. My eyes grow wide as she breezes over to Gallant's table.

"Aurora!" Gallant rises to his feet and embraces her.

This is Aurora? I swallow so hard I almost choke. She's blond and gorgeous! A female version of Gallant! Like attracts like! I feel sick to my stomach.

A beaming Gallant graciously pulls out a chair out for her. "I'm so glad you could make it, darling."

Darling? He called her "darling?" Sweat is pouring from every crevice of my body. *Stay calm. Don't blow your cover.* Wiping my brow, I accidentally knock off one of my chocolate moles. It lands on their table.

"Don't eat that!" I spit out the words and hastily brush the chocolate bit off the tablecloth.

Gallant eyes me strangely. "Server, we shall have some tea and a couple of cupcakes. Surprise us." He clasps Aurora's slender hands in his.

My stomach twists into a ball while my heart gallops. I can't leave the two of them alone!

"Um, nice weather," I stammer. *Procrastinate!* "Um, do the two of you come here often?"

"Can you get our order now, please?" Gallant looks and sounds annoyed. "We are in a bit of a hurry."

He can't wait to do it with her! The thought of them naked, entangled in bed, completely paralyzes me. I can't breathe! I can't move!

Gallant furrows his brows. "Server, please do not force me to talk to the manager. We would like our order."

"Um, right away," I finally sputter. I don't know how I manage to get my two feet to walk.

When I return with their order, Aurora is holding up a sheet of parchment. She studies it. Admiration fills her eyes, followed by tinge of melancholy that makes her look even more glamorous—and seductive.

"I love it!" she exclaims.

Holding the tray with their order, I peer over her shoulder. Oh my God! It's a sketch of Aurora showing off her amazing body in a skimpy pair of lacy briefs and a matching brassiere. I recognize the setting instantly. It's the Wonderland blue lagoon—where Gallant and I made passionate love for the first time!

I am shaking like a flickering flame on its way out. I barely have the strength to stand up. The tray plunges from my hand. CRASH! Aurora lets out a yelp. A cup of hot tea has landed on her lap while the other teacup and the plates with the cupcakes have smashed to pieces on the ground.

"Look what you've done!" says Gallant, his voice harsh.

It's all your fault, you scumbag! I want to scream back.

He rushes to Aurora's side. "Darling, are you all right?"

"I'm fine," she says calmly and looks down at her dress. "Just a little tea stain. Thank goodness, nothing happened to the sketch!" She gazes at it again and smiles. I want to rip it into a thousand pieces and bury her with the scraps.

Gallant grabs her hand. "Come, darling. Let me take you to The Ballgown Emporium. Buying you a new dress is the least I can do."

What! He's going to take *her* shopping for a new gorgeous gown! With *our* money! At *my* fairy godmother's boutique!

To add insult to injury, he marches out of Sparkles—with the man-eater on his arm—without leaving me a tip.

I'm fuming. This is war! There's no time to waste. It's time to take the enemy on. Clad in my ridiculous jester getup, I take off after them. I've only gotten five steps beyond Sparkles when someone tackles me from behind and knocks me hard to the pavement. It's the manager.

"Where do you think you're going, young man?" he barks.

"Shopping," I snap back at him in my normal voice.

The man yanks me to my feet and steers me by the elbow back to Sparkles' kitchen.

"Don't you know you can go to jail for harassment?" I scream, my voice shrill. My former co-workers gaze at me, perplexed.

The scowling manager shrugs and thrusts a broom into my hand. "You need to clean up the mess you've made and pay for the damage you've caused. And then you're fired!"

Quitting is not an option.

———◆———

After paying for the broken plates and the two smooshed cupcakes, I sprint out the door, promising the disgruntled manager I will wash and return the jester costume. The Ballgown Emporium is just a few stores away. With luck, I can still catch them. While running, my fake nose falls off. Gallant will recognize me, but I no longer care.

Breathlessly, I storm into the store and search everywhere for Gallant and Aurora. They're nowhere in sight. Dragonballs! How could she have found something new to wear so fast?

"My dear, what are you doing here?" I'd recognize that booming voice anywhere. I spin around. It's The Queen.

Taken aback, I make a nervous little "hello" gesture with

my fingers. The Queen circles around me, scrutinizing me from head to toe.

"I simply love what you are wearing! A jumpsuit! It is so fashion forward! You must tell me where you got it!"

"It's mail order," I stammer. "Actually, it's not my style. You can have it!"

"Wonderful!" beams The Queen. "I shall send for it later. I may even wear it to Gallant's retrospective."

"Have you seen Gallant?" I ask.

"You just missed him. He was here shopping with Aurora."

She knows Aurora? Of course, she and Gallant were childhood sweethearts.

"It has been years since I last saw her. She and Gallant used to be so close. I always hoped that he would marry a girl just like her."

Gallant's mother wanted him to marry her! I've heard enough.

"I am so delighted he is bringing her to the retrospective."

A painful knot forms in my stomach. He's taking *her* to the most important event in his career? Instead of me? Just when and how is he going to break the news to me?

"Aurora said he has a big surprise in store for everyone."

A burning sensation rips through my heart. It'll be official. Gallant is going to announce that he's leaving me for Aurora. His first true love. The woman he would have married had he had the chance.

"And Dear, by the way, what are those horrible growths on your face? You must really see a doctor and get them taken care of before the gala."

The Queen wanders off. I've heard *more* than enough. I'm about to blow!

"Dahling!" comes an effusive, nearby voice. It's my fairy godmother, Emperor Armando. Heading my way, he gives me his signature double-cheek kiss. He licks his lips. Holy crap! He's eaten one of my fake moles.

"Armando, did you just see my husband with a tall blond

woman?" I ask anxiously. I can't bring myself to say beautiful.

"You mean Aurora?"

The hair on the back of my neck stands up. Armando knows her too?

"Dahling, he bought her a fabulous dress from my new ready-to-wear collection." He hooks his arm in mine and squires me over to a rack of gorgeous gowns that are perfect for both everyday wear and glamorous balls.

"I can't keep them in stock. They sell out as fast as I make them," he beams.

"Which one did he buy her?" The words fly out of my mouth.

Armando pulls out a stunning silk magenta gown with a large white satin collar. "She took the 4 and wore it out the store."

"I'll take it in 6."

Armando gives me the once-over. "Dahling, I'd recommend the 8. Maybe, even to go with the 10."

I buy the 8. Magenta isn't even my color.

"He also bought her this." Armando sashays over to another rack.

What? He bought her another gown? My blood is boiling.

The Emperor returns, holding up a magnificent black taffeta gown. "They've been flying out the store!"

My jaw drops. The long full skirt billows like a cloud. On the backside, there is an enormous batwing bow, that makes the dress look like it can actually fly, and a long, dramatic train. I can feel my face reddening and my temperature rising. The asshole bought *her* a dress that is *so me!*

"She looked drop-dead gorgeous in it," gushes the Emperor.

Drop dead are the only two words that resonate with me.

"Gallant insisted that she wear it to the museum gala. Especially since all eyes are going to be on her."

My heart sinks to my stomach. Armando has essentially confirmed what The Queen just told me. Gallant is going to announce his engagement to Aurora at the museum opening! Our marriage is over! I blow a breath of air that's as fiery as a dragon's.

"Dahling, are you sure you're okay?" asks Armando.

"I'll take it," I snap.

"But dahling, this one is a sample Size 6, and it runs small. Really, you should go with the 10." He scans my body again and shakes his head in dismay. "Maybe even the 12."

I snatch the dress from him.

"Dahling, is there anything you want to tell me?" ask Armando.

"Charge everything to The Prince," I say as I tear out of the store. Or should I say ex-husband?

I'm so mad I can kill. Weaving my way to the valet, I know I look insane. Children regard me with terror in their eyes and grip the hands of their mothers, who hastily move away. It doesn't help that I'm still wearing the jester getup. And that I'm picking off the remaining chocolate moles from my face. The faster I get out of here, the better.

When I get to the valet, my body stiffens, and my eyes almost pop out of their sockets. I don't believe it! She's standing in line! Aurora, the mistress of evil! Although her back is to me, making it impossible to see her face, her shimmering cascade of golden hair is unmistakable, and she's wearing the magenta gown. And in her hand is an oversized Ballgown Emporium shopping bag.

I feel like a falcon that's found her prey. Without wasting a second, I tackle her from behind, knocking her facedown to the ground.

Straddling her back to hold her down, I pull her hair and claw at her dress. Screaming, she struggles to free herself and manages to roll over. Her face is contorted and in shock. And so is mine. Holy Shit! It's *not* Aurora!

Suddenly, two sharp pointed objects press deep into my temples. And then, someone practically yanks my arms out of their sockets, jolting me to a standing position. My eyes dart left and right. I'm being held prisoner by four armed guards, two of which are holding spears to my head. They look authoritative and scary mean.

"She attacked me!" cries the would-be Aurora, her eyes brimming with contempt. After one of the guards helps her to her feet, she gathers her shopping bag and mounts her coach.

"You're under arrest!" barks one of the guards.

Oh no! I'm going back to that dark dreary dungeon where I wrongly spent seven years of my life for Snow White's attempted murder. I can already see the headline in tomorrow's *Fairytale Tattler*: *"Mall Madness: Ex-Evil Queen Attacks Shopping Beauty!"*

Oh, God. How is this going to look? How am I going to explain this to everyone I know? The King? The Queen? Sweet Calla? Even worse, I've made it so easy for Gallant to marry his Sleeping Beauty! Insanity… the perfect grounds for a divorce.

"Wait! You don't know who I am!" I plea. "I can explain everything!"

The guards respond with look that says: we don't give a flying fairy's ass who you are.

In desperation, I struggle to break loose of their grip, writhing and kicking. Defending himself, one of the armed guards slams me to the ground. My eyes look up. A five-foot blade is about to penetrate my skull! *Say good-bye to your life, Jane!*

"Okay, okay, take me away!" I say as submissively as I can.

———

The dungeon is exactly how I remember it. Dark and dreary. Even that green ogre, who brought me my meals and told me I was going to Faraway, is still here.

"Nice to see you again," he says.

I give him one of those big fakes smiles I so detest. There's a reason he's never gotten a promotion, I think to myself.

"I'll be back with your dinner."

I'm sure the food still sucks. At least, I'll shed a few pounds while I'm here.

I pace the crammed cell and begin to angst out. Poor Calla! She must be freaking out, not knowing where I am. What if she thinks something terrible happened to me? My thoughts turn angry, and I seethe. Gallant's probably too busy with Aurora to even notice I'm not around.

The ogre returns. But instead of carrying a tray, he's holding a large metal key.

"You're getting out of here."

Did I hear that right? He unlocks the cell door and sets me free.

"Hello, dahling!" comes a very familiar voice. It's Emperor Armando. I run over to hug him. When I wrap my arms around his bearish body, my anger gives way to tears of relief. It's the first time all day I feel comforted. I bury my head against his pillowy chest.

"How did you know I was here?" I sniffle.

He tilts up my chin with his large hand. "Dahling, have you forgotten that I *am* your fairy godmother?"

Magic.

"I told these lovely people that these silly little skirmishes happen all the time. Women are always fighting over my creations."

"And they believed you?" I ask, my tears subsiding.

"Of course, dahling, especially after I offered to invite their wives to a private 80% off event. No one can resist a sale."

I hug my fairy godmother again, even harder. I'm so lucky to have her. I mean, him. He tells me not to worry about the two gowns; he'll have them delivered to my palace. To tell the truth, I totally forgot about them.

"Jane, dahling, are you sure there's nothing you want to tell me?"

I shake my head. "I just want to go home."

I'm too exhausted to dwell on Size 4 Aurora.

———❦———

It's almost midnight when I get back to the palace. Holding a candle, I tiptoe upstairs and check on Calla; she's sleeping peacefully. Lady Jane is in her arms, and Henry the Frog is in his cage on the nightstand next to her bed. He lets out a ribbit.

I pad down the hallway and peek into the chamber I share with Gallant. The bed is empty. My heart should sink with sorrow but instead pounds with rage. He must still be with Sleeping Beauty. I hate her! I hate her! For taking Gallant away from me. And for almost costing me years of my life.

Rage gives way to fatigue. Barely able to keep my eyes open, I retreat to my private chamber. I drift off quickly, but the nightmare of my stillborn awakens me. Cold sweat soaks my body, and I hug myself to ward off the chill that ripples through me.

This has been definitely been the worst day of my marriage. And it's all because of Aurora. With the force of a tidal wave, depression washes over me. I succumb to what I've needed to do all day. I sob.

CHAPTER 13

Mommy, where were you last night?" Calla asks me as she packs her school bag. "I was worried."

"Mommy was out having fun." I serve my sweet little girl her breakfast. "Who put you to bed?"

"Papa did," she says with a dimpled smile.

So, the swine came home and left again to be with the Sleeping Slut, leaving Calla in the care of our servants.

"Was Papa worried about me?"

"Papa told me not to worry. He said bad things don't happen to good people."

HA! He thinks I'm good? Evil is seeping back into my veins like a speeding bullet.

Not long after Calla departs for school, a loud rap sounds at the front door. My heart quivers. Can it be that egghead reporter from the *Fairytale Tattler* here to get the scoop on my arrest? Or another secret love letter from Aurora?

Not this time. It's an elfin messenger with a large, meticulously wrapped package for me. My eyes widen, and my heartbeat accelerates. Has Gallant finally come to his senses? Has he bought me an extravagant present to mend our relationship? To prove it's me he loves, not her.

I sign for the box and rip off the wrapping. Inside, under layers of delicate tissue paper, there's a sealed letter and a stunning black gown with shimmering layers of tulle. A stunning *familiar* gown that used to hang in my closet. I tear open the letter.

Dear Jane~

I needed to write this to get things off my chest. Your preoccupation with Aurora is getting in the way of our friendship. Your insistence that I sympathize with you is too demanding and unfair. It would be best if we don't see each other for a while.

Yours~

Winnie

PS I am returning herewith the black dress you lent me for the museum gala.

I read the letter again. What nerve! Two can play at this game. Tossing both the dress and letter onto the floor, I scurry to my desk. I'm going to give Winnie a piece of my mind. Taking a stylus to a sheet of parchment, I scrawl:

Winnie:

I regret that I have had to come to this decision. You and I can no longer be friends. We no longer see eye to eye. As you well know, I've been going through a major crisis in my marriage, and you have not been there for me. Not one bit!

Your former friend,

Jane

PS You can keep the black dress. I don't want it.

HA! I'm a much better writer than she is. When she gets my letter—with the black dress—she's going to get what she deserves. Pain!

I stuff the dress along with the letter back into Winnie's box, X-out my address, replacing it with hers, and run out the front door to catch the messenger. Unfortunately, he's already gone. I'll just bring it to the postal office after my appointment with Shrink.

I head back inside, stopping in the doorway for a long moment. A slew of emotions bombards my head. Sadness. Anger. Remorse. Despair. First, Gallant. Now Winnie. How much more pain can I bear?

———◆———

Sitting upright in the chaise, I tell Shrink everything about yesterday. Minus the little trip to the dungeon. I've met the man-eater. I've witnessed Gallant's amorous behavior with her. And I have confirmation from The Queen herself that they've been in love forever and are planning to announce their engagement at Gallant's museum gala.

Shrink buzzes around her office. I grow impatient for a response. What more can I possibly say or do to prove that Gallant is having an affair with Aurora?

She settles on the arm of the chaise and crosses her tiny legs. Her wings flutter.

"Jane, *why* do you think Gallant is having an affair?" she asks matter-of-factly.

Her question throws me for a loop; I wasn't expecting it. I haven't given this much thought.

"Because he's found someone younger and prettier," I falter. Who am I kidding? She's gorgeous! A mirror image of Gallant!

"Has Gallant not ever found you attractive?"

It's true. While I'm definitely no longer *Fairest of All,* he's always told me how beautiful I am. Just not lately. Before

I can respond, Shrink fires another question.

"Can you think of another reason?"

"I'm not rich enough for him. We've had to depend on his parents to support his painting career." I fidget with my locket. "She's a princess millionairess."

"Has money ever been source of friction in your marriage?"

Not really. I shake my head.

"Has sex been disappointing for the two of you?"

Hey! That's none of her business. But the answer is no. Making love with Gallant has been pure magic. For both of us.

"Can you think of anything else?"

I don't have to think hard. "I haven't been able to give him a baby," I blurt out. "He's given up on me."

"Has he ever told you that he's frustrated with your inability to conceive?"

I shake my head side to side again. I'm getting irritable. Where is she going with these questions?

Shrink takes another spin around the room and then hovers over me. She looks straight into my eyes with unsettling intensity.

"Jane, you've been focusing on finding evidence proving that Gallant is having an affair. Quite frankly, I am more interested in evidence proving that Gallant *wants* to have an affair."

I've done all this hard work, even risked my life with that fire-breathing dragon, to prove that Gallant is having an affair. And now this flying bug of a woman who calls herself a therapist is asking me to go down a whole different road?

The chime sounds. I bolt off the chaise. I've had it with Gallant! I've had it with Winnie. And now, I've had it with Shrink. I've made up my mind. I'm going to stop seeing her. My next visit will be my last.

Fuming, I storm out of Shrink's office and run smack into

Winnie! HA! So, the end of our friendship has driven her to see Shrink. Desperation is scrawled on her face. Serves her right!

The good news is I no longer have to go to the postal office. I can just hand my ex-BFF my resignation letter and the black gown. Dragonballs! I've left the package in Shrink's office. As I turn back for it, Winnie tugs at my arm.

"Jane, Wait! I've been looking all over for you." Her voice is panicky.

I swivel my head and meet her gaze. What does *she* want? We haven't talked to or seen each other for almost a week. Which in girlfriend time is like a year. And to tell the truth, I'm not so sure I want her back in my life. Friends are supposed to be there for you. Support you. Make you feel better. Help you solve your problems. Let you cry on their shoulder. Agree with you when you tell them someone has been a shit, right? Well, Winnie's done none of these things. Not one. All she's done is challenge Gallant's affair with Aurora and make me feel stupid.

"What's up?" I ask frostily.

Tears fill Winnie's eyes. Sheesh. She's resorted to crying so that we can be friends again. I'm not going to fall for her manipulative drama queen tactic.

"It's Elz," she splutters. "She may lose her baby and needs you."

Oh my God! Poor Elz! This can't be happening!

"Let's take my coach," I say. "It's faster."

———◦———

The coach ride to Elz's house seems like eternity. Even though it's only a few miles away. Winnie and I face each other in silence. My head is spinning. I'm beyond worried about Elz, yet I can't help wondering what's going on inside Winnie's head. Is she thinking about Elz or about how much she hates me? Oddly, the last thing on my mind is Gallant.

At last, Winnie breaks the strained silence.

"Hansel told me he has a crush on Calla."

More silence. I gaze out the window and then face her. Our eyes connect.

"He'd better stand in line. Calla has a crush on a frog," I say bluntly.

Silence again. Winnie looks at me blankly. Suddenly, she bursts out in laughter.

"A frog!?" she manages to say between hysterics.

"Honestly!" Winnie's laughter is contagious. I can barely contain myself or get the words out. "Yes, she thinks this frog she's found is cursed with an evil spell and will turn into a prince when she kisses him."

"An enchanted frog!?" Winnie is bent over with laughter. "That's the funniest thing I've ever heard."

"Totally!" I howl, laughing even harder. And before I know it, I'm laughing so hard I'm crying. Really crying. Burning-hot, remorseful tears. And Winnie is doing the same.

"Winnie, I couldn't live with you," I splutter.

"The same," says Winnie, wiping my tears and then hers. "I'm sorry I haven't been a good friend."

"No, don't be sorry. It's my fault. I've been too wrapped up with myself." I blink back more tears and clasp her hands in mine. "I didn't even celebrate Elz's pregnancy with you."

Winnie's face grows solemn, and she squeezes my hand. "She might lose the baby."

"What happened?" I ask anxiously.

Winnie tells me how she and Elz were window shopping for baby clothes when suddenly Elz fell ill. By the time, Winnie got her home, poor Elz was experiencing terrible, gut-wrenching cramps. Winnie stayed with her while Rump took off to summon Dr. Grimm.

"Faster, driver!" I yell.

Silently, I pray for Elz. And thank God that Winnie is back in my life. Leaving the package with the letter and the dress behind in Shrink's office was fortuitous. I'll send someone to retrieve it later and give the dress back to Winnie the next time I see her. As for the letter, I'm going to burn it.

———

Elz's crystal palace is fabled throughout Lalaland. She designed it herself and had the Seven Dwarfs build it according to her plans.

There was no way she was going to live with Rump in her late mother, Lady Germaine's house, which she inherited. It was too big, too dark, and too rundown. And it had too many bad memories. So she tore it down and, with the fortune she made from her shoe empire, she built her dream house.

Much like her flagship boutique, The Glass Slipper, it's a little gem. Because the entire palace is made of crystal, light shines through it everywhere. Sparkly chandeliers dangle from the high ceilings and create dancing rainbows on the sleek white furnishings when the sun bounces off them. All the main rooms, including the bedrooms are on the first level; Elz didn't want Rump to have to climb up a flight of stairs with his bad leg. Upstairs is her design studio. You can see right up to it because the floors are crystal clear.

As Winnie and I pull up to the palace, Dr. Grimm is departing. Hunched over and head down, he looks downtrodden. Like he's lost his quest to take over the world. Holding hands, we jump out of the coach.

The little doctor takes off his spectacles and rubs his tired, sunken eyes. Without their sparkle, he looks a lot like his morose brother. His eyes meet ours. I squeeze Winnie's hand tightly, and my heart hammers.

He shakes his head glumly. "I did all I could, but I'm not a magician."

Oh no! Elz has died! Tears flood my eyes.

"She lost a lot of blood, but she'll be alright."

I breathe a loud sigh of relief; Winnie does the same.

"What about the baby?" I ask anxiously.

Dr. Grimm shakes his head. He cannot mask his disappointment. "She needs you now." He solemnly mounts his delivery coach, a traveling advertisement for his practice. *"Where Fairy Tales are Born."* Not this time.

The brightness of Elz's palace creates an odd disconnect with the dark tragedy that has just taken place inside. Rump looks terrible. His eyes are bloodshot, his face blotchy, and his limp is more pronounced than usual. The little man looks like the whole world has come tumbling down upon him.

His tear-soaked eyes meet mine. Tears roll down my cheeks as I run over to hug him. What a special place he holds in my heart. He was one of my first friends at Faraway. He made me keepsake name bracelets, my most treasured being the gift Calla gave me on the day of my marriage to Gallant. The one that has "Mommy" woven into the golden threads. Sadly, he won't be making a Mommy-bracelet for his beloved Elz.

"It's all m-my f-fault," stammers Rump, agonizing to get the words out. He has regressed to stuttering so badly that it's painful to watch and listen to him.

Winnie pulls me aside and whispers in my ear that Rump is blaming himself for Elz's miscarriage. That he's being punished for once trying to extort the firstborn of a kindly queen. Now, by a twist of fate, God has claimed *his* first child.

Poor Rump! He's paid a thousand times over for his crime. After the queen outsmarted him by fortuitously discovering his complicated name, Rumpelstiltskin, he furiously stamped his foot deep into the earth, leaving him a cripple and an amnesiac who couldn't even remember his name until Faraway helped come to grips with his tainted childhood. A painful, twisted childhood filled with mockery and bullying that drove the deformed troll to become an evil trickster. And as if the limp was not a big enough reminder of his sins, the amnesia left him with a permanent stammer. But neither of these physical hardships has gotten in the way of his road to recovery. The former troubled trickster has become one of the kindest, most selfless people in all of Lalaland. Honestly, he would give his life to anyone! Everyone adores him. And now, he has to suffer again. Life is so unfair. My poor sweet Rump!

"Rump, you must stop blaming yourself," I tell him, brushing away his tears.

"I've told him it's meant to be," says Winnie. "That nature has her way of making things happen for a reason."

I'm not sure it's meant to be, but I do believe that God took Elz and Rump's firstborn for a good reason. Not as a punishment. But as a blessing.

"Rump, there was something not right with the baby. Elz lost it so that it did not have to come into this world and bear the pain you bore as a child."

Rump's forlorn eyes look up at me, and I can tell that he's replaying memories of his childhood, many of which he's shared in our EPA meetings. Years of mean-spirited youngsters mocking him for his deformities—his dwarfed body, big bulbous nose, and large protruding ears. No, Rump would not want to have a child who had to endure his pain.

For the first time, Rump smiles. It's a faint smile, but nonetheless a smile. Winnie and I exchange a look of relief.

"Jane," says Rump, "I b-beg you to talk to Elzmerelda." His stuttering has lessened. "She's in-c-consolable. She won't even talk to m-me."

I draw the little man close to me. "Give me ten minutes and then go to her."

———

Elz is in the bedroom she shares with Rump, her pillar-like body bundled under a fluffy white comforter. Her face is wan and tear-stained. Her sobs are needles in my heart.

Quietly, I slip into bed with her. Under the covers. Just like I did when her mother died at Faraway. Her long, limp body is cold. Like something inside her has died.

"Elz, you must stop crying," I say softly, smoothing her

damp, matted hair.

She bawls louder. "Rump wanted the baby so badly," she splutters between sobs. "I've let him down."

"No, no, you haven't. He thinks it's all his fault."

Elz abruptly stops crying. "It's *not* his fault!" She jerks herself up to a sitting position.

I hastily plump up pillows and gently lower her to a resting position. "Elz, it's no one's fault. Sometimes these things happen for a good reason."

"Jane, what was your miscarriage like?" she asks weakly.

My miscarriage. The blood, the pain, the sorrow. I relive it almost every night. A sickening feeling sweeps over me.

"Elz, what you've gone through is tragic and not any less tragic than what I went through. But thank goodness, you didn't have to give birth to a stillborn child. Hold its lifeless little body in your arms and then have it taken away from you forever." My eyes grow watery. I take a deep breath to stifle an onslaught of tears.

"Jane, you poor thing!" cries Elz. It's just like Elz to think more about others than herself in her moment of need. Still weak, she bolsters herself up and wraps her spindly arms around me. I draw her close to me, and we rest our heads on each other's shoulders. We're bonded like sisters.

Elz looks up at me. "We didn't have a girl's name picked out, but were going to name the baby, if it was a boy—"

"Bob," says Rump as he swings open the bedroom door and teeter-totters toward us.

"Bob?" I exclaim as I slip out of the bed. "That's one of the funniest name I've ever heard."

Elz immediately comes to Rump's defense. "Rump wanted our son to have a name that was easy to say, and everyone could remember. Even if you spell it backward, it's still Bob."

B-O-B. B-O-B. What do you know, she's right.

Rump climbs onto the bed and runs his stumpy fingers through Elz's long mousy hair. Their eyes meet and then they kiss. A passionate kiss that has no shame. My skin prickles. They make such an odd couple but such a perfect one.

"Elzy, we're going to have Baby Bob one day," declares Rump without a trace of a stutter.

"Rumpster, maybe we should think of another name," says Elz in her almost back to normal singsong voice.

I slip out of the room, leaving the two lovebirds alone. Embracing. They don't notice me leaving.

My short-lived sense of relief is replaced by malaise as I head back to Winnie. How lucky Elz is to have Rump. A man who loves her unconditionally! Who yearns to have her baby! Gallant and I don't even have cute nicknames for each other.

Winnie and I decide to walk home. After the all the drama with Elz, we both need some fresh air. And besides, the day is beautiful. The leaves have changed into hues of orange, yellow, and red, and the crisp autumn air is refreshing. Plus, a walk will give the two of us a chance to catch up.

Winnie bends over to pick up a large orange-red leaf that closely matches the color of her flaming hair. She hooks her arm in mine.

"What are you doing for Calla's birthday?"

She reminds me. Calla's turning nine tomorrow. All the drama in my life has put her birthday on the back burner. Damn Gallant!

"I'm not sure yet," I say, trying to hide my guilt. "Whatever we do, it's not going to be grand. Maybe just a few kids from her class."

"I hope Hansel, Gretel, and Curley are invited."

"Of course!" I laugh. Winnie's children and Calla are best friends. Their closeness has made the two of us even closer.

Winnie twirls her leaf and smiles. "Hansel is planning on proposing. He even had Rump make a love bracelet—H+C4EVER."

Forever. Nothing is forever. Especially love. I'm too jaded to appreciate the charm of this innocent infatuation.

"Well, he'd better plan on having his heart broken because Calla's in love with Henry."

"Henry?"

"Her enchanted frog."

Winnie grins. "I think he can handle the competition."

If only I could handle my competition. We pass an orchard full of trees bearing bright red apples. One of them is all I need to eliminate her.

"Don't go there," says a loud voice in my head.

Winnie picks up another leaf. This time, one that's toasty brown, like the color of her freckles. "Let me know if I can do anything to help."

"Thanks. I will." It's a relief to know that my event-planner friend is still always there for me. I love Winnie.

For the next half-hour or so, we stroll through the countryside in silence. Winnie stoops occasionally to pick up a fanciful leaf to add to her collection. I should be focusing on Calla's birthday—I still haven't even bought her a present—but instead all I can think about is Gallant and Aurora. Thoughts swirl around in my head like the autumn leaves. What kinds of thing do they talk about? What is she like in bed? Does Gallant make her explode like he does me?

"Don't go there," that voice inside my head whispers. A strong gust of wind stops my mind from wandering dangerously and breaks our silence.

"What's going on with you and Gallant?" asks Winnie, adjusting her cloak.

A chill rushes through my body. I thought she was deliberately avoiding this delicate subject. The source of our rift.

For a minute, I think about changing the subject but instead find myself spewing out everything that's happened since the last time we saw each other. I spend considerable time on yesterday's events at The Trove.

Winnie listens without interrupting me once. When I'm

done catching her up, I take a deep breath. Sharing all this negative stuff with Winnie has had cathartic effect on me. I feel better. Now, I must prepare myself for Winnie's response. She's going to tell me again that I'm jumping to conclusions. *Okay, Winnie, lay it on. I can handle it.*

I turn to her, anxiously awaiting a response. Her pretty profile is pensive, almost solemn. Unexpectedly, she turns to me and envelops me in her arms.

"You poor thing!" she says, like a mother comforting a child who's scraped her knee.

Tears trickle down my face. I'm not sure if I'm crying because of Gallant's infidelity or Winnie's reaction. Or a combination of both.

Winnie brushes away the tears with her cloak. "What are you going to do?"

"I don't know." I shake my head. "What do you think I should do?" Winnie with all her wisdom will have the answer.

Winnie takes a deep inhale and tosses her leaves into the air. She gazes up at them as they waltz around the sky.

"Jane, I have to tell you something." She pauses. "Something I've never told anyone."

I look at her, perplexed. I thought we kept no secrets from each other.

She takes another deep breath. "John once had an affair."

I'm shocked. Virtually speechless. How awful that she's kept her husband's indiscretion inside her so long. No wonder she's had such a hard time listening to me blabber on about Gallant's affair. It probably triggered memories of a time she's wanted to forget.

"Did you confront him?" I ask at last.

"No, I never let him know that I knew." She sighs. "I can't blame him. I was a two-hundred pound bitter woman."

John's lack of attention toward Winnie drove her to become an emotional overeater. I wonder if his affair made her fatter and bitter. "What was she like?" I ask cautiously.

"She was really a no-one. A plain goose girl who had a reputation of being a shrew. John was not her only conquest."

"How did you know John was having an affair with her?" My curiosity is getting the better of me.

"I was suspicious and hired someone to follow him. The investigator caught them embracing in his cobbler shop. At least, he had the decency not to bring her into our house with the children."

Rage is racing through me. I battle the urge to stomp to Winnie's house and punch John out.

Winnie's eyes grow watery. She takes another deep breath.

"Jane, I let it go."

"Why?" *How could she?*

"Because I loved him. And I believed deep inside he loved me."

I listen intently, speechless.

"Jane, John and I have been married for fifteen years. A marriage is a lot of work. There are good times and bad times. But at the end of the day, you have to decide if this is the man whose hand you want to hold for the rest of your life and with whom you want raise your children."

I digest her words. "Are you happy you stayed with John?" I ask tentatively.

A wide smile spreads across her freckled face. "Yes. We've never been happier."

I flashback to visitor's day at Faraway, the day Winnie and John reconciled in front of all us in Dr. Grimm's group session. How for the first time in my life I witnessed what I believed was true love when he took her in his arms and begged her to come home. To be his wife and the mother of their children. I believe her.

The sun starts to set, and I silently admire the blushing autumn sky. Leaves continue to fall lazily to the ground all around us. We trod on in silence until we reach a fork in the road; one path leads to Winnie's house, the other to mine. We hold each other in a hug for a long time and finally say goodbye.

The air gets chillier. I hug myself to keep warm and wonder which road I need to take with Gallant.

CHAPTER 14

"Mommy, they're here!" Shouts Calla as I finish braiding her golden tresses. Her big brown eyes are popping with excitement.

Leaving Lady Jane and caged up Henry behind, she skips downstairs to greet Hansel, Gretel, and Curley. She didn't even give me a chance to hug her and wish her a Happy Birthday. Nine! I guess she's reached the age where she'd rather spend more time with her peers than with her family. Peering out her chamber window, I smile as I watch her play chase with her friends. My fragile flower is on the verge of blooming into a beautiful adolescent. A pang of sadness sneaks up on me. I wonder how many more birthdays I'll get to celebrate with her. Or will this be the last?

I'm glad that she was okay with a small, after-school celebration. Winnie, thank goodness, helped me put together a last-minute scavenger hunt around the property. Gallant, who made a quick appearance at breakfast, was no help at all, claiming that he had to work 24-7 in preparation for his retrospective, now only four days away. I'll be surprised if he shows up any time again today. Yesterday's conversation with Winnie has haunted me. I don't know how I can stay with the man who has broken my heart.

"How's Elz doing?" I ask Winnie while the children are off

searching for clues on their scavenger hunt. The two of us are seated at a small wrought iron table in our garden, sharing some wine. A celebration of our friendship.

"She's much stronger. She wants to get back to work, but Rump and I both told her that she needs to rest."

Rest is not part of Elz's vocabulary. She's a workaholic. And frankly, getting back to work might just be the medicine she needs to get her mind off her miscarriage.

The unmistakable sound of a child crying cuts our conversation short. We exchange an alarmed look, fearing the worst. Something terrible has happened to one of the children!

Hansel is running toward us. His flushed freckled face is almost the color of his hair, and tears are streaming down his cheeks. Winnie leaps to her feet, her own freckled face blanching. My heart hammers as the child buries his face against his mother.

"What happened, my sweet boy?" asks Winnie. Her voice is bordering on panic.

"I asked Calla to marry me," he blubbers. "And she said no."

Winnie and I exchange a quick glance and a sigh. I personally don't know whether to laugh or cry. Winnie may feel the same, but she draws her son close to her and gently wipes away his tears.

"My poor little man." She gives him a hug.

"Mama, she wouldn't even take the love bracelet that I had Rump make for her." Still sniffling, he pulls it out of one of his knickers pockets and flings it to the ground. "She told me she's in love with some prince named Henry."

I pick it up and hand it back to him.

"I think you should hold on to this." Compassion swells inside me. I know what it's like to have your heart broken. "Calla may one day find out that Henry is not the prince she hoped for."

Hansel gazes up at me with his hazel brown eyes. They're so soulful. So beyond his years. "Auntie Jane, do you really think there's a chance that Calla might love me one day?"

I nod with a smile and ruffle his wavy ginger hair with my hand. "Honestly, I do."

He stares at the bracelet in his hand and then slips it back into his pocket.

"I won the scavenger hunt!" It's Calla. Hansel smiles at the sight of her, filled with renewed hope. She's skipping toward us, holding Gretel's hand. Chubby Curly trails behind them, trying hard to keep up.

"What's my prize?" Calla asks eagerly. My sweet little girl is so competitive, much like me. "And where's Papa?" She gives me a long searching look.

Gallant. Where the hell is he? Rage sweeps through me. Not so much because he's blown off another one of Calla's birthday parties, but because I know he's with her. The tramp. His Sleeping Beauty.

Winnie stops me from letting my imagination go wild. "Let's open presents!" she insists.

The children race over to a stone bench where a pile of presents is scattered. They're all beautifully wrapped. Except for mine. What can I tell you? I'm the world's worst wrapper, and doing things last minute was no help.

Calla immediately reaches for the biggest box. It's about the length of one of my outstretched arms and exquisitely wrapped with pink princess-themed paper and a humongous matching bow. I'm sure it's from Winnie.

Calla eagerly tears off the paper and opens the box. Under sheets of delicate pale pink tissue paper is the most magnificent gown I've ever seen. At least for a young girl. It's a confection of ivory tulle, accented with a large sash and tiny hand-sewn roses—exactly the color of Calla's rosebud lips. It must have cost a small fortune. Calla holds it up and gasps.

"You shouldn't have spent so much money," I whisper to Winnie.

"I didn't," she replies. "That's not from me."

What? Calla finds a note inside the box and reads it aloud.

My Darling Calla~

I hope you love your new dress. Happy Birthday!

Love and kisses~

Aurora

Love and kisses, Aurora! I snatch the note out of Calla's hand and read it for myself. It's her! I'd recognize that distinctive flowery handwriting anywhere. Every nerve in my body is sizzling. I'm going to implode!

Calla slips the dress over what she's wearing and twirls around. "Oh Mommy, isn't it the prettiest dress you've ever seen?"

"How did Aurora know what to get you?" I stammer. All I want to do is tear the dress off her and shred it into pieces. Winnie reads my mind and steps hard on my foot.

Calla waltzes around the garden in the gorgeous dress. "Papa took me The Trove to one of his meetings with her."

Gallant has already introduced her to the slut? A giant lump forms in my throat. I can hardly swallow. Or breathe.

"We walked around the mall, and I saw this dress in the window of Forever Princess. I really, really wanted it. But Papa said 'no' because it was too expensive."

Calla holds out the layers of tulle and gazes down at the dress in awe. "I can't believe Aurora bought it for me!"

"What does she look like?" I snap. Winnie steps on my foot again, even harder, but it's too late.

"She's so beautiful," beams Calla.

"What color hair?" I can't get the words out fast enough.

"She has the prettiest hair in the whole wide world. It's blond and super long."

She sounds just like the tramp that was at Sparkles!

"Let's open more presents," urges Winnie, trying

desperately to change the subject. Forget it! I want to know more!

"What is she like?"

"She is sooo nice!" replies Calla, dreamily.

Nice! I hate nice. I hate the homewrecker even more.

"When I turn thirteen, she's going to take me shopping at her store, Aurora's Secret, and let me pick out anything I want!"

What! The child molester is going to turn *my* daughter into a slut?

"Aurora says I'm almost like a daughter to her!"

Almost like a daughter to her? The words whirl around in my head and sicken me. I clutch my stomach. It's only a matter of time. Gallant is going to marry Aurora. And I'm going to lose Calla!

Calla skips back to the bench. "Mommy, which one is your present?" She gazes up at me. "Are you okay? You look sick."

"I'm fine." Am I kidding? I may not make it through this day.

Trembling, I hand her my pathetically wrapped present. She tears it open and looks at it blankly.

"It's a book of fairy tales by my editor, Charles Perrault. They're written in French. I thought you'd like to read them."

She shrugs and then tosses the book back on the bench without even a kiss or a *merci.* She hates it! Why shouldn't she! It was a thoughtless, last minute gift—a leftover from some children's book fair I attended—and can't compare to the magnificent dress from Aurora. *Her new mommy!*

Desperation overtakes me. "Maybe, you'd like to read the stories to Lady Jane."

Calla shoots me an indignant wide-eyed look. "*Mon dieu!* I'm going on ten now. I can't play with dolls anymore!"

My heart sinks. She no longer loves her treasured doll. The very first gift I bought her. Up until now, they've been inseparable.

"Face it, Jane," a voice inside my head snickers. "It's not even just the book she hates. She's done with you!" I fight back the tears that threaten to rush down my face.

"Look, there's Gallant." Winnie tugs at my sleeve and points his way. He's dismounting his white steed and holding a large straw basket in his right hand.

My heart pounds and my legs wobble. The thought of his pending marriage to Aurora is all too much for me. My whole world is coming apart. I grip Winnie's arm for support as he strides toward us.

"Papa!" screams Calla with joy. "Is that my present you've got?"

"Yes, my sweet princess" replies Gallant, taking faster, longer steps. "Please forgive me for being so late. I have been working around the clock."

Dragon dung! He's bursting with radiant energy. Not like a man who's been working 24-7. More like someone who's just had the best all-night sex in his life. I want to puke.

"What is it?" ask Calla full of excitement. She opens the lid of the basket and peeks inside. She shrieks.

"It's a puppy!"

What! That cheating asshole got her a puppy! The one thing in life that Calla's wanted as much as a little brother or sister. Well, almost. We were supposed to pick out one all together. From The Queen's rescue sanctuary. Why did Gallant do this to me?

Calla holds the little dog in her arms. He's mostly white except for a bandit-like black mask around his eyes and a heart-shaped brown marking on his backside. He wags his tail and licks her face. Reminiscent of my beloved childhood rescue Bambi, he's the cutest pup I've ever seen.

"He looks just like Aurora's dog, Beauty!" exclaims Calla.

Aurora's dog? Okay, taking her to the mall was one thing. But taking an innocent little girl to the house of his mistress is another. How could he be so indiscreet! Bile rushes to the back of my throat.

The swine chuckles. "Aurora didn't want to tell you that Beauty recently had a litter. We kept it a secret."

Gulp! They're already a "we." In no time, they'll be the perfect family, dogs and all. A giant wave of nausea washes over me. I can't help it. I puke. Winnie grips my trembling hand. And I puke again.

"Jane, are you okay?" asks Gallant, making a face of disgust. He despises me.

"She's looked sick all day," chimes in Calla. She doesn't even call me "mommy."

"Calla's right," I mumble. "I must be coming down with something." I wipe my forehead. I'm feverish. I've got to lie down.

As I stagger back inside the house, Calla makes an announcement.

"I'm going to name him Secret."

Like in Aurora's Secret. And Gallant's.

I don't know how my legs manage to get me to my bed.

———— ❧ ————

Once inside my private chamber, I crawl into bed and shiver under the thick down duvet. Waves of nausea come and go. My distended stomach spasms. It's as if someone's trapped inside and pounding the wall to get out. Maybe, I'm *really* sick.

A loud knock sounds at the door. For a wishful moment, I think it's Gallant. He's come to check in on me because he's concerned about my health. Because he loves me so much. And couldn't live without me. I *must* be delusional with fever.

The door swing opens. It's Winnie. She's holding a tray with a tea caddy and cup. Her presence warms me like a blanket.

"I wanted to make sure you're okay." She sets the tray next to me on the bed. "I made you some chamomile tea. Have some."

I smile weakly. It's just like Winnie to check in on me.

My mind flashes back to the time at Faraway she brought me tea after my near-death escape. I knew then what a wonderful mother she was. And friend.

She puts a palm to my forehead. "I don't think you have temperature. That's good."

But I'm burning up inside. My life as I know it is about to be over.

Managing to sit up, I sip the tea that Winnie's poured for me. It's soothing and actually lessens my nausea.

Winnie plumps up some pillows behind me. "Jane, I know you don't want to hear this. But I've thought a lot about everything you've told me. Just because Gallant met Aurora at Sparkles, bought her a dress, and gave Calla a puppy from her dog's litter, still doesn't mean they're having an affair."

I sigh. Here we go again. What about Lalaland and the sketch of the tramp practically naked? Sleeping Nudie! The truth is, I'm too weary to fight her, and I don't want to destroy our friendship again. I just don't know what it'll take to prove I'm right about the two of them. And then, it comes to me.

"Winnie, what was the name of the private investigator you hired to follow John?"

"She goes by the name, The Potato Sack Princess."

I take another sip of the tea and immediately feel a lot better. What I have to do is catch Gallant sleeping with the beauty. Except I'm not going to be the one to do it.

CHAPTER 15

In the morning, warm, wet flutter kisses awaken me. Gallant? I snap open my eyes and find Secret in my face.

Okay. Confession. I left the door ajar after Winnie left. Hoping that Gallant would, at least, check on me. Wishful thinking. He didn't. A wrenching pain stabs me in the gut. I have to face the truth. He's over me. *So* over me. Despite his despicable auspices, the little dog's unconditional love is the one bright spot in my sea of gloom.

The pup follows me as I stumble out of bed and manage to get dressed. Though I'm still nauseated, I have no time to waste. I've got to track down that private investigator. Dragonballs! What's her name? *Think, Jane, think. The Paper Bag Princess?*

"There you are, you naughty boy! I've been looking all over for you!"

Calla darts into my bedroom. She scoops up Secret and smothers him with kisses. She doesn't ask how I'm feeling. Or call me "mommy."

"Hurry," she says impatiently. "Grampy's waiting for us. Remember, he promised to take me fishing for my birthday."

I totally forgot Calla has a day off from school due to a teacher conference, and we are spending it with my father. Stinky fish. Slimy worms. Patience. I'll have to put my search for that private investigator on hold. Another wave of nausea washes over me and then more gut wrenching pain. I run to the bathroom.

I have to admit it's a perfect day to spend at Lake Sunshine. There is not a cloud in the sky, and the crisp autumn air does me good. I, however, bow out of fishing and instead sit along the shore, minding Secret and Calla's frog Henry, who tagged along last minute. Secret is off-leash, chasing butterflies amidst the flowers and playing an approach-avoidance game with the gentle waves that wash up on shore. Henry is in his little gilded cage, ribbiting and staring at the water.

This lake has special memories for me. Located on the edge of our property, this is where Calla and I first bonded over a fart of all things. And this is where I first fell in love with Gallant after he rescued us both from drowning. My fingertips tingle at the memory of wrapping my arms around his bare, rippled chest as he carried us back to the palace on his handsome white steed.

Stop it, Jane! I take a deep breath and sigh. I need to get Gallant out of my mind. Playing with a twig, I turn my attention to my father, The Huntsman, who is teaching Calla how to fish. He's such a good teacher. Patient. Funny. Loving. He adores her as if she were his grandchild by blood. Calla is lucky to have him in her life. I often wish I'd had him in my life when I was a child. A pang of sadness pricks me as I watch the two of them laughing. I hope he'll be able to stay part of my sweet little girl's life when she moves on to her new family.

Calla squeals when she catches her first fish. She unhooks the wiggly sliver of silver and throws him back into the water. She's an animal lover like me. Tears threaten my eyes. I'm going to miss her so much.

My father heads my way, leaving Calla alone by the shoreline. Thank goodness, I no longer have to worry so much about her drowning. I taught her how to swim. Like me, she's now an excellent swimmer.

"My dear, you don't look yourself," says my father, crouching on the sand next to me. "Are you alright?"

I tell my father I have a touch of the flu. No big deal. I don't want to worry him with my marital problems that have made me physically and emotionally sick.

His concerned green eyes connect with mine. "How's your friend with the cheating husband doing?"

His question takes me by surprise, but I manage to hammer out a response.

"I told her your story, but she refuses to believe that her husband is having just a little fling. She wants to hire a private investigator to follow him."

"I know just the person," says my father brightly, happy that he can help.

My ears perk up. It makes sense that my father, The Huntsman—Mr. Law and Order—would know someone in this field. "Who?" I ask, trying hard to mask my eagerness to find out.

"Her real name is Princess Lisbon. But professionally, she goes by the name, The Potato Sack Princess."

HA! *That's* her name. That's who Winnie used.

My father takes off his red-feathered pelted hat and strokes his bristly beard. "She's a strange one, but she's quite good at what she does. She even helped me bring a few fairy-tale outlaws to justice."

"What's her background?" I ask with curiosity. Out of the corner of my eye, I check on Calla. She's given up on fishing and is contently collecting rocks. I listen intently as my father launches into the story of Princess Lisbon, aka The Potato Sack Princess.

Once a beautiful princess in love with a handsome prince named Roland, Lisbon lived in a fabulous castle and had a fabulous wardrobe. From what my father tells me, she must have been a regular at Armando's Ballgown Emporium. Then one day, a fierce dragon smashed her castle, destroying all her princess clothes with one fiery breath, and carried off Roland.

I interrupt my father. "By chance was this dragon really an evil fairy named Malevolence?"

My father's face hardens. "It's possible. What do you know about Malevolence?"

"I've heard she's Lalaland's most wanted outlaw."

"This is true. I have never been able to bring her to justice." I can detect anger and frustration in my father's gruff voice. "But one day, I will."

Whoa! If he's out to get Malevolence, he must know The Sleeping Slut. "Father, do you, by chance, know Princess Aurora?"

My father's green eyes glisten. "Of course. Malevolence tried to destroy her. However, to be truthful, I haven't seen her for years. She must be about your age, maybe a little younger. She was quite a beauty."

Again, I have to hear about her beauty. Rage and jealousy seep through my veins. My Evil Queen persona is busting out of my skin. I swear if one more person tells me how beautiful Aurora is I'm going to ask my father to take her into the woods… and bring me back her heart.

I eye the foot-long dagger my father keeps in a satchel attached to his belt as he gets back on track with The Potato Sack Princess story.

"So, to make a long story short, Lisbon put on a potato sack—the only thing that survived the dragon's inferno—and embarked on a quest to find her beloved Prince Roland. She finally found him and rescued him by outsmarting the deadly dragon."

"So she and her prince ended up happily ever after?"

My father shakes his head. "Hardly. Roland thought she looked like a tramp and told her to come back after she bought some new clothes worthy of a princess."

Asshole. He and Gallant should get together and form a club. "So what did Lisbon do?"

"My dear, she basically told her Prince to go to hell."

I'm liking this princess more and more. She's got balls.

Certainly more than I do.

"Did she ever marry?" I ask out of curiosity.

He shakes his head again. "No, she decided to become a private investigator and help others find their lost loves."

"Father, she's perfect for my friend!" I exclaim. "How can I... I mean, my friend find her?"

I'm praying that he knows.

"She lives somewhere on the grounds of her former castle. She's quite a recluse and still wears that same potato sack."

My father picks up a stick and draws a map in the sand. "It's quite a journey from here. And a dangerous one."

I study the map. In fact, memorize it. I think I know how to get there.

"Thank you so much, Father, for sharing this information. I know my friend will be so appreciative." *I am! I am!*

Calla runs up to us. I almost forgot about her! I *am* a terrible mother. She pays me back by paying no attention to me.

She hugs only my father. "Grampy, this was so much fun, but I need to get back home to do my homework."

My father smiles proudly. "Good girl. Homework always comes first." Calla pirouettes across the grassy area behind us to collect Secret, who is now happily chasing after a rabbit.

She skips back to us with the pup in her arms and then screams. "Henry's gone!"

I gaze down at the little gilded cage. My mouth drops open. There's no frog inside. He must have squeezed through the bars and escaped.

Calla bursts into tears. "We have to find him!"

"Sweetheart, we'll find him," says my father already on his feet, slashing brush behind us with his dagger.

Spreading out, we frantically look everywhere for Henry. While Calla, holding Secret, searches the shoreline, I get down on my hands and knees, shouting out his name. No stone is unturned. But he's nowhere to be found. Guilt crescendos inside me. It's all my fault. I wasn't paying attention to the frog. How will I explain what happened to Gallant? It'll just give him more ammunition to expedite our divorce proceedings. And give me less time, if any, to see Calla after we're officially separated. I'm a lousy mother and wife. My heart quivers with despair.

Just as we're about to give up, Secret barks. He jumps out of Calla's arms and scampers over to a marsh. All three of us chase after him and then come to a dead halt.

Perched on a lily pad is Henry the Frog. Happily gulping right next to him is another frog with red spots.

"That's a female Bufo punctatus he's sitting next to," says my father, The Huntsman, an expert on all kinds of species.

Calla's rosebud lips part, and her eyes blink rapidly. The telltale signs that she's going to cry again.

"Henry's in love with someone else!" The dam holding back her tears bursts, and they pour down her face.

I wrap an arm around her heaving shoulders, drawing her close to me. I feel her pain. In fact, I share it.

"My sweet girl, sometimes the people we love the most are not the ones who are meant to be." Tears well up in my eyes too.

With the back of my other hand, I wipe away her tears. And then my own. She'll get over Henry, but I will miss Gallant forever.

"Will I ever love someone else as much?" my sweet girl sniffles.

"Of course," I stammer.

Calla looks up at me. Her chocolate eyes pierce me as if they can see right through me. "You're a big fat liar!" Still sobbing, she runs away.

My father runs after her.

I crouch down on the sand and bury my head in my arms. Little Secret tries desperately to give me kisses I don't deserve.

Calla's right. I *am* a big fat liar. Who am I kidding? I will never love someone as much as I've loved Gallant. *Never.*

When I return to the castle, Gallant is at his desk, nursing a drink. His presence rips apart my already torn heart. Emotionally, I'm not prepared to deal with him. I quickly pivot on my heels before he notices me, but it's too late.

"Jane. What are you doing here?"

I could ask him the same question. I turn to face him, but words stay trapped in my throat.

His eyes are bloodshot and heavy lidded, and paint covers his hands, obscuring his wedding band that he might as well stop wearing. Secret jumps out of my arms and onto his lap. He doesn't mind and pats the pup's head. A dimpled smile crosses his lips.

I battle the me that's ready to melt. *Jane, be the Ice Queen.*

"Did you talk to Calla?" I ask frostily.

"I just got home," he says with a weary sigh. It must be exhausting juggling a marriage, career… and an affair.

"She's beside herself. Henry ran away."

He takes a swig of his drink. "Who is Henry?"

"Her frog!"

"I didn't know he had a name. She'll get over it."

Rage rushes through my bloodstream. I want to take his drink and splash it in his face; I ball my fists to hold back. His affair is bad enough, but to have such a laissez faire attitude toward his daughter is another thing. Obviously, the person he cares about the most is Aurora.

I'm not going to let him get away with this indignant behavior. "You should go upstairs and check in on her."

"I can't. I must leave. A coach will be here any minute to fetch me."

"What do you mean?" I ask, my voice shrill.

"I have another business trip. It should be the last one before the retrospective."

"Fine." I stab the word at him. "Where are you going?"

He hesitates. "I can't really tell you," he says at last.

Truthfully, there's no need for him to tell me. I *know* where he's going.

Gallant marches upstairs, and when he returns, he's carrying a small overnight valise.

Outside, the sound of a horse-drawn coach gets nearer.

"Give Calla my love," he says hastily, dashing to the front door. I tag behind him.

Parked outside is an elegant coach. Made of rich polished wood with gold inlays and hitched to two stylishly outfitted white horses. The kind that belongs to royalty.

A coachman opens the gilded carriage door. Gallant steps inside, not turning to see the tears oozing from my eyes. As the coach pulls away, my eyes stay riveted on a large, flowery scarlet "A" that is inscribed on the rear side. I recognize the font. It's "A" for Aurora.

After my emotions settle down, I trudge upstairs to check on to Calla. Her chamber door is bolted, and she won't let me in no matter how hard I knock or beg. I even try to bribe her with Secret, who has not left my side. Finally, her sobbing stops, and I give up. Her refusal to let me comfort her adds to my dejection. I'm losing a husband *and* a daughter.

With a heavy heart, I tread downstairs, Secret tagging right behind me. I desperately need to imbibe some wine but end up brewing tea in our kitchen. I take the teacup to our great room and do something I haven't done for a very long time. With Secret curled up in my lap, I close my eyes. And meditate. The crackling fire in the hearth warms my soul as it travels to higher place where Gallant doesn't exist.

When I blink open my eyes, Secret is sound asleep. All is clear. Tomorrow I will visit The Potato Sack Princess and hire her to follow Gallant—and provide me with the final piece of evidence I need to prove he's having an affair with Aurora. The ammunition I need to move my life forward.

CHAPTER 16

Morning comes. Secret, who once again snuggled with me, awakens me with more face-licking kisses. His puppy-breath warms my cheeks. Physically, I'm a lot stronger—the nausea is gone—and, for the first time in a long while, I feel driven and purposeful. I hop out of bed, eager to meet with The Potato Sack Princess. Before heading downstairs, I check on Calla.

I sigh with relief when I find her chamber door unlocked. Cautiously, I venture inside. Wagging his tail, Secret follows me.

Calla is still in bed, bundled under her covers, when she should be getting ready for school. Her eyes are swollen-red from crying. Secret jumps onto the bed and slathers her face with wet kisses. To my dismay, my sweet little girl shows no sign of cheering up.

"Mommy, I don't want to go to school today." Her voice is tearful. "Please, pretty please?"

How can I force her? Her heart is broken.

Let her stay in bed. She probably didn't sleep a wink last night, and school will just be wasted on her. My poor little girl! There's no way I can leave her. The Potato Sack Princess will just have to wait until tomorrow.

I head back downstairs. I need a distraction. I know. I'll work on my next children's book. With Gallant's affair, it's been the last thing on my mind.

At my desk, I tear out a sheet of parchment and stare at

the blank page. The clock strikes nine... Then ten... Then eleven. No brilliant ideas fill my head. No words fill the page. Not even "once upon a time." Tears well up in my eyes. I simply can no longer live a fairy tale of lies.

When the clock tells me it's noon, I head to the kitchen where I make Calla's favorite soup—my famous Potage de Meeshmash. The magical vegetable soup that made Gallant fall in love with my cooking. And with me. As I stir the ingredients in a cauldron, a tear escapes my eye and falls into the simmering mixture. A dash of salt. The delicious aroma wafts through the air. Calla hasn't eaten a thing since yesterday. Perhaps this will nourish both her body and soul. If only it could mine.

Holding a tray with a bowl of soup, I clamber back upstairs. To my surprise, when I enter Calla's chamber, she's out of bed, dressed in her school uniform—a simple white blouse and a long navy wool jumper with a small gold crown—the Midas family crest—embroidered in gold threads on the upper left pocket.

"I've changed my mind," she says, brushing her hair. "I want to go to school."

I inwardly breathe a sigh of relief. I'm glad she's decided to go to school. Being around other children will help get her mind off Henry. Trust me, hanging around me all day would do her no good.

Calla scoffs down the soup as Secret looks on with puppy-eyed envy.

—————◆—————

No matter how many times I've been to Calla's school, The Midas Center for Early Education, over the last two years, I can't believe it used to be my castle. The chambers have been converted into classrooms; the apple orchard into a nature learning center; my throne room into a theater for the performing arts; and my dungeon, where I conjured Snow

White's poison apple, into a science lab. Where my courtyard once stood, The Seven Dwarfs constructed a playground under Winnie's supervision. And thanks to dear Pinocchio, it's filled with toys, playhouses, and a jungle gym.

My castle—I mean, the school—is perched high on a cliff. At first, parents and their kids had to hike to the top, but thanks to Headmaster Diggs, they now have a fun ride to transport them up and down. A hot air balloon, from his wizardry days for which he no longer had any use. Students look forward to going to school every day just to take a ride in the balloon. As Calla and I launch into the sky and float upward to the clouds, I'm overwhelmed with sense of wonderment. The flight is exhilarating. And the view of Lalaland, with its enchanted hills and vales, charming thatched-roof villages, and dotted castles, is spectacular.

Greeting us at the landing is Headmaster Diggs himself. Formerly the Wizard of Oz, a Faraway inmate who suffered from delusions of grandeur, he decided he wasn't really ready for retirement after constantly losing croquet matches to The Queen. So, when Midas offered him the headmaster job, he grabbed it. "I always loved working with munchkins," he said in his inauguration speech.

Clad in his habitual black broadcloth doublet and fanciful polka dot bowtie, Diggs gives Calla a stern look.

"Nice for you to finally show up, young lady."

Calla cowers and sheepishly scurries to the school's entrance. Diggs winks at me. Letting me know that all is okay. I smile and follow Calla.

Little of my former palace remains inside. It's almost unrecognizable. The halls are painted in bright primary colors instead of drab shades of gray, and children's colorful paintings have replaced gloomy ancestral portraits. A change for the better.

On our way in, several children say hi to Calla. My sweet little girl is very popular.

The children who attend the school are, for the most

part, the sweetest kids you'll ever meet. Midas didn't want to build an exclusive school for spoiled princes and princesses and hence declared the school public—open to royals and non-royals alike. The school uniforms, designed by Emperor Armando, help maintain equality and discipline. There's a no-tolerance policy for bullying, elitist behavior, or discrimination of any kind. Once, Calla told me about a classmate, a snotty prince, who picked on a pixie-sized boy named Tom Thumb. He was immediately expelled. His royal parents offered to build a new wing if the boy was readmitted, but Midas said no and told them to spend their money on therapy for their son.

Wouldn't you know that Calla's classroom was once the secret chamber that housed my "magic" mirror. It's located on the top level. Calla races up the seemingly never-ending spiral staircase that leads to it while I wind up it behind her, panting every step of the way. Silently, I curse the weight I've put on, especially over the last few days. Damn that Gallant for turning me into an emotional overeater. And a wreck.

When we get to Calla's classroom, boys and girls, in two parallel lines, are exiting into the hallway. Mrs. Hubbard, Calla's teacher, stands at the doorway, supervising them. She brightens when she sees Calla, one of her star students.

"Calla! You're just in time for recess. Hurry now and join the others."

Flashing a smile, Calla skitters to catch up to her classmates. Hansel's face lights up when she gets in line next to him.

Mrs. Hubbard is a wonderful teacher and mother. Before she began teaching at the school, she was a destitute widow who could barely feed her own twelve children. She would have had to sell her house—maybe even have turned to a life of begging—had not Midas offered her a job. Now, she's living comfortably, and her kids ranging in age from five to eighteen—each one as sweet as can be—are enrolled in various grades at the school.

"Is Calla alright?" she asks with genuine concern.

I take a deep breath. "Do you have some time to talk?"

She invites me into her classroom. Taking a seat at one of the student's desks, I survey my surroundings. My eyes immediately gravitate to a charming painting that's hanging on the back wall. It's a self-portrait of Calla. She's a gifted artist just like her father. My eyes travel to the front of the room where math problems and exemplary cursive letters are scrawled on the chalkboard. I swear that's where my "magic" mirror once hung. I can practically hear it talking. Except it's not telling me that I'm the *Fairest of All.* It's telling me that I'm fat, stressed, and tired. Okay. My mirror was always brutally honest, even if it was just my sub-conscience making me face reality. Thank goodness, it ended up in a dumpster, cracked beyond repair.

"Calla is having some issues," I begin. I tell Mrs. Hubbard about her infatuation with Henry the Frog Prince.

Mrs. Hubbard smiles. "It's part of growing up," she says warmly. "Like an imaginary friend."

She pauses. "But perhaps her extreme reaction to Henry's abandonment is symptomatic of something else that's going on at home."

I take another deep breath and just blurt it out. "Prince Gallant and I are about to get a divorce."

Mrs. Hubbard's eyes flutter with shock. "I'm quite frankly very surprised. Calla's always given me the feeling that you're wonderful, loving parents."

Well, we maybe we've done okay in the parenting department, but as a couple, we suck, I think to myself.

Mrs. Hubbard's eyes meet mine. "Does Calla know?"

"Not yet."

"The important thing is that you don't fight in front of her. And that you both give her all the love you can. Children are more resilient than you think."

I impulsively hug this incredible woman, teacher, and single-mother of twelve.

Mrs. Hubbard places her motherly hands on my shoulders and looks straight into my eyes. "I hope you and The Prince can work it out. For the sake of Calla."

A sharp pain stabs me in my gut. She has a point.

When I return home, there's a letter waiting for me. Lately, every delivery has made me edgy, even those addressed to me. The handwriting on the envelope looks official. My heart skips a beat. It's from a magistrate. For sure, Gallant's sent me divorce papers. With trembling hands, I rip open the envelope and read the contents.

> *Dear Client:*
>
> *This is a formal reminder that your next children's book, per your agreement, is past due. Although we recognize that you are the daughter-in-law of our esteemed founder, we regret to inform you that we will be forced to terminate your contract if we do not receive it shortly.*
>
> *Yours sincerely,*
>
> *Midas Publishing, Children's Division*

My stomach churns. Not only is my marriage going to be over. So is my career! By the time they review my request for an extension, King Midas will no longer be my father-in-law.

I'd better get to work. *Dewitched* was a big success. How hard can it really be to write another fairy tale? That's what my readers expect of me. It should be a piece of cake.

With Secret curled up at my feet, I sit down at my desk and begin to write. *"Once upon a time..."* Okay, a good start, but now what? Once again, words won't come. No matter how hard I labor.

I crumple up the sheet of parchment and try again. Nothing. By the time, Calla comes home, I've gone through an entire ream of parchment. And not a word more. I can no longer write a happily ever after fairy tale.

———

My writer's block has put in an even fouler mood, so Calla's return from school is a welcomed distraction. She's like a whole new child. Cheerful and energetic. Secret, who hasn't left my side all afternoon, dances circles around her, his tail wagging madly.

"Look what Hansel gave me!" She proudly holds up her wrist, showing off the bracelet Rump wove.

"It's beautiful!" I gush.

"Do you think he likes me?" Calla looks up at me with her big brown eyes, the eyes that remind me so much of Gallant, despite their difference in color.

My eyes meet hers and I smile. "I think he does."

Calla scoops up the puppy. "We're going to play outside. I'm going to teach Secret a trick."

Not a word about Henry. Thank goodness, she's over him. My eyes follow her as she merrily skips out the French doors that lead to the garden. A pang of envy shoots through me. How lucky to be so young! And to recover so quickly from heartbreak. I wonder again if I'll *ever* be able to rebound from my first true love. Gallant.

CHAPTER 17

How quickly the week has gone by. It's Saturday again. Calla is eager to go on her weekly playdate at Winnie's house. Hansel's woven bracelet still circles her wrist, and she's wearing Aurora's dress.

"Do you think Hansel will like it?" she asks with a little twirl.

"He'll love it," I reply although the sight of it makes my stomach muscles clench.

The good news is that Calla will be at Winnie's all day; I'll be able to visit The Potato Sack Princess. After Calla skips into the courtyard with Secret, I prepare for my journey. The private investigator will surely need some information to help her identify the royal adulterers.

Heading over to Gallant's desk, I slide open the top drawer and search for the small self-portrait I came across before discovering Aurora's love letter. I find it right away in his stack of doodles. My heart sinks to my stomach as I study it. It's a slightly younger Gallant, but his piercing blue eyes, tousled flaxen hair, and dimpled smile are unmistakable. Holding it, I feel My Prince slipping out of my fingers. I take a deep, painful breath and refocus on my mission.

I rifle through the desk with hope of finding that sketch of Sleeping Nudie. It's not here. A description of Aurora will have to do. Grabbing a sheet of parchment and a stylus, I scribble: *Tall, thin, blond, blue-eyed, and beautiful. Very princessy.*

After packing the portrait and description in my purse,

right next to my list of evidence and the original incriminating evidence, Aurora's love letter, I ask one of our servants to saddle up my horse. I'm going to make the trip alone. It's better that no one knows where I'm going, including our help. Who knows? They could blow my whole plan by telling Gallant, the last person I want to find out.

———⚬———

Mentally retracing my father's map in my head, I lead my horse across an unfamiliar route, filled with dense, overgrown foliage. Signs of human life are far and few between. An occasional cottage; nothing more. A chill runs through me as the wind kicks up. This would definitely not be a good place to have an accident. Soon, all traces of human life disappear.

My woolen cloak flaps loudly against the brisk air as the horse gallops. My mind races, filling with impending doom. Maybe this wasn't such a good idea. Finally, after about three hours, I pull up to a weather-beaten sign.

BEWARE!
You are now entering the Forbidden Forest!
Proceed at your own risk!

A shiver runs down to the base of my spine. I didn't realize that The Potato Sack Princess lived in this remote and perilous part of Lalaland. Few people have ever been here, and even fewer have ever returned upon venturing on its soil. Lore has it that it's home to hordes of horrific creatures—boggarts, goblins, gremlins, and other evil forest spirits. And didn't the Badass Fairies say that this is where Malevolence hangs out? With my luck, I'll run smack into her. She'll turn into a fire-breathing dragon and barbecue me in one breath. And then a brainstorm hits me. If I encounter her, I'll bargain for my life. "Let me go and I'll lead you to Aurora." That's who she really wants. It'll be a win-win for the both of us. Dragon or no dragon, I've come this far, and I'm not turning back.

Trotting slowly, my horse and I enter the foreboding forest. At first, it's what you'd expect any forest to be—a dense, verdant array of tall aromatic trees. My eyes dart back and forth like a pendulum, watchful for the unexpected and hopeful for a sign of The Potato Sack Princess's castle. Nothing. The fresh, invigorating scent of evergreens soon gives way to the rancid smell of rotting wood, and I notice dead logs in our path. Soon, there is not a sign of greenery anywhere. Everything is charcoal black. Burnt to a crisp. It looks and smells as if a terrible fire has rampaged the forest.

My childhood fear of being alone in a dark forest comes back to haunt me with a vengeance. My imagination goes wild, scaring me silly. Any minute I expect the seared, sinewy trees to turn into monsters and wrap their gnarly charred branches around me. Or one of those frightful creatures I've heard about to jump out of nowhere and attack me. And, of course, there's the possibility of a fire-breathing dragon, be it Malevolence or another, swooping down upon me. I shudder to think that a dragon's fiery breath caused so much devastation.

All of my senses are on high alert. I give my horse a kick to go faster. The horse whinnies and bolts. Without warning, dozens of grotesque imps with large pointed ears tumble out of the trees. They're all over me! Pinching me, pulling at my clothes, and nit picking my hair with their sharp dirty nails. Shrieking, I swat at them frantically, trying to flick them off. No matter what I do, I can't get rid of them. *Okay, Jane. It's time to panic.*

"Leave me alone!" I scream. "My father-in-law is the King of Lalaland, and I can have you arrested!"

The revolting creatures continue their vicious assault and jabber in a strange high-pitched gibberish. Great! They don't even speak the same language.

Think, Jane, think. I know. Maybe I can befriend them or, at least, bargain with them.

"Hi," I say in the sweetest voice I can muster.

What do you know! They calm down, and their cacophony quiets to a hum. One of them, the apparent leader, says something and points to the purse that's slung across my cloak.

"You want my purse?" Hesitantly, I pantomime handing it over to them.

The insipid imps jump up and down. Their drone once again turns dissonant and deafening.

"Fine." *Not fine.* All my money is in there, along with the Gallant's self-portrait, my evidence list, the description of Aurora, and her love letter. But I have no choice—my life trumps my purse. I slide the purse over my head and hand it to the leader.

With great curiosity, he examines the bag. I hold my breath as he unlatches it and shakes it upside down. Dozens of gold coins fall to the blackened ground while the rest of the contents blow away with wind. Everything I needed for The Potato Sack Princess is gone!

Like a flock of hungry ducks who have discovered breadcrumbs, the imps jump off me and scuttle to the coins. They gather them up and scamper off with their booty. I'm free of them, but penniless. I suppose this was a small price to pay for my life.

Gloom sweeps over me. Worse than being broke, I no longer have Gallant's self-portrait. The list of evidence and description of Aurora—and even her original love letter—are not that important, but how will The Potato Sack Princess find Gallant without knowing what he looks like?

Disheartened, I dismount my horse to retrieve my purse. This whole journey has been pointless. Not meant to be, as Winnie would say. As I crouch down to pick up my purse, something flies into my face. I peel it off. What do you know! Gallant's self-portrait! With renewed purpose, I place it my purse and climb back up on my horse.

The rest of the journey is uneventful, although I don't let my guard down for a second. At any time, an evil creature, as tall as a tree or as small as a blade of grass, can strike. Most of all, I fear a dragon encounter. Malevolence.

At last, through the tangles of blackened branches, an imposing castle comes into view. Or should I say what little remains of an imposing castle. It, too, looks like it's been rampaged by a massive fire. It's still smoldering, and a thick layer of black soot covers the decaying façade.

I've followed the map to a tee. This must be my destination. The headquarters of The Potato Sack Princess. Yet, it's not humanly possible for anyone to inhabit this wreck of a castle. Especially a princess.

I dismount my horse. My feet sink into the sooty, ash-covered ground, and I immediately wish I had worn a pair of old hiking boots instead of Elz's gorgeous custom-made leather riding boots. I swear if they get ruined, I'm going to deduct the cost of their replacement from The Potato Sack Princess's bill.

Someone royal and privileged must have indeed once lived here, I think as I tread on the charred remnants of a past life. Chunks of blackened gilded frames, smoky mirrors, and scattered crystals, and even the seared, tattered remains of what was likely once a beautiful gown. A life of luxury that went up in smoke. A tinge of sadness pains me. Princess Lisbon, like me, lost everything that was dear to her. A crunchy sound makes my skin crawl. I look down—the remains of a human skull are beneath the soles of my boots. That's it. I'm out of here. I'll find another way to prove that Gallant is having an affair with Aurora.

As I turn around, a raspy voice stops me. "Over to the left." My eyes swish to a slightly ajar arched door that's carved into a massive tree trunk. It has a huge metal knocker and a sign above it that reads:

The Potato Sack Princess: Finder of Lost Loves
ENTER AT YOUR OWN RISK!

Okay. I've indeed found her. A voice in my head tells me to get back on my horse and get the hell out of here. I take a deep breath. "GO!" the voice says louder, as sure as death. I ignore it. I've come this far. There's no going back.

The minute I step foot in the dark, cavernous trunk, I have second thoughts. A cloud of smoke envelops me. My eyes sting, and I can't stop coughing That's it. I'm out of here!

But before I can pivot around, the door bolts behind me, and I'm shoved onto a super-sized, sooty, tattered chair. I think the remains of what must have once been a throne. Standing before me is petite woman who's wearing nothing more than a soiled potato sack and a partially melted gold crown atop her head. Her scrawny limbs are covered with soot; her fingernails are ragged and filthy, and her scraggily ash-brown hair looks like it's been singed. And she stinks. I can't help wondering when was the last time she went to a spa. Or even took a bath.

She gives me a scathing look and hands me a card.

THE POTATO SACK PRINCESS

Experienced. Expedient. Expensive.

"I'm a very busy princess, so get straight to the point," she rasps, her hoarse voice I'm sure the result of living in this smoke-filled hellhole. Sheesh! Doesn't she know that smoke is bad for your health? That it can lead to birth defects or even death? On second thought, she must since the sign on her door says "Enter at Your Own Risk."

I spew the words as fast as I can. "I believe my husband is having an affair with a princess named Aurora. I need concrete proof that he's sleeping with her."

"What does she look like?"

I recite the description I wrote down verbatim.

She rolls her eyes. "Another beautiful blonde. They're a dime a dozen. What about him?"

Reaching into my purse, I hand her Gallant's self-portrait.

With her head bowed down and brows furrowed, she paces the cave and studies it. The unreadable look on her face is angsting me out. What's her problem? She wants the case or she doesn't. Finally, she hands me back the portrait.

My heart sinks. She's not going to help me.

"I usually don't take on cases like this, but I'll make an exception."

My heart lifts. Yes! She'll do it!

"I need a down payment," she says testily.

Shit! Those pesky imps took all my money! "What about full payment in cash when the job's done?" I try to negotiate.

"No deal!" She scans me up and down with her dark beady eyes. Her gaze narrows, and she points a grubby finger at me. "What's that you're wearing around your neck?"

I look down and grasp Shrink's mirrored locket. No! I can't give her this!

"Hand it over," she says, rubbing her fingertips together, "or say good-bye."

I take a deep breath and have another coughing fit. Slowly, *very* slowly, I slip the necklace over my head. To my shock, a giant raven sweeps down and snags it in his beak. He flaps over to The Potato Sack Princess. She snatches the necklace from him.

"Good boy, Amigo." The Potato Sack Princess admires the locket.

The bird squawks loudly and circles around my head. He's terrifying me. I crouch, protectively folding my arms over my head.

"Don't be afraid of him," says The Potato Sack Princess. "He's a very sweet bird, and you might as well get used to him because he works for me."

She signals the bird with a double snap of her fingers. "Come here, good boy."

The bird zooms over to her and sits on her shoulder.

"He's a rescue bird. I found him in the forest and nursed him back to health. That damn fire-breathing dragon—the one that destroyed my castle—burnt off half his feathers. Some chick named Malevolence posted a sign for his return—she called him Deevil—but there was no way in hell that I was going to give him back."

She turns her head and looks lovingly at the giant bird still perched on her shoulder. "Finders keepers, right Amigo honey?"

The bird squawks happily and flaps its wide wings. I, on the other hand, am quivering at the mention of Malevolence's name. I dread the thought of the ride home.

The Potato Sack Princess returns her attention to my locket. Holding it in her palm, she fidgets with the lock.

"Hey, careful with that!" I protest. "That locket means a lot to me."

"Don't worry, sister. I'll give it back to you when you pay me."

She struggles to open the gold locket with her dirty, ragged fingernails.

Shit! She's going to break it. My heart pounds with dread. Finally, she snaps it open.

She gazes at herself in the mirror inside it and makes a face. "Do you know someone who will come out this way and give me a haircut?"

Gothel's name immediately comes to mind. She could work wonders. But I just shake my head "no."

She slips the locket over her head; it grazes her grungy potato sack. "There's one other thing you should know about me if we're going to be working together."

There are probably hundreds of things I should know about her. But to be truthful, I've heard enough.

"I prefer the company of women to men."

Cripes! Now I'm also going to have to give her sexual favors.

"Don't worry. I never mix business with pleasure. And besides, you're not my type. I like them fat. Like my bank account."

With the way my weight's been soaring, I might be right up her alley by tomorrow. Another reason to go on a diet. I hope she never hit on Winnie.

We finally get down to business. I fill her in on everything I know about Aurora and Gallant, focusing on the present and not their past.

"Your husband's an artist? He sounds like a bum, just like my Roland."

Roland... the handsome prince for whom she risked her life, only to be rejected by him because she didn't look princessy enough. I detect bitterness in her voice. I have to admit I feel sorry for her. And can even understand her sexual preference. I wonder if I'll go that way.

"You'll be very pleased with the results of my investigation." She smugly snaps the locket shut. "I'll give you a full detailed report with the evidence."

All of a sudden, I'm not so sure if I'm doing the right thing. Not so much the spying on my husband part; I'm okay with that. It's the report that's making my heart go boom, boom, boom. Truthfully, I don't know if I can bear hearing what Gallant is like in bed with Aurora. For the first time, a vision of their long, lean, athletic bodies tangled up together floats in my head. The sound of them moaning and groaning with pleasure fills my ears. What if he does things to her that he does to me? And more? And she turns out to be a better lover than I've ever been? But the biggest question of all is: Then what? A painful knot forms in my stomach.

The Potato Sack Princess plays with *her* new locket— okay, it's just a down payment, I assure myself—and shows me out the door. It bolt-locks behind me.

A deal is a deal. I only hope I don't live to regret it.

CHAPTER 18

I get back to Lalaland safely without a hitch. Just in time for my afternoon appointment with Dr. Grimm.

Truthfully, I thought my last appointment with Dr. Grimm would be my last. But as I headed back to Lalaland, I decided I wanted to personally tell the kind man that I no longer need his services.

His waiting room is packed with pretty princesses with baby bumps, cheerfully exchanging pregnancy stories and baby names and comparing answers to that stupid motherhood quiz. Thank goodness, Dr. Grimm is able to see me right away.

"Well, well, well, my dear. How did you do with the herbs and birthing stones?"

"Um, good," I mutter. I'm not going to tell him that I threw them away.

"Excellent," he beams. "Let's do a pea test."

A pea test? I thought that was a princess test for baby girls. Maybe it's also some kind of genetic test. Mystified, I await twenty elves to parade through the door, each schlepping a mattress and a featherbed. What a waste of time and energy! Trust me, I'm no princess.

Dr. Grimm hands me a flask.

"I'd like you to *pee* in this."

What? He wants me to pee into a jar? Now, I'm really confused. He leaves the room. I lift up my layers of petticoats and put the jar where it needs to be. Piss vinegar! Nothing comes out. Finally, I relax my muscles and manage to squeeze out a few drops. I don't need to be doing this. I'm definitely telling Dr. Grimm that this is my last visit. I'll just tell him that Gallant and I have decided that we don't want a child. I'll spare him the gory details. He can read all about the breakup and divorce in the *Fairytale Tattler.*

Dr. Grimm teeters back into the room and examines the flask. Using a dropper, he puts of few drops of some strange powder into the pee. I scrunch my nose. It stinks! Turning his back, he heads over to one of his wired up lab stations.

I utter a little attention-getting cough. "Dr. Grimm, I actually came here to tell you that Gallant and I—"

Dr. Grimm cuts me off. "My dear, come here and see this." He sounds excited.

I slide off the examining table and head over to the gurgling flask. My eyes grow as round as marbles. Worms are growing inside it!

My pulse races. "What's wrong with me?"

He grins. "Nothing, my dear."

I breathe a loud sigh of relief.

"Except you're pregnant."

"I'm pregnant?" I squeak. The words echo in my head, but no matter how many times I hear them, they don't register.

"And judging by the size of these critters, I'd say you're well into your eighth month."

I'm eight months pregnant? I still can't register the shock. But the more I think about it, it makes sense. I should have known. The mood swings. The sleeplessness. The maternal instincts. The nausea. And... the weight gain.

"You had us all fooled," chuckles Dr. Grimm. "You were actually pregnant before you started seeing me six months ago."

I do the math. He's right. All his magic—the birthing stones, chants, prayers, herbs, and potions—did not make me pregnant. Gallant did. With *his* magic.

"Why didn't you this test before?" My voice is in panic mode.

"My dear, it's a sudden breakthrough in modern medicine."

"What about the on and off bleeding I've had?" With my irregular few and far between periods, I thought I was menstruating.

"I suspect, given how strong your pee test reaction is, you were going to have multiples. I think you lost one early on."

Two? One is bad enough. Reality plunges into me. I'm losing My Prince! I can't have this baby. His baby! Not now! Not ever!

"Dr. Grimm, we'll have to do something about the baby because Gallant and I have decided that we *strongly* don't want any more children." Desperation underlies every word, and I practically scream "strongly."

Grimm shakes his head. Not a good sign. My stomach churns. "My dear, there is nothing we can do. You are way too far along."

I swallow hard. I'm having a baby. Gallant's.

I stumble into Dr. Grimm's waiting room in a trance. I gaze numbly at the mural of baby lambs jumping over the rainbow. My numbness succumbs to glumness as my eyes shift up to the fertility doctor's motto. *"Where Fairy Tales are Born."* Believe me, this is no fairy tale hiding out in my body. It's a horror story!

The bevy of pregnant princesses still sitting in the waiting room is one giant blur. I can't even hear the sound of their chatter. The deafening chaos in my head overpowers it. I desperately need some fresh air. To clear my head.

I leave my horse behind—I'll send someone to fetch him later—and just start walking. The unusual late afternoon haze mirrors my mental state. Questions without answers whirl around in my head. What am I going to do with this child? How am I going to raise it alone? How will I ever love it knowing it's Gallant's?

Wait! I don't need any answers. The child will be stillborn. Just like my first baby, the one I had when I was only thirteen-years-old after Snow White's father's lustful assault. And this time, I won't survive the horrific birthing.

A strange spasm rocks my stomach. I place my hand on my swollen belly. Another spasm, but this time I can actually feel a flutter beneath my palm. The baby is kicking. It's trying to tell me something. Of course, it could hear all my horrible thoughts. It's upset and getting back at me. Treating my womb like a punching bag. It kicks me hard again as if acknowledging I've guessed right. And then out of nowhere, I have something that approaches an outer body experience. An indescribable mixture of wonderment, excitement, determination, and fear fills every fiber of my being. Tears pour from my eyes. Holy shit! This is not supposed to happen. I'm bonding with my baby.

My stomach gurgles. A hunger pang. I'm ravenous, not having eaten a thing all day. The baby jabs me again. Hard. Of course, it's hungry too.

I'm beginning to think that my baby is very smart and that we're going to get along just fine. "Come on, kid, let's get a bite to eat. There's this really yummy cupcake place at The Trove that's not too far away. You're going to love the double fudge chocolate chip cupcakes. They're my favorite." And then it hits me. I'm talking out loud to my baby!

The Trove, as usual, is packed with beautiful princesses bustling in and out of stores. My eyes gravitate to several pushing elegant prams. I follow one of them. She pivots around and gives me a dirty look. She must think I'm a stalker and hastily moves away from me. Sheesh. I just want to ask her where she got her carriage.

On the way to Sparkles, I pass Jack and Jill, *the* store for baby royals. I press my nose against the window, ogling the most gorgeous handmade baby clothes I've ever seen. I can't resist going inside.

"Can I help you?" asks a very prim and proper nanny type in a condescending tone. She eyes me up and down. I'm sure she's checking me out to determine if I'm royalty and can afford the exorbitantly priced merchandise.

I pick up a delicate white dressing gown, trimmed with lace, that would be perfect for either a baby girl or boy. "How much is this?" I ask.

"I don't think you can afford it," she scoffs.

I put down the little gown and give her the cold, haughty stare that I perfected in my "magic" mirror.

"And I don't think *you* can afford to have that attitude," I say dismissively.

The stout woman gives me a who-do-you-think-you-are look. She's about to find out.

"My father-in-law, King Midas, owns this mall." Well, at least for now, he's my father-in-law. "And I would you say you're about to be fired."

The saleswoman's eyes widen with shock. A wicked smirk spreads across my face as I saunter out the store. Yes, sometimes, it pays to be evil. The baby gives me a little kick. *Touché!*

Next stop: Barons and Nobles to get something to read.

As I step into the bookstore, a bookwormy sales maiden intercepts me.

"Perhaps, I can interest you in this." She hands me a thick hardcover book. *The Princess Guide to Raising a Royal Baby.* I guess it's obvious I'm pregnant.

I flip through it. Interesting… it recommends using your husband's monogrammed hankies for burping cloths to save time and money. Good idea. I'll be sure to pack all of Gallant's before he runs off with the homewrecker.

"I'll take it," I tell the woman.

By the time I leave Barons and Nobles, I've purchased a dozen books on pregnancy and baby care, including one with the top royal baby names. Having not a penny to my name, I charge them all to Gallant. By the time he gets the bill and questions it, I'll no longer be in his life. A pang of sadness runs through me.

At Sparkles, I find a table for two outdoors. A server, in one of those ridiculous jester getups, takes my order. Having personally experienced what it's like to have this demeaning job (and wear that god-awful outfit), I treat him with dignity and promise myself to leave him a fat tip, charging it to Gallant's account.

"Will it just be you?" he asks politely.

"No, there will be two of us," I say with a smile. The baby kicks. *Yes, you and me, kid.*

I order some tea and a platter of cupcakes—enough to feed a large family. I randomly pull out the baby-naming book from the bag full of books. Opening up the book to the middle of the "A" section, I begin to read.

Ariel... meaning "lion of God"... Aurora... meaning "dawn"

With a shudder, I slam the book shut. I just can't get away from her. She ruined my marriage. But I'm not going to let her ruin my child. I make a mental note for the child custody hearing. No visitation rights with Aurora. Wait! What if Gallant fights me for custody of our child? No, it's *my* child! I'm not going to let him do that to me! I'll resort to evil if I have to! I know. I'll send an anonymous bottle of champagne to Mr. and Mrs. Unfaithful to congratulate them on their nuptials. One sip, and they'll both be history. And this time I'll get away with it!

My machinations are cut short by a familiar voice.

"Can I join you? I'm on my break." It's Gothel. Without waiting for an answer, she straddles her long, leather-clad legs over the empty chair across from mine. The cupcakes come, and she helps herself to two. Let's talk about rude!

"You're pregnant aren't you?" she says in her deep husky voice.

Damn it! The baby-naming book is on the table, right in her face. I nervously toss it back into the shopping bag.

"Don't worry, I knew it when I did your hair. I'd say about seven or eight months."

My eyes widen. How does she know this? Maybe she's a witch.

She bites into a cupcake and looks straight at me with her fierce violet eyes. We look enough alike to be sisters. Except for the nose ring and her C-cup chest.

"I was pregnant once."

She launches into her story. It turns out that she used to be married, and her husband, a lord, desperately wanted a child. After many years and visits to Dr. Grimm, Lady Gothel, as she was known then, finally conceived. Except just before she was due, she fell down a flight of stairs and lost the child.

"Grimm had to cut the baby out of me." She plays with a knife. "A son."

A chill runs up my spine. Memories of my stillborn child flicker in my head.

"My husband couldn't forgive me for losing the child. I tried to give him another child. I did everything. Herbs. Candles. Chants. Magic potions. Birthing stones… "

"Love baths?" I interrupt.

"Babe, you name it, I did it. But no baby. My husband had enough. The bastard took up with another woman, some chick he met at a pub."

Suddenly, it becomes crystal clear to me. Duh! Of course, that's why Gallant went back to Aurora. Because I couldn't give him a child. But now, all has changed. The baby gives me an assertive kick. HA! I'm right!

"What happened?" I ask, eager to hear more after my ah-ha moment.

"I wanted my man back." Gothel's violet eyes grow

hooded, and there's sadness in her voice, something I've never heard before.

"I thought that if I could present my husband with a baby, he'd come back to me."

"What did you do?" Maybe she can help me win back Gallant.

Gothel digs into another cupcake. I grab one before she eats them all.

She continues her story. She lost all friends who were married and starting families. Lonely and barren, she befriended a poor childless young couple that moved into the guesthouse on her property. Gothel was happy to have the extra income and the companionship. Plus to keep their rent down, the husband, an aspiring dragonslayer, maintained the garden and even gave Gothel dragon slaying lessons.

"The lessons got my mind off my husband and got me into great shape."

She still has an amazing body, especially those arms. As she pours herself a cup of tea, she flexes her tattooed biceps. I glance down at my untoned arm; jealousy gnaws away at me.

"Did your husband come back to you again because you looked so good?"

"As a matter of fact he did. We fucked our brains out. And then he went off to war. I knew that if I didn't present him with an heir by the time he came back, it would be over again."

I'm all ears. "Did you get pregnant again?"

"Nah. But the dragonslayer's wife got pregnant."

"How did you feel about that?" I ask, sounding rather Shrink-like.

"Fucked. It happened like that." Gothel snaps her purple-lacquered fingertips. "She didn't even have to spend a fortune on 'magic' fertility treatments. I couldn't bear to look at her."

"Why didn't you just get rid of them?"

Gothel snorts. "I wanted to but they had a lease."

Smart move on their part.

"One day, Mrs. Dragonslayer had a hankering for

rampion, a rare green that grew in my garden."

Rampion, also known as rapunzel. At Faraway, we grew the beautiful flowering plant in The Enchanted Garden and used it in the salads we fixed.

Gothel goes on. "Mr. and Mrs. Dragonslayer couldn't afford to buy it at the market. They begged me for some— even a few leaves—but I told them to take a hike and grow their own garden."

Oooh! She's moving into her evil phase.

"The wife craved it like someone craving a drug, so one night, her husband snuck into my garden and stole a rampion plant. Bad move. I caught the fucker."

I wonder where the hell this story is going. The baby gives me a hard kick. I think it's getting bored. Plus, I don't think it's good for it to be exposed to all these bad words.

Gothel picks up where she left off. "And then I had a brainstorm. The answer to my problem."

She pauses. Her violet eyes narrow.

"I told the dragonslayer to say goodbye to his wife and career. That I was going to turn him in and get him life in a prison. In a dark, dreary dungeon where he could never see his wife again."

She's getting eviler.

"But I made him a deal. I told him if he gave me his firstborn, I would look the other way."

Now, I think I know where this story is going. Gothel digs into another cupcake and continues.

"He didn't want to accept my offer, but his wife made him do it."

She must have really loved him. Would I have done the same for Gallant? Maybe, a year ago. But not now. A pang of sadness stabs me.

Gothel continues. "And so, I got their baby. A beautiful little girl. I even helped deliver her. She was breech. So, I had to cut her out with a knife. Just like this."

Grabbing a sharp knife, Gothel slashes a cupcake and

cuts out the cream. Now, she's scaring me. I'm relieved when she puts the knife down and plays with her nose ring.

"Now that I had a baby, I was sure my husband would stay with me when he came back from war. But I was fearful that Mr. and Mrs. Dragonslayer would come after the child. So I hid her in a stairless one-window tower in a remote part of the forest and named her—"

"Rapunzel," I say, knowingly. "The girl with the legendary mile-long hair."

"Yes, Rupunzel." A melancholic smile crosses Gothel's face. "People still think I mistreated her, but I didn't. I loved her like a daughter."

Come on. She kept the poor girl locked up in a tower with no escape. She even one-upped me. At least, I let Snow White to go outdoors and dream about escaping by a wishing well.

"Rapunzel even called me Mother Gothel." Gothel's violet eyes grow watery. "I gave her everything."

I'm still not buying her good mother act.

"How did you get up there if there were no stairs?"

"Simple. I would yell up to her: 'Rapunzel, Rapunzel, let down your hair.' She'd drop down her braids from the window, and I would climb up."

That explains how she got those wicked arm muscles. Whoof! All that climbing!

"I always brought her one of her favorite things." Tears roll down her high cheekbones. "Sweets, music boxes, art supplies, books, and gowns fit for a princess. Anything she wanted except—"

"Except what?"

Gothel sobs the words. "Except access to the world. Freedom."

I'm near tears now myself and regret that I misjudged her. She *did* love Rapunzel like a daughter. Unlike me who treated Snow White like a servant and dressed her in rags, depriving her of every material thing possible. My baby kicks me hard again. *Don't worry, kid, I won't do that to you; I promise.*

I rub my tummy and look into Gothel's eyes. "I don't understand why you wouldn't let her leave the tower."

"I was afraid of losing her. That she'd leave me. And then when my husband returned, he'd leave me again because I didn't have a child."

So all this time she thought her husband would come back to her. "What happened?" I ask, anxious to hear the end of the story.

"I discovered that I wasn't the only one climbing up Rapunzel's braids. She had another visitor—some local prince—with whom she was plotting to run away. I told Rapunzel to say bye-bye to her braids and her beloved." She picks up the sharp knife again, grabs my hair, and slices off two small clumps. I tremble. "With two snips, the braids were gone and so was her hair-climbing prince."

"What happened to him?" I ask, my eyes wide.

"The prick tumbled into a thorny rose bush and was blinded."

So, the prick got pricked, no pun intended. "Did he live?"

Gothel's eyes grow fierce again. "Yes! And he got me arrested. By that damn Huntsman!"

My father! Though I don't appreciate the insult, it's yet another ironic connection.

"I got life in a windowless dungeon."

"Was the guard a stupid green ogre?"

"Yeah, how did you know?"

"I spent some time there too." It's odd how much we have in common. "What happened to the prince and Rapunzel?"

"What do you think? The prick got his eyesight back, and they got married."

Yet another happily ever after story. But not for Gothel.

"How did you end up at Faraway?"

"Rapunzel forgave me. She got why I kept her prisoner all those years. So, she sprung me from the hellhole dungeon and sent me there for rehab."

An image of Snow White pleading for leniency at my

sentencing flashes into my head. How ironic that the ones we hurt the most are often those who are there for us the most... And the ones we love the most, those who hurt us the most.

Shocking me out of my thoughts, Gothel takes her knife and stabs it into the table. She sobs. "I should have never kept her locked up." Her tear-stained violet eyes meet mine. "I deserved to die, not to live."

The very words I used when I found out that the Huntsman spared my life after I had tried to escape Faraway. I'm moved by Gothel's story. Near tears myself. And amazed how similar our lives have been. But there's something she's left out.

"Did your husband ever come back?" *I need to know.*

Fury falls fast and fiercely over Gothel's face. "Yes, the fucker came back. But not for me."

"Why did you tell me this story?" I ask, holding back tears. "Are you trying to tell me that I shouldn't have my baby? That it's futile. That Gallant will never leave Aurora?"

Gothel knits her arched brows. "What the hell are you talking about?"

Wait. She doesn't know about Gallant's affair? I just assumed she did. That by now, everybody did.

"My husband is having an affair with Princess Aurora." Tears escape my eyes. "It's just a matter of time before he leaves me."

"That sucks." She gazes at me, her violet eyes filled with compassion instead of their usual fierceness. And then she does something unexpected. She clasps my hands in hers and gives them a gentle squeeze. I'm full of remorse—sorry that I thought she was trying to hurt me or mess with my head.

She surveys my bump. "You're tiny. Does Gallant even know that you're pregnant?"

I shake my head. Tears stream down my cheeks. I'm so emotional. So out of control.

"You should tell him."

The tears keep coming. What's the use? He's in love with Aurora. He's going to announce the end of our marriage at his retrospective tomorrow night. A deep shudder runs through me.

Gothel flicks off my tears with her sinewy fingers. "Trust me, he'll never leave you if you're giving him a child."

How can she be so sure? Her husband never came back to her.

Gothel glances down at fob that's chained to her black leather leggings. "My break is over. I've got to split."

"Please don't tell anyone about Gallant and Aurora," I say anxiously, well aware that if their affair becomes the talk of My Fair Hair, the entire kingdom will know.

"Trust me, I won't." She picks up the bill and throws some coins on the table. "My treat."

"Thanks." I'm surprised she treated. And grateful.

"Come see me at My Fair Hair tomorrow. I'll book you an appointment for Gallant's retrospective."

My stomach flutters as fast as my heart. Oh God. The museum gala! Questions pummel me, each one coming at me faster than the one before. Will I be able to face Gallant and his new wife to be? How am I going to handle their announcement? And what about the baby? That's a whole new wrinkle. Should I or shouldn't I tell Gallant?

"Chill, babe. I'll make you beautiful. He won't be able to resist you."

As she gets up to leave, I can't resist asking her one question.

"Does Hook know your story?"

Gothel presses her full lips into a thin line. "You're the only person I've ever told it to, outside of Shrink."

"Why me?" I ask curiously.

"I don't know." She plays with her nose ring again. "It just came out."

I understand. Sometimes, we just need to tell our story. I felt that way when I was writing *Dewitched*. Plus, we're kindred spirits. I knew that the minute I met her at Faraway.

The baby gives me a little kick. Just one final question

before I go to see Shrink.

"Have you ever slain a dragon?"

"Not yet, but I know how," Gothel boasts with a sly smile.

"Good."

———————

It feels good to relax in Shrink's chaise. After all this walking, I could use a little rest. The baby is calm too. I haven't felt a kick for a while. It must be sleeping. A funny thought crosses my mind. My baby isn't even born, and it's in therapy.

My weary eyes are about to close when Shrink comes flying in, showering me—and the baby—with a burst of fairy dust.

"I see you're not wearing the mirrored locket I gave you," she begins.

Damn! She's observant.

"Um, I'm having it professionally cleaned," I splutter absently. There's no way in hell that I'm going to tell her that I gave it to some whacked-out private investigator.

Shrink looks at me dubiously, but quickly changes the subject. "How is your investigation going?"

"I hired someone to follow Gallant." I plan to tell her as little as possible about The Potato Sack Princess. The less she knows, the better.

"And why is that?"

"She's going to provide me with the final piece of evidence I need to prove that he's having an affair with Aurora."

"And what might that be?"

"That they're engaged in extramarital sexual activity," I say, trying to sound as scientific as I can. It does sound better than fucking their brains out.

"I see. And what are you going to do with this finding?"

I'm taken aback by her question. My lips part, but my tongue is tied.

"Are you going to add it to your so called 'Growing List

of Evidence'?" Shrink's voice sounds threatening. I don't like the tone of it.

"Um… "

"And when, Jane, are you planning on confronting Gallant with all this evidence?" She's building her case like a fortress, brick by brick.

A painful lump forms in my throat. The truth is, I've never thought about confronting Gallant with the evidence. I've never once fantasized that scenario or rehearsed the moment. Or imagined the consequences.

Shrink continues. "I find it interesting that you've discovered such an abundance of evidence 'proving' that your husband is having an affair with another woman. And yet, you've never put it under his nose."

She's right! I do have so much incriminating evidence. I could have even hit him up with Aurora's first love letter but…

"You've never had the courage to confront him." Shrink finishes my thought.

Tears trickle down my cheeks. Damn Shrink for being so right!

"Do you know why you are afraid?" she asks, her tone a little gentler.

I shake my head. My tears are blinding me.

"Because, Jane, you are afraid of losing him."

Her words pierce my heart.

"And afraid of losing love."

I wipe my watering eyes but can't stop the flurry of tears. My whole life has been a quest for love. For the love I coveted but never had. My mother's and then that of Snow White's father who squired my stillborn and then deserted me. And when I finally found it with Gallant—and Calla—happiness was mine for the first time. Now, it's all going away. Sadness devours me. I bury my face in my hands and sob until it hurts.

"Jane, look at me." Shrink's voice is soothing yet commanding.

Blinking back my burning tears, I lift my head and gaze at

the tiny fairy, hovering over me like a hummingbird.

"I don't believe you want to end your marriage to Gallant."

"I love him so much," I cry out from some place deep in my soul.

My shoulders heave with pain. Raw and reckless. My new reality gives me a hard kick in the gut.

"And I'm having his baby!" I blurt out, unable to keep it in any longer.

For the first time since she's been here in Lalaland, Shrink is speechless.

The chime rings, signaling that our time is up.

And for the first time, Shrink doesn't flit out the door.

"Jane, I must tell you something."

I gaze up at her with a glint of hope. That she'll have the solution to this fucked up life of mine.

"I'm going on a vacation to Neverland with my sister Tink for three weeks. I leave tomorrow."

What! How could she do this to me? My marriage is about to collapse, and I'm carrying the child of the man who's betrayed me. "What should I do?" I scream out in desperation, needing Shrink more than ever.

"You once ruled a kingdom. Now rule your heart." She zooms out the door. Her trail of fairy dust smothers me.

"Don't forget to write." I choke out the words.

Oh God! What am I going to do?

CHAPTER 19

The long awaited opening of The Midas Museum of Art is just hours away. Everyone who is anyone will be there. I won't.

The last twenty-four hours have been pure hell. While life kicks against the walls of my womb, all the blood inside me is draining. I haven't seen Gallant since Calla's birthday. And the truth is, I can't bear to see him. After he announces his engagement tonight to Aurora, he will be out of my life. Forever.

At my desk, I stare absently at a sheet of parchment. The great thing about a blank sheet is that the possibilities are endless. You're starting from scratch. You can write down anything you want. You can rewrite your life.

A little flutter kick inside me reminds me that, at least, I'll have company. I'm going to have a child. My Prince's child. Without him. Alone. A tear escapes my eye and falls onto the parchment. A sad beginning.

Calla's cheery voice cuts into my gloom. "Mommy, I'm ready!"

My sweet little girl skips into my office. She's wearing a red woolen cape and carrying a small suitcase. Secret trails behind her.

I almost forgot. My darling daughter is sleeping over Winnie's house tonight. She didn't want to go to the grand opening of the museum, even though both Gallant and I told her she could a while back. Spending an evening "with a bunch of boring adults" that she didn't know was not her idea of fun. Now, knowing that Gallant and Aurora will be announcing their engagement, I'm glad she's not going.

Maybe, I should tell Calla I'm staying home, and that there's no need for a sleepover. I could use her company. And Secret's too. The truth is, I can't. She's been so looking forward to spending the night at Winnie's house. I think her blossoming "friendship" with Hansel has something to do with it. Winnie told me not to worry. Her husband John, who loathes big events like the gala, is staying home with the kids and will keep a watchful eye on them. He has a whole evening of fun and games planned. Just no kissing games.

Calla gives me a reproachful look. "Why aren't you ready?"

My eyes meet hers, and melancholy sweeps over me. What a lovely, independent young woman she's turning into. I'm so going to miss her when she's no longer an everyday part of my life. I hope she and the baby will become close even if Gallant and I will no longer be together. Another tear trickles down my cheek.

"What's wrong, Mommy?" Worry fills Calla's big brown eyes.

"Nothing, my sweet girl." *Everything* would be closer to the truth.

Stifling my tears, I grab my cloak and the boxed-up black gown I've been meaning to give back to Winnie. Calla's birthday party was a missed opportunity. But understandably so. I was not in my right mind.

As we mount the coach, Calla remembers that she's left something important behind.

"Hurry, my sweet girl!" I call out to her as she races back inside our palace.

When she returns, she is cradling Lady Jane in her arms. A smile spreads across my face despite my misery. God! I'm going to miss her!

Winnie's house is a charming gingerbread-style two-story cottage that her husband John built from scratch. They used to live in a smaller house in another part of Lalaland, but it held too many painful memories—Winnie's obesity, her crumbling marriage, and her psychotic breakdown that led her to almost eat her children. Winnie and John and their family needed to move away and let the past go with a fresh beginning.

They certainly could have afforded a much larger house— even a small palace—thanks to Winnie's successful event planning business and cobbler John's partnership in Elz's shoe empire. But that's not how Winnie wanted to raise her kids. All they needed was enough space for all of them to live comfortably—and an adequate, state-of-the art kitchen for Winnie to indulge her passion for cooking, and enough land to cultivate a garden full of vegetables, fruits, and flowers.

As soon as we arrive, Calla immediately runs off to play with Hansel, Gretel, and Curly in the beautiful garden. Secret, wagging his tail, follows her.

Winnie's house always smells delicious, and today is no different. She leads me to her wonderful kitchen where platter after platter of delectable salads, tortes, and pastries line the counters. I inhale deeply. The unmistakable aroma of baking bread arouses warm memories. At Faraway, Winnie and I bonded over baking a loaf. She taught me that baking bread was a lot like making love.

Wearing a large apron and her long red hair pinned up, Winnie stirs a pudding that's bubbling in a giant cauldron and then checks on the bread that's baking in her palatial hearth.

This must be some extravagant birthday party she's catering. Then I remember. She's handling tonight's opening of The Midas Museum of Art. Gallant's retrospective! Aurora's coming out party! Their announcement! My heart drops to the floor.

Back to stirring the pudding, Winnie wipes sweat off her

brow with the back of her free hand. "Your mother-in-law is so demanding."

"I thought you never wanted to work for Her Royal Bossiness again after the Princess Swan nightmare," I manage.

"Don't the words 'off with your head' mean anything to you yet?" Winnie sighs, now arranging a platter of sparkling star-shaped cookies.

I crack a faint smile. Inside, the baby kicks madly.

"Try one." Winnie stuffs a cookie into my mouth. Although I'm sure it's melt-in-your-mouth scrumptious, my taste buds are numb.

"The theme of the gala is 'Reach for the Stars.' The Queen wants it to be the ultimate celebration of Gallant's creativity."

How creative has he been with Aurora? The Potato Sack Princess will have the answer for me soon. I swallow hard. The masticated pastry mingles with bile in the back of my throat.

In need of a break, Winnie artfully assembles a small tray of pastries, along with pot of chamomile tea, and leads me to the cozy parlor that's adjacent to the kitchen.

"This is for you." Before lowering myself to the comfy floral couch, I hand her the box containing my black dress. As usual, it's disastrously gift-wrapped.

Winnie unwraps it and gasps.

My lips curl into a smile. "It's yours, and besides it doesn't fit me anymore."

Winnie gives me a warm hug. "Oh, Jane. Thank you. I'm going to wear it to the gala." She holds up the dress against her. "What are you wearing?"

"I'm not going." I spit out the words, blinking back tears.

Winnie's eyes flare. "You have to. Everyone in the kingdom is expecting to see you there."

"I can't." Tears spill into my tea. "I know that you and John made things work, but that's not what's in my stars. I'm positive Gallant's going to announce that he's leaving me for Aurora."

Silence. For the first time, Winnie doesn't challenge me. Maybe like me, she's figured out our friendship is worth too much. Or she finally believes me. She hugs her arms around me, but her warmth cannot melt the chill coursing through my body.

A sharp pain zaps abdomen, and I wince.

"Jane, what's the matter?" asks Winnie, wide-eyed with worry.

The pain strikes again, and I wince even louder. I grab Winnie's hand and squeeze it.

And then, I just breakdown. Unabashedly, uncontrollably breakdown. Tears storm down my face. My sobbing is so loud that Winnie runs to close the double doors leading the garden so that the children won't hear me and grow frightened.

Returning to the couch, Winnie clasps my hands in hers and looks at me intensely. "Jane, you must tell me what's going on. No man is worth this many tears."

Again, the awful pain strikes and goes away as quickly as it came. And then, the words shoot out.

"Winnie, I'm pregnant!"

Winnie ponders the news, the look on her face unreadable. I continue to bawl. Finally, her lips part.

"That changes everything." Her tone is no-nonsense and straightforward. She dabs my tears with a lace-trimmed napkin. I take it from her and blow my nose.

"What do you mean?" I blubber.

"Jane, you're going to go to the gala, and you're going to tell Gallant about the baby," she says with authority. "And then you're going to fight for your man." She pauses and looks straight at me. "The man you love."

She's right. Just like Shrink. Even though My Prince's heart has strayed, I've never stopped loving him. *Never*. Another round of tears makes its way down my cheeks.

"It's too late," I bawl. "Gallant's made is mind up."

Winnie places her hands firmly on my shoulder and looks hard into my eyes. "It's never too late. You're a fighter, Jane.

You fought for Gallant once, and now you're just going to have to fight for him again."

In my volatile state, the prospect of battling Aurora makes my stomach heave. "But what if, I don't win and Gallant chooses her over me?"

"Jane, there are *no* what-ifs." Her eyes burn into mine. "You and Gallant are meant to be."

For once, Winnie's meant-to be attitude resonates with me. I want to believe it. I do!

"It's as simple as this. Aurora is moving in on the father of your child. The man you love. And *you* have to stop her."

Without warning, the baby kicks up a storm. And poison apples dance in my head. "Yes, I'm going to do it for you, kid," I say to myself, smiling.

"Do you want to feel the baby?" I ask Winnie, gently placing her hand on my swollen belly.

Winnie flashes a cheek-to-cheek smile. "That's a fighter in there for sure. How many weeks pregnant are you?"

"You mean, months. Eight."

A little jolt of surprise is followed by a big hug. "Shame on me. I didn't even congratulate you. You're going to be an incredible mother; in fact, you already are."

"Thanks, Winnie," I say humbly. That's a real compliment, coming from her. The best mother I know.

She loops an arm in mine, and we stroll outdoors through the French doors to check on the children.

They are playing a game of tag around the wishing well in the middle of Winnie's garden. Even Secret is part of the antics, chasing after chubby Curly. Barks mix with giggles. A chorus of pure happiness. The charming scene freezes in my mind like one of those beautiful illustrations you'd find in a children's book. The beginnings of a nursery rhyme fall into place.

> *Four children ran around a wishing well*
> *Chasing each other 'til one fell.*

"Make a wish...

'Hi, Mommy!" yells a sprinting Calla, putting an end to my mental ramblings.

"Guess what Calla wished for?" shouts out Hansel, about to tag her.

Please... not another frog prince.

"Don't tell!" screams Calla, but it's too late.

"A new brother or sister!"

Winnie and I exchange a knowing glance.

I so want to tell Calla about the baby, but instead stop her in her tracks to kiss her good-bye. I remind her to be mindful and polite. And to take good care of Secret. And Lady Jane.

Now, it's time to get ready for a showdown.

CHAPTER 20

Life can often boil down to a simple series of equations. Looking Good = Self-Confidence. Self-Confidence = Winner. Winner = Prize.

As my coach pulls out of Winnie's cottage, a thought crosses my mind. If I'm going to win Gallant back, I'll need to look good at the gala. Damn good! I order the driver to take me to The Trove. I'll go to the Enchanted Spa for a sauna and massage, but, on second thought, those treatments may be harmful to the baby. Also, lying face down on my big belly for an hour is not going to be easy. If fact, it's probably impossible.

I know. I'll take Gothel up on her offer to do my hair. Aurora has fabulous hair. Mine will be more fabulous. I smile wickedly. All is fair in love and war.

My Fair Hair is packed with gossiping princesses getting their hair done for the gala. I ask the receptionist, a cheery hair fairy I've never seen before, for Gothel. My eyes search the salon; I don't see her.

"You must be Jane," she says in a high-pitched pixie voice.

I nod, not sure how she knows my name.

"Gothel's working from home today. She wants you to meet her there."

The hairy fairy's wings hum as she hands me a parchment

scroll. I unroll it. It's a map.

"Gothel told me to tell you that her house is on the right at the end of Forest Lawn Drive. You can't miss it."

The hair fairy was right. It's hard to miss Gothel's house. After traveling miles along a winding path through a lush forest, my coach comes to a dead end—and the first and only residence on the road. A soaring stone tower. I bet this is where she kept Rapunzel.

The tower is surrounded by hundreds of rose bushes. I meander through the prickly bushes to the front door. Except there is no front door. I should have known that. My eyes look up. There's just one small round widow near the top of the tower. I scream out Gothel's name at the top of my lungs. It works. She pops her head out the window.

"Hold on," she shouts down to me. She disappears, and then two tower-length golden braids slowly lower to the ground. Gothel reappears at the window. "Grab onto them and enjoy the ride."

Is she kidding? Reluctantly, I grab a braid in each hand and find myself being hoisted up to the top of the tower. My heart pounds. I keep eyes my focused ahead of me. *Hold on tight and don't look down.* The baby flutter kicks me; at least, one of us is having fun.

When I reach my destination, I sigh with relief. What was probably a five-minute ride felt like eternity. Gothel helps me through the window. With my big belly, let's put it this way: it's not my most graceful entrance.

"Glad you could make it. Let's get to work," she says, coiling the braids around a giant spool that's bolted to the floor.

I straighten myself up and take in my surroundings. My eyes grow wide. Gothel's home is no beauty parlor. It's a three-story-high arsenal filled with every weapon imaginable. Swords, spears, knives, and daggers of all different lengths and widths. Shiny shields of all sizes and shapes, some with dents and scratches. Plus armor and leather trappings. Suddenly, I'm nervous. Very nervous. Perhaps, she's lured me here to kill me. It's a set up to make sure I'm out of Hook's life once and for all. My eyes dart from corner to corner and then back to the window. Holy crap! There's no way out! Unless I jump!

"Relax, babe," says Rapunzel. "This is my dragonslayer studio."

I don't relax. My eyes roam anxiously around the vast interior. In addition to all the scary dragon slaying paraphernalia, there are diagrams of different types of dragons scattered on the walls. One of them, black and bigger than the others, looks especially fierce and menacing with its outstretched wings and razor-sharp fangs. Against the far wall, there's a shelf filled with books like *Dragon Slaying for Dummies* and *What to Expect When You're Expecting a Dragon*. And cattycornered on an another is a case full of first aid supplies—bandages, ointments, and adhesives.

"Have you ever gotten hurt?" I ask her nervously.

My eyes widen as Gothel yanks down her skintight leather britches, revealing her taut, muscular butt. My jaw drops in shock. Covering most of her of left buttock cheek is a hideous, asymmetric red scar. The expression on her face grows fierce, her violet eyes narrowing into blades.

"A souvenir from that bitch she-dragon Malevolence. She seared my ass."

The mention of her name sends a chill down my spine. No matter what I do, everything leads back to Aurora.

Gothel inches up her tight leather pants. "One day I'm going to burn *her* sorry ass and finish her!" She reaches for a shiny sword and then charges toward the illustration of the black dragon. With an explosive grunt, she slashes the beast. The hair on the back of my neck bristles. This is one scary chick.

"Is this where you kept Rapunzel?" I ask, eager to change

the subject. What a terrifying place to keep a child, I think to myself.

"No, she had her own room."

I look around. There is no other room. Or any doors leading to one.

"I gave her dragon slaying lessons here," says Gothel, brandishing the sword. God, I wish she'd put it down.

Gothel explains that she wanted Rapunzel to be able to defend herself in the world in case she ever escaped. She was a great student, having likely inherited her father's dragon slaying talent.

"Ready?" *Ready for what?* Without warning, Gothel lunges at me with the sword. With a gasp, I jump back and stumble to the stone floor. Madame Dragonslayer looms over me, pointing the sword at my heart. Her full lips curl into snarl, and her purple eyes grow fierce.

"I'm sick and tired of pathetic princesses waiting for some handsome prince to show up and rescue them," she growls.

She lowers the tip of the sword closer to me. I'm an inch away from death! My heart thuds in my ear. I was right. She did lure me here to kill me. Fear mingles with despair. If I die, will my baby die too?

As the sharp tip of the sword presses into my chest, the image of Gallant flashes through my head... magically charging through the walls on his majestic white steed... scooping me up... and saving *us* from doom.

Gothel snorts. "Women have to take charge of themselves and save their own lives." With a sharp whack, she slashes the button off my cloak; it goes flying across the room. "And, babe, that's what you've got to do tonight."

She puts her sword to the side and yanks me up with her free hand to a standing position. My buttonless cloak slides to the stone floor as I breathe a sigh of relief. While I take several more calming breaths, she swaggers over to her weapons rack. She returns with another sword and a shield. "These are for you, babe."

Hesitantly, I take the sword in one hand, the shield in the other. They're much heavier than I expected.

Gothel gives me the once-over. I can feel her eyes mocking me as she says, "I'm going to give you three pointers:

1. Hold on to your weapon and be prepared to replace it if you lose it.

2. Go for the heart; it's smack in the middle of every dragon's torso.

3. Most important of all, always keep your mind in the fight."

Okay. I got it. *Dragon Slaying for Dummies*. Now what?

"Now babe, pretend I'm a dragon and try to kill me."

Crap! What have I gotten myself into? All I wanted was to get my hair done.

Gothel's expression again grows fierce. Her eyes morph into sharp slivers of violet glass, and her mouth opens wide. She lets out a roar so loud, it echoes off the walls. I shudder with fear.

Awaiting a breath of fire, I impulsively lunge at her with my sword. She dodges me, and I miss.

"Don't stop!" snickers Gothel. She's enjoying this little game of hers and twirls her nose ring. "C'mon, bitch, bring it on!"

Damn her for calling me a bitch! Mad as hell, I lunge at her again. And this time I slash her muscular upper arm. The sound of ripping skin sickens me. Blood trickles from the wound over the tattoo on her bicep and down her forearm. Oh no! I hope I haven't hurt her too badly.

"Nice one," snorts Gothel. "Don't worry, it's just a little scratch."

I rest my sword and take a victorious breather. HA! I'm not bad at this.

"FIRE!" screams Gothel.

I instantly let go of my sword; it falls to the floor with a clank. My eyes dart around the room, and panic grips me. There's no way out.

As I contemplate diving through the window (maybe my driver will catch me!), two hands wrap round my neck, squeezing it tight. Gothel! My eyes clash with hers as I gasp for air. I'm either going to choke to death or burn. Either way, I'm going to be toast, although I don't see or smell any smoke.

"Gotcha!" smirks Gothel. "There is no fire." She releases me.

What! She tricked me? My blood is bubbling with rage.

"See what happens when you don't keep your mind in the fight."

Damn it! She's right. I got distracted. And let myself be taken.

Gothel's violet eyes flicker with victory. "Enough fun and games. Let's get to the salon."

Salon? I survey the room again. I still don't see any doors to another chamber. And then, a chilling thought runs through my mind. She's going to style my hair with her weapons. Goose bumps pop along my arms.

My theory is confirmed when Gothel strides over to her weapons rack and yanks out a long spear. Good for parting and curling? To my surprise and relief, she hurls it upward. When the spear hits the ceiling, a trap door drops down along with a long makeshift ladder made of woven strands of golden hair. I gape one more time. More of Rapunzel's hair!

"Follow me," says Gothel.

While long-legged Gothel navigates the ladder like a trapeze artist, I take one uncertain step at a time, clinging to the shaky rungs. I've had enough climbing today to last me a lifetime. My palms sting from rope burn—I mean, hair burn—and I'm panting like a dog from the baby weight. And talking about baby, it's kicking up a storm. Doesn't this child ever sleep?

"Hang in there, babe," Gothel shouts out, several rungs ahead of me. "You're almost there."

When she gets to the top and can climb no more, Gothel hoists herself through the opening in the ceiling. Her long, sinewy arms reach down to pull me through.

My eyes pop. Gothel's private hair salon is a far cry from her dragon slaying studio. Everything, illuminated by candle-lit crystal sconces, is pink and beautiful. There's a canopied four-poster bed adorned with a satin duvet, matching monogrammed "R" pillows and a bevy of adorable stuffed animals... a plush velvety rug... a tall, hand-painted bookshelf lined with charming music boxes and every fairy tale imaginable... and even a charming table and chairs, set for a tea party. Gilt-framed child-like drawings are scattered on the walls. Calla would love this place! It's a dream house fit for a young fairy-tale princess, except there are no windows anywhere. Of course, this is the dungeon where Rapunzel once lived.

Gothel escorts me to a throne-like armchair, carved in gilt and richly upholstered in pink velvet. In front of it is an exquisite gold-leafed standing mirror and to the right, a small pink chest of drawers.

"This is where I used to braid Rapunzel's hair," she says, her voice dripping with melancholy. "I've always been good with hair."

She runs her sinewy fingers through my tresses. "Let's give you an upsweep for tonight." She gestures to the pink velvet chair. "Sit."

Lowering myself to the chair, I glimpse myself in the mirror. There are no voices in my head telling me that I'm the *Fairest of All*. My fair skin is wan; my green eyes sunken, and my jet-black hair limp. I need help.

Removing a hairbrush from the chest of drawers, Gothel runs it through my hair. Her firm, powerful strokes feel good against my scalp.

"Why do you still live here?" I ask, attempting to make

some friendly conversation.

"I got a bum deal. After Rapunzel sprung me from that dungeon, her shrewd prince forced me to give them my manor house and her parents my guesthouse. As part of the deal, I was confined to live in this tower for the rest of my life."

So the vengeful prince wanted to give her a taste of her own medicine. He *was* a prick. "That's awful."

"The truth is, I like it here." Her eyes circle around the room, and a smile forms on her lips. I think the truth is more she can't let go. Gothel is even more complicated than I thought.

"Why did you spoil Rapunzel?" I ask.

"Because I wanted her to have everything that was taken away from me as a child."

In the mirror, sadness sweeps over Gothel's reflection as she begins to arrange my hair on top of my head.

"What was your childhood like?" I venture, treading dangerous territory. I thought she came from royalty.

"It frickin' sucked."

"Your mother was wicked?" I ask cautiously.

"Hell no." I observe a faint, wistful smile on her face in the mirror. "My mother was an angel. Beautiful and loving."

Surprised by her response, I'm all ears.

"When I turned five, a dark fairy snatched me from her." Her violet eyes grow cold and distant. As if she's reliving that terrible moment. I try to imagine what it was like. A beautiful little girl clinging to the arms of her mother... a mother screaming... a child sobbing... evil having no mercy.

"The fairy handed me over to a wicked woman in a faraway kingdom who worked as courtesan for a local lord."

"What happened?" I ask, gripped by her new story.

"All Mother Evil wanted was money. Money to buy her riches. She threatened me that if I ever wanted to see my real mother again, I had to do what she told me. She made me beg for money, even on the coldest of nights. The only way I kept warm was by lighting matches. I got to be known as 'The

Little Match Girl.'"

How awful! And how strangely similar her childhood was to mine! I shudder at the memory of my evil mother.

Gothel goes on. "One brutally cold night, I almost froze to death. Had not the Lord himself not discovered me and taken me in, I would have died."

Poor Gothel!

She continues to pin up my hair as she reminisces. "The Lord exiled my mother from his royal court and offered me a job as a servant. He had a son about my age. We fell in love… and you know the rest."

We share a stretch of silence. While I reflect on her challenging, tragic life, I watch her examine the back of my neck in the mirror. She leans in closer, furrowing her black as night arched brows.

"That's weird. I have the very same mark in the very same place."

"What are you talking about?" My curiosity is piqued.

She comes around the chair and bends her spiky-haired head down. On the nape of her neck is a small, red heart-shaped birthmark.

She straightens up and pulls out a jewel-encrusted hand mirror from the top drawer of the chest.

"Stand up and face your back to the mirror." I do what she orders. She holds up the hand mirror to my face.

I'm shocked by what I see behind me in the large standing mirror. A red heart, identical to hers, on the nape of my neck. I never knew I had it. Up until I entered Faraway, my hair cascaded down my back to my butt, covering my neck. And since then, I've spent as little time as possible regarding myself in a mirror. Strangely, no one's ever mentioned it to me. Not even Gallant.

A question races into my head. It's just too uncanny. Can Gothel and I be related? Possibly be sisters? It makes sense. I mean, the way we've clicked, and all the things we have in common. We even look a lot alike, not to mention that Hook was attracted to both of us.

"What was the name of the woman who adopted you?" I ask, my heart pounding with anticipation.

"Bitch," snarls Gothel.

I suppose that could be my mother's name too.

"I don't know what happened to her. And to be dead honest, I don't give a dragon's ass."

"What was your real mother's name?"

"Ellena," says Gothel softly. "If you look it up in your baby naming book, you'll find out it means 'shining light.'" Gothel pauses, and I swear her eyes are watering. "She *was* a shining light. A ray of sunshine."

My mother, Nelle, on the other hand, was the darkest of clouds. I guess the birthmark is just a coincidence and drop the subject. Gothel puts the finishing touches on my hair, pulling a few wispy tendrils onto my forehead.

"What do you think?" she asks.

"I love it!"

I admire my new upswept hairstyle in the mirror. My hair is piled high on my head in cascading curls, with a few thick tendrils curling around my long neck. Gothel's done her magic once again. I'm going to look hot tonight at Gallant's gala! My confidence is soaring. I can't wait to take on the man-eater!

I reach into a pocket and offer Gothel a handful of gold coins. She hesitates at first about taking them, but ultimately snatches them and slips them inside her tight leather bustier.

"Thanks, babe." As I rise to my feet, her fierce violet eyes meet mine. "Just remember what I told you. Keep your mind in the fight."

The baby, who's been quiet all this time, gives me a couple of fighting kicks. We're in this together.

CHAPTER 21

I rush home, eager to get ready for the gala. Winnie's right as usual. I need to tell Gallant about the baby. *Our* baby. I'm going to spring the news to him before he announces our separation and his pending marriage to Aurora. The more I've thought about it, the more I'm confident he'll come back to me. With arms wide open. Maybe I won't forget about his affair, but I'll forgive him. Things will go back to being just like they were. All "lovey dovey" as Elz would say. All perfect.

Taking a quick bath, I gently slather soap around my extended belly. I swear, it's bigger than it was this morning. Our baby is growing. A warm feeling saturates my body as I marvel at this miracle of life inside me.

Stepping out of the tub, I take a deep breath and bundle myself in fluffy robe. I've never felt so ready for a showdown. I'm going to take on Aurora. My hair looks amazing, and if Aurora dares to attack me, I know what to do thanks to Gothel's self-defense lesson. The man-eater may not be a dragon, but she's still a monster to be reckoned with. There may even be bloodshed. I hope not too much. Nothing's worth losing the life of my child. *Nothing.*

My genius plan will make her easy prey. I'm going to wear my new black taffeta gown—the one that's identical to the one Gallant bought for her at The Ballgown Emporium. There's nothing more humiliating, more horrifying, or more debilitating than seeing another woman in the same dress at a Lalaland gala. When she sees me in her gown, it'll unnerve her. She'll be defenseless. Gone with the wind. At the end of the night, Gallant will be mine again!

After slapping on some makeup, I dash to my closet and pull out the black gown. Holding it up, I admire it. The fabric is rich and the detailing exquisite. And that super-sized batwing bow on the backside and sweeping train are to die for. I'm glad I bought it. Even for the wrong reason.

I carefully step into it and inch it up over the layers of petticoats I've put on first. So far, so good. I even manage to get over my hips. The full skirt falls nicely, hiding all my imperfections. But when it I get to my waist, the bodice will not budge. I try wiggling into it. Stretching the fabric. Holding in my swollen tummy and butt. Nothing works. It no longer fits! The baby kicks. "Stop it!" I yell. "This is not a good time to be acting up!"

I refuse to give up. If only I had a corset, I could lace it tightly around my middle and badda bing. Hopeful, I suck in my tummy one more time—until it hurts and I can't breathe. Using both hands, I yank the dress up over the baby bump. Success! But what was that weird screechy noise? Gazing down, my eyes shift left, then right. Oh no! The side seams have burst! The dress is unwearable. Armando was right. I should have taken the dress in Size 10. Or maybe Size 12. Okay, a 14.

Plan B. I frantically comb my closet for something else to wear to the gala. I tear through dress after dress. What's the point! Everything is Size 6 and nipped at the waist. I have absolutely nothing to wear to Gallant's retrospective! My heart sinks to my stomach. I can't go!

Slumping toward the closet door, I eye my ivory tulle wedding dress crumpled on the floor. The magnificent work of art that Armando designed for my wedding to Gallant. The *Fairytale Tattler* called it the ultimate princess dress for the ultimate fairy-tale wedding. Gazing at the gown, I hear a voice in my head. It's the dress—begging me to hang it up. I give it hard kick, shoving it into the corner of the closet.

"After tonight, you're nothing to me!" I yell back at it and kick it again and again. Tears tumble down my cheeks and onto the dress. I'm going to lose My Prince. I cannot stop crying or kicking the dress. A hard kick from the baby finally makes me stop.

Still wearing the torn black taffeta gown and blurry-eyed from my tears, I stumble down the stairs and lumber to the kitchen. The cackling fire in the hearth illuminates the dark room. I head straight away to the pantry and madly start consuming everything in sight. I'm not going to the gala. No gala. No Gallant. I might as well just get fatter.

As I'm stuffing my mouth with raw oats, a strange ruffling sound startles me. My eyes dart from corner to corner and then I look up. There's something flying around the room. Crap! A bat? It lets out a screeching squawk. I recognize it immediately. It's The Potato Sack Princess's obnoxious raven. Amigo. Né Deevil. There's nothing friendly about this bird.

He's carrying something in his beak. A large singed leaf. The bird zooms toward me, getting too close for comfort. I throw a jar of jam at it. I miss.

"Beat it," I scream. The bird squawks angrily. Shit! It's going to attack me. Gothel's dragon slaying lesson flashes into my head. "Reach for the nearest weapon." Yes, that's what she said... or something like that. The same philosophy must apply to slaying a crazy bird. I hastily survey the kitchen and grab the first weapon I see—a large frying pan. I chase after the bird, trying to swat it. But it's too fast for me. The bird hovers in a corner and then, to my wide-eyed horror, makes a beeline for me. I hold the pan up to my face like a shield to protect myself. Something hot dribbles onto my scalp. I know what it is and clench my fists so tightly my nails dig into my flesh. The damn bird has pooped on me! He's ruined my hair! Now, it's personal.

"I'm going to get you!" I lunge for it with the pan.

To my frustration, the big bird squawks in mockery and flies out the open window, leaving me a few souvenir feathers and the leaf he was carrying in his beak.

Well, at least, it's gone. Cleaning up, I pick up the leaf it's left behind. On it is a scribbled note from The Potato Sack Princess. I step closer to the blazing hearth to read it.

TO: Jane Yvel
FROM: The Potato Sack Princess, P.I.
RE: Prince Gallant Affair
DATE: Once Upon a Time

After extensive investigation, I am pleased to inform you that your husband, Prince Gallant, and a princess by the name of Aurora are indeed having a very mutually rewarding affair. I will shortly bring you the proof you requested—their love child.

Their love child! Oh my God! Gallant and Aurora had a baby together? A mix of shock and rage races through my blood. I'm hyperventilating. My legs are like jelly. This is beyond my wildest imagination. My hand shaking, I crumple up the note and hurl it into the hearth. As the red-hot flames eat it up, every muscle in my body twitches. I don't even know how my legs are holding me up. Somehow, I manage to stumble to the butcher-block table where Calla and I often take our meals. I collapse into a chair.

I bury my hands in my arms and tears explode. My wails echo in my ears. It's futile! What's the use of telling Gallant about the baby! He already has one! With his Sleeping Beauty. My marriage is over!

My shoulders heave as I sob harder. Gallant must be making his grand entrance with the slut on his arm right about now, and soon he'll be announcing to the world that he's leaving me and marrying her, his first true love. Everyone will gasp, I'm sure, but when they see how perfectly matched they are—how radiant they are together—they'll just see me as a little filler-inner. Of course, The Prince was grieving over the loss of Snow White and needed me for temporary relief. Until, his first true love came along. And then he'll tell everyone about their love child. The heir he *thought* I could never give him. A kick jabs my womb, then another and another. I look down at my swollen, fluttering belly and let my tempest of tears pour down upon it.

Gallant! I wish I had had never met him! I wish I had never fallen in love with him! I wish I had never married him! I wish I had never become preg—

Before I can finish my thought, the baby kicks me hard. As if to say, SHUT UP!

"I'm sorry," I sniffle. I rub my belly gently, and the baby stops kicking.

As my hand continues to circle my belly, a montage of memories drifts through my head. My first encounter with Gallant... Our first kiss... Our fairy-tale wedding... Our romantic honeymoon. Yes, that unforgettable night I made beautiful love with him for the very first time, and he whispered in my ear, "Jane, let's make a baby."

On that magical night, I vowed that I'd never leave him. And I believed he would never leave me. That our life would be happily ever after. That our love would be forever. As the memories fade, the should haves become could haves. Oh, what my life with Gallant could have been! How much joy this baby could have brought us!

Gut-wrenching chokes replace my sobs. Damn, damn, damn it! I wish Aurora never existed! I wish that Gallant were still mine! But forever is over. I yank at my gold wedding band; there's no use for it anymore. It belongs in the hearth. Let it melt away with my heart. But it won't budge over my knuckle, no matter how hard I twist and turn it. My finger is too swollen from the baby weight. I give up and bury my head in my arms again on the table, drenching it with my tears. "It's just you and me, kid," I sob aloud.

"So not true." A familiar voice startles me. I lift my head, and a portly figure stands before my blurry, tear-soaked eyes. It's Emperor Armando. My fairy godmother!

He's clad in a glittery caftan and matching cap. A large Ballgown Emporium shopping bag dangles from one hand. "Dahling, you can't miss the gala!"

"You're too late," I wail. "Gallant is going to divorce me and marry his childhood sweetheart, Aurora. They even have a baby." Burning tears storm down my cheeks. "It's their destiny."

"Puh-lease. Fate is so overrated."

I blink my watery eyes several times. "How do you know that?"

"Dahling, just trust me and get dressed." He scrutinizes my torn gown and shakes his head in dismay. "You can't go looking like that."

"Nothing fits! I'm pregnant!"

"It's about time you told me," Armando pouts.

My eyes grow wide. "You knew all along?"

"Of course, dahling. *I'm* your fairy godmother! I know everything!"

"Am I having a boy or a girl?" I blurt out.

"Dahling, I didn't say I was fortune teller," he says, rolling his eyes.

I glance down at the torn black taffeta gown and then at his shopping bag "You bought me another dress in Size 12?" I hate to admit that he was right about the size I needed.

"Sorry. Sold out, dahling," He scans my body from head to foot and shakes his head again. "I'm afraid that nothing at The Ballgown Emporium would fit you."

He's right. I look down at my tummy. It looks like I'm baking a large round loaf of bread inside it.

"We need to get creative," says Armando, surveying the kitchen. His eyes dart from corner to corner and then he grins.

"Perfect! Bring me that potato sack."

A potato sack? My eyes widen. Mystified, I cross the room and retrieve the burlap sack.

Armando takes the sack from me and turns it upside down. Two large potatoes roll onto the stone floor. Sashaying over to a counter with the sack folded over his arm, he grabs a pair of meat scissors and heads back to me. My eyes stay riveted on him as he cuts a half-circle on the top seam of the sack and two more on each side.

"Dahling, put this over your head." Is he kidding? He wants to me wear this to Gallant's gala? I'll be the laughing stock. A Potato Sack Princess! Just like Princess Lisbon, whose true love Prince Roland ditched her for wearing such a hideous outfit. Gallant will scorn me too!

"How could I be married to *that!*" he'll proclaim to the kingdom, and then he'll introduce my replacement, Princess Aurora, looking perfectly princessy in her black taffeta ball gown. Yes, they'll boo me and sing her praises! I can see and hear it now! Inside, I'm shriveling.

Reluctantly, I put the potato sack over my head and pull it down over my distorted body. My head eases through the top aperture, and I slip my arms through the two side ones. It fits over my big tummy and extends to my ankles. I have to admit, except for being a little scratchy, it's quite comfortable. But there's no way, I'm going to let Gallant see me in it.

"I can't go to the gala like this," I sulk.

"Of course not, dahling. The fashion police would arrest you!"

He reaches into his shopping bag. Of course, he's brought me a fabulous dress. A custom-made creation. He was probably just playing with my head when he said The Ballgown Emporium had nothing in my size.

My heart sinks with disappointment when he pulls out a small, shiny pin. He surveys the kitchen again. Now, I'm confused. His eyes land on an ivory lace doily on the butcher-block table.

"I love it!" he exclaims with a little clap of his hands. He picks up the dainty doily and pins it onto the back of the potato sack. A flourish? I grow even more confused. And impatient. He dips his hand into the shopping bag again and pulls out a long glowing stick. His magic wand! Waving it in the air, he chants:

> "Bippity boppity boo,
> Potatoes and paper won't do.
> Whip them together
> To look good with a feather;
> Bippity boppity boo."

Suddenly, a whirling dervish of sparkling dust spins around me. I cover my eyes with my hands. When the storm of dust finally dies down, I flutter them open.

GASP! Armando has done it again. He's magically transformed the potato sack into a stunning oatmeal-colored silk sheath that loosely frames my pregnant body, camouflaging my baby bump. An elegant train of ivory lace—formerly the doily—drapes down the back and reaches almost to the kitchen door. A masterpiece of understated elegance. The gown is beautiful enough to be a wedding dress.

Armando circles around the dress, straightens the train, and makes a few other minor adjustments.

"Dahling, what does the baby think?"

"It's magnificent!" The baby is actually kicking up a storm. I give my fairy godmother a big hug and gaze down at the dress in awe. My feet are bare.

Armando lowers his eyes and looks pensively at my bare feet. "Dahling, you really should treat yourself to pedicure," he tisks as he digs a hand once more into his "magic" shopping bag. He pulls out a pair of stunning six-inch high stiletto heels. They're the same color of my dress and encrusted with crystals. Smiling, I already know whom they're from as Armando hands me a gift card from inside one of them.

Dear Jane~

*Kick Aurora's butt! I'll be there tonight with
Winnie to watch your
back.*

XOXO~ Your BFF

Of course, the shoes are from Elz—custom-made Glass
Slipper works of art. My size—6. Yes, I'll let Aurora know
how I feel about her stealing Gallant from me. From taking
him away from *our* baby. I *am* going to kick her butt. And
that's just the beginning.

I pluck the shoes from Armando and place them on the
floor. Holding on to The Emperor's broad shoulder, I slip my
feet inside them. Except I can't get my feet into them. I try
harder, squeezing them as far in as I can get them before I
groan. And that's only half-way. Dragonballs! My feet have
swelled up from my pregnancy.

"Time for Plan B," tisks Armando. He gazes at my
swollen belly, which is actually not that noticeable under
the flattering gown he's created for me. "Honestly, dahling,
you're in no condition to be strutting around in six-inch heels.
Heaven help me, if you fell and something happened to *my*
fairy grandchild." He places a hand on the bump, and I feel
the baby flutter kick inside. "Oooh, a feisty one!" exclaims
The Emperor, pulling his hand away.

Twirling his magic wand, Armando sashays over to the
two potatoes that fell out of the sack. He waves the wand over
them. Before my eyes, they transform into chic pair of beige
leather ballet flats. Where there were once spuds, there are
now pearls.

Armando slips them onto my feet. They fit like a glove
and, honestly, are the most comfortable shoes I've ever worn.

"Who said you can't have sensible shoes with style?"
gloats Armando. "Dahling you're good to go!"

But wait! I can't go with bird poop all over my hair.
Serves me right for wishing Cinderella to get caught in storm

of pooping birds at our EPA meeting. Just proves what goes around comes around. I'm literally about to kick myself when Armando brandishes his magic wand in the air yet again. My eyes grow wide as Amigo's souvenir feathers rise from the floor and float toward me; they hover above me. The Emperor waves his wand again, this time high over my head. I close my eyes as fairy dust enshrouds me. When I flutter them open, I can tell something's sitting on my head. I run my hands over it. It's a tiara with jewels and feathers. I can't wait to see what it looks like and reach for Shrink's mirrored locket to take a peek. And then I remember—I loaned it to The Potato Sack Princess. My blood curdles.

"Don't worry, dahling. You look like a princess," Armando says effusively.

He locks his elbow in mine and escorts me outside. Waiting for us in the courtyard is an ornate golden sleigh with two handsome white stallions hitched to it side by side.

"After you, dahling, and my new fairy grandchild." Armando helps me into the spacious sleigh. The plush velvet seat is roomy enough for the two of us, which given my girth and his, is a welcomed blessing.

"Don't you just love my new cross-country sleigh," gushes the Emperor. "Riding horseback is so uncomfy, and chariots are so yesterday."

I have to admit this vehicle is amazing. I'm just not sure how it's going to cross the hilly terrain of Lalaland without wheels.

"Tell baby to prepare for takeoff." The Emperor yanks the reins, and the horses sprout spreading wings. The sleigh soars into the starlit sky. We're flying!

This is the third time I've flown, each experience more magical than the time before. I look down and below me is a spectacular view of all of Lalaland. The magnificence of the panorama makes me at once exhilarated and light-headed. All my worries evaporate into thin air.

As we race past the golden moon, the baby kicks

vivaciously. HA! The baby likes extreme rides. What a vision we must be from the earth below with my long lace train sailing in the sky like a comet.

Out of nowhere, a blast of hot air assaults me. A flash of light lights up the night sky. It's followed by a thunderous roar that sends a shiver up my spine.

I look over my shoulder. Two flickering yellow eyes meet mine as a breath of fire heats up my face. We're being attacked by a dragon! My heart leaps to my throat. Malevolence?

"Hold on, dahling!" yells Armando.

He pulls the horses' reins hard, and the vehicle nosedives at least one hundred feet. Blood rushes to my head, and my stomach sinks. Oh, God! I'm going to throw up.

As Armando races full throttle ahead, I steal another glance behind us. Shit! The dragon is still on our tail. The heat of its fiery breath scorches my back.

"How is my fairy grandchild doing?" asks Armando, shooting me an anxious glance.

"Fine." To be dead honest, I'm sick to my stomach. And sick with worry. The dragon's hot pursuit has taken a toll on my body, and I fear the baby's too.

"Hang in there, kid," I say to myself.

Suddenly, we're going up again. Higher and higher. Our vertical angle is so sharp, I'm virtually upside down. Stars shine in my eyes. I grip the side of the sleigh and scrunch my eyes shut so tightly it hurts. I don't want to see myself tumble light years to the Earth below.

"We're almost there," shouts Armando.

And then finally, we're level and cruising at an acceptable speed. Yet, I still feel extreme heat. The dragon must still be right behind to us. I dare to peel open an eye. A large ball of fire blinds me. But it's not a dragon! It's a star! We're in space!

A beaming Armando tells me that we've lost the beast. It turns out he's a sea of knowledge when it comes to dragons. Dragons, because of their massive size, cannot fly this high. Gravity is one of their few enemies. Water is the other. They cannot swim and fear it. Why didn't Gothel tell me these facts?

Though it's hard to breathe, I'm mesmerized by my surroundings. I take in all the stars——how bright and huge they look up here——and gaze down at the Earth below. How tiny it looks! What a microcosm we are in this vast and mysterious universe! As we float through space, a sense of peacefulness ripples through me, transcending anything I've ever felt before.

Armando points out other planets as we begin our descent. Soon, Lalaland comes into view, its glistening towers and spires tickling the sky. We cruise toward a monumental building that, from my vantage point, resembles a giant gold crown. It must be The Midas Museum of Art.

As we prepare to land, reality sets in. I quiver with fear, having no idea how this night is going to play out. The stakes are high. There's everything to gain. And everything to lose. Including My Prince and my baby.

CHAPTER 22

I've heard a lot about the museum from The King and Queen, but nothing has prepared me for what to expect upon entering. In a word, it's breathtaking. Seven gilt and marble stories high, a single spiraling ramp connects the main level with the top floor. My eyes follow the ramp upward to a magnificent domed rotunda and enormous skylight. Stars and moonlight beam through it, illuminating the interior. And all of Gallant's magnificent paintings that are hanging throughout on the white marble walls.

Everyone who's anyone in Lalaland is here. And so are many of my Faraway friends. Pinocchio (holding hands with Peter Pan), Headmaster Diggs and, of course, Elz, Rump, Winnie, and my father, The Huntsman. Also milling around the crowd, with a notebook and stylus in his hand, is that egghead reporter from the *Fairytale Tattler*, Humpty Dumpty. He must be covering the event. Guests are admiring Gallant's masterpieces or stuffing their faces at the candlelit buffet. Armando immediately mingles with the crowd. Virtually every princess is wearing one of his magnificent creations, each itself a work of art. I don't, however, see Aurora. Or Gallant.

A jingling sound diverts my attention.

"Hello, dear. Everyone loves what I'm wearing and wants to know where I got it!"

It's The Queen. I don't believe my eyes. She's actually stuffed her blubbery body into the stretchy jester outfit. Every roll and bulge is visible. And on top of her head, she's wearing that ridiculous four-pointed hat with the bells. I'm sure no one here has dared to tell her how frighteningly absurd she looks in fear of losing their head.

"You simply must try the pâté," she says, shoveling a heaping forkful into her mouth.

"Have you seen Gallant?" I ask her anxiously.

"Oh, he's somewhere around rehearsing his speech." She pauses to take another bite of the pâté. "He's going to unveil something very important. I understand it involves Aurora."

My heart practically leaps out of my chest. Aurora's here! And he's preparing his announcement that our marriage is to be dissolved so that he can marry her. His first true love. The woman he was meant to marry! *That's* the real reason Humpty is here. To break the story! So that everyone can read about it in tomorrow's *Fairytale Tattler*. The headline flashes into my head: *"EXTRA! Prince to Wed New Baby Mama"!* A giant wave of nausea washes over me. Barely recovered from the harrowing dragon encounter, I'm close to throwing up. *Please don't barf now! Hang in there, Jane!*

The baby gives me a kick, and somehow my nausea subsides enough for me to focus. My eyes dart around the museum. Gallant is still nowhere in sight. Panic grips me. Where is he? I need to tell him about the baby before his speech! *I must!*

"Jane, are you okay?" I wheel around to a welcomed familiar voice. It's Winnie, looking positively stunning in my black gown. Elz, dressed in rose, is standing beside her and looks radiant. You'd never know that just a few days ago she endured a traumatic miscarriage.

I breathe a sigh of relief. Just what I needed. My best friends. After hugs all around, I quickly catch them up on the events of the night—Armando's fairy godmother magic, the life-and-death dragon encounter, *and* my discovery of Gallant and Aurora's secret love child. The latter makes them gasp in unison.

"You poor thing," singsongs Elz, giving me another sympathetic hug. "At least, you're going down looking beautiful."

Winnie shoots her a look of disbelief and then directs her attention at me. "Jane, there are no ifs or buts. You have to tell Gallant about *your* baby before he makes the announcement."

Elz flashes me a wide-eyed look of surprise. Realizing what she's just said, Winnie bites her lip. She must have forgotten to tell Elz about my pregnancy. Or didn't want to in light of her miscarriage.

Elz bursts into tears. She must be thinking about her loss. A pang of pity stabs me.

To my surprise, they turn out to be tears of joy. She's thrilled for me and gives me another big hug. I let her feel the baby. A genuine smile spreads across her face. Unlike me, there's not a jealous bone in her body.

"Promise you won't name the baby Bob," she sniffles. "Even if it's a girl."

Relieved, Winnie and I share a laugh. And then, Winnie gets serious again.

"Jane, you keep looking for Gallant; we'll spread out and look for Aurora; he could be with her."

Leave it to Winnie to come up with a plan of attack. I describe Aurora to my posse and give them a detailed description of the black taffeta gown she's likely wearing.

"Oooh! It sounds just like something you'd wear," beams Elz.

My fists clench. I love Elz, but sometimes I just want to put a sock in her mouth. Another kick from the baby stops me from saying something I'll regret.

Elz and Winnie split up, leaving me alone. I take in the scene and am mesmerized by the beauty all around me. Gallant's paintings touch me in a way that no words can describe. I'm overwhelmed. Dizzied. Confused. And saddened. My mind flashes back to the first time I ventured to his studio and discovered his secret talent. How awed I was by his brilliance. How moved I was by his passion. I knew right then my heart belonged to him forever. I blink my eyes several times to fight back tears.

A loud growl emanating from my stomach brings me back into the moment. Despite my queasiness, my body—and my baby—are calling out for food. Keeping my eyes peeled for Gallant, I head over to the buffet. It's a grand, candlelit display of vegetables, fruits, breads, and other delicacies that Winnie has artfully prepared. I bypass everything and make a beeline for a platter of peas, for which I have a sudden odd craving. I pile my plate high with a mountain of the green legumes.

"You should get used to eating for one," comes a women's voice from behind me. Startled, I spin around.

It's her! The homewrecker. The man-eater. The whore. Aurora!

And she's wearing the black taffeta gown along with an extravagant matching bow ornament that holds back her long golden locks.

Narrowing her eyes, she sneers at me. I can feel her venom. Unable to control myself, I sweep my free hand toward her face, ready to slap her, but she darts off, and I miss. With my plate of peas in hand, I dash after her, but the dense crowd, combined with my swollen belly, makes it impossible for me to catch up to her. Plus, too many well-wishers stop me to congratulate me on Gallant's success. Each time someone refers to Gallant as my husband, I grow more enraged. And more determined to eliminate the wench.

In no time, I lose sight of her. Damn it!

As my eyes flicker around the room in desperation, a cold metal object hooks around my neck and swivels me around.

"Yo, Ho, Ho, babe. Looking mighty fine although I might say a few pounds heavy."

It's Hook in his pirate finest. It's not surprising he's here since he's now a good friend of Gallant's.

"Have you seen Gallant?" I ask, ignoring his obnoxious comment.

"Nope, haven't seen my matey yet." His blue grey eyes wander around the room. "Gothel should be here soon. I heard she did your hair." He gives my updo a once-over. "Looking good, babe." He winks at me.

I want to take that hook of his and hang him by his eyeballs. No, balls.

"Have you heard the news about Aurora?"

My heart skips a beat. "What do you know about her?" The words fly out of my mouth.

Hook gives me one of his smarmy smiles I so detest. "Gallant told me everything." He twirls his newly grown mustache and moves uncomfortably close to me. "He wanted to surprise everyone, including you."

Hook knows about their affair! Gallant confided in him but kept it secret from me. My stomach knots up, and my legs become jelly. I resist holding on to Hook for support.

As I steady myself, the orchestra breaks into to the kingdom's anthem. All eyes follow King Midas and The Queen of Hearts as they march, arm-in-arm, up the spiraling ramp to a podium on the museum's top level. Two tall torches flank the podium. Behind it, there is a massive backdrop draped in red velvet. The music stops.

Midas welcomes the glittering crowd to the opening of the museum and thanks the Seven Dwarfs, who are in the crowd, for constructing this magnificent showcase.

"At last my son's masterpieces will have a home and can be enjoyed by everyone in Lalaland."

Everyone, except me, if I don't find Gallant fast and tell him about the baby. My eyes search desperately for him.

The Queen takes over and, in her bellowing voice, announces the end of cultural illiteracy in Lalaland. Her heart-shaped lips break into a proud smile.

"Ladies and gentleman of Lalaland, on behalf of my son Gallant, who will be making an announcement shortly, I thank you for your support and present to you his latest, never before seen masterpiece."

An announcement? Shortly? I feel like I'm going over a cliff again. My heart's falling into a bottomless pit. It's over! My marriage is over!

The King and Queen step apart and together remove the velvet covering on the backdrop behind them.

Oh my God!

"Aurora's Secret!" roars The Queen.

The crowd gasps. I want to die.

It's a monumental, full-blown painting of the sketch I saw at Sparkles! Against the lush backdrop of Wonderland's blue lagoon, Aurora, stands seductively on a giant seashell, clad only in lacy briefs. Her golden mane cascades over her full breasts, and she tilts her head up just slightly. Her lush lips are pursed, and her smoldering blue-green eyes gaze straight at me. The painting talks to me! I can hear her poisonous sweet voice.

"Jane, say good-bye to your prince! Forever!"

The words swirl around in my head. Around and around until I am dizzy. My heart beats erratically. My legs wobble. And then the whole room starts swaying. I'm about to faint.

Helplessly and hopelessly, I feel myself going down. Except before I drop to the floor, I fall into strong, familiar arms.

"Darling, are you okay?" It's Gallant!

"Put me down," I scream at him.

"What is wrong with you?" He raises his brows. A mystified expression falls over his breathtaking face.

"How could you do this to me?" Sobbing, I pound my fists against his rock-hard chest. I am too weak to free myself from his arms.

"What are you talking about?" His voice registers even more surprise and a touch of anger.

"I know *your* secret!"

"My secret?" he says nervously. "Darling, I have never kept any secrets from you," he stammers.

"Don't lie to me! I know about your affair with Aurora!" I choke. Angry tears roll down my cheeks.

"My affair with Aurora?" Gallant furrows his brows as if he's stunned, but I'm not falling for it. No way! My tear-soaked eyes meet his and narrow into sharp slithers of glass. Finally, I've confronted him. *Finally!* And, now, I'm ready to take him on full force.

"YES! And I can prove it!"

Composing myself, I start from the beginning with the love letter I found in his desk... move on to my trip to Faraway where I learned about their childhood romance from the Badass Fairies... then on to my escapade at Sparkles where I, undercover, witnessed their romantic tryst.

Gallant cuts me off. "That awful server at Sparkles was you?" And then he does something I could never imagine. He bursts into laughter. Uninhibited, uncontrollable laughter. He laughs so hard he cries.

"STOP laughing!" I scream at him. "This is no joking matter." I can't believe he's laughing his head off while I'm exploding with rage. His reaction has totally unnerved me.

He tries to say something, but his hysterics won't let him. Wiping his eyes, he finally manages.

"Darling, Aurora is *not* my first love. Or my lover. She's my first cousin!"

His first cousin? He carries me over to a secluded velvet settee. Still in his arms, I listen in a state of total numbness as he explains how their fathers are brothers... how he, as a young child, witnessed Malevolence put her curse of death on newborn Aurora and overheard The Good Fairies' plan to hide her in the forest... how he and Aurora soon became secret best friends... how he wrote her letters, giving her the code name "Briar Rose" so no one would discover her whereabouts... how he introduced his other best friend, Prince Phillip to Aurora, who instantly fell in love with him... how he secretly followed his friend into the forest on his quest to bring Aurora out of her deep sleep... which was a fortuitous thing because when vengeful Malevolence made her surprise appearance and transformed into a deadly black dragon, Gallant was there to fight her off and save the lives of both Phillip and Aurora.

I'm in shock. Complete and utter shock. My Prince is not an adulterer; he's a hero! As Gallant continues his story, a horrible guilt devours me. I'm speechless.

Aurora married her true love Phillip shortly after he awoke from her deep sleep with a kiss, and they went off to live in her father's distant kingdom. Over time, Gallant lost touch with his two best friends. Until enterprising Aurora opened up a lingerie store at The Trove. Aurora's Secret—*"For the Sleeping Beauty"*—playing off her moniker and fame. The cousins got together a couple of times, and when Aurora learned of Gallant's talent as an artist, she came to him with an idea. With the success of Aurora's Secret at The Trove, she decided temporarily to leave Phillip (Eeks! So, that was the split up!) to open a second store in Wonderland. A perfect place for a women's lingerie store given that the resort was a honeymooner's paradise. She had an interesting strategy. Why not lure men into the store to buy their princess brides lingerie? She commissioned Gallant to create a large painting of a beautiful woman wearing her seductive undergarments to be the centerpiece of the store. When Gallant told her he needed a model, she volunteered herself. Why not? Aurora was blessed with beauty (and a perfect body!), and there was no one better at selling her lingerie.

Holy shit! So, that explains everything. Gallant was not at in Wonderland having an affair with Aurora. He was merely there working on the painting of his cousin and helping her open her new store. The plan was for the painting to debut at the museum opening and then move it to her new store. That was going to be his "big announcement." Crap! I can't believe misjudged everything and jumped to such a horribly wrong conclusion.

I grow limp in Gallant's powerful arms and avert his gaze. I feel sick-to-my stomach awful. I'm overflowing with guilt and can't stop cursing stupid, stupid me. Self-hatred consumes me. How could I have ever doubted my beloved husband Gallant? Ever!

But wait! Aurora practically told me herself earlier tonight that Gallant was leaving me for her. *Start eating for one.* Her sinister words whirl around in my head.

"She was vicious, I swear," I tell Gallant after relaying my nasty encounter with her.

"Darling, you must have heard what you wanted to hear. There is not a chance that Aurora would say something like that. In fact, she is so looking forward to meeting you tonight."

He's probably right. Given my volatile state, I probably hallucinated the entire thing.

Gallant gently brushes his fingertips through my upswept hair and gazes at me tenderly. His piercing blue eyes penetrate my heart.

"Darling, do you still love me?" I ask feebly, too afraid to look him into the eyes.

Gallant smiles warmly. His dimpled cheeks give me goose bumps.

"Jane, my darling, I cannot paint beauty without thinking of you. You have been my life force and inspiration. I love you more than life itself."

Tears stream down my face. How could I have ever mistrusted him? Doubted his love? I don't deserve someone as wonderful as Gallant. I don't!

I gaze up at him and our eyes connect. Slowly, his mouth moves toward mine. The mists of our breaths become one. He lowers his eyelids and parts his lips, pressing them against mine. My lips melt into his, and we kiss like we've never kissed before. It's passionate, all-encompassing, and delicious.

A sharp kick from the baby takes me by surprise. I pull away from Gallant.

"Darling, what's wrong?" asks my alarmed prince.

The baby won't stop kicking And then I feel a strange but familiar contraction.

"I have a little secret," I splutter.

Gallant looks taken aback. "I have one too."

My eyes widen. So much for a husband and wife claiming to have no secrets from each other. I tell him to spill the beans first.

"Darling, do you recall all those overnight business trips?"

"Of course. You went to Wonderland to help Aurora," I reply matter-of-factly.

Gallant looks at me sheepishly. Oh no! He's going to tell me he's been having an affair with someone else!

"I was going to Faraway to see Dr. Grimm," he says, spitting out the words.

I breathe a sigh of relief. Therapy! No big deal!

"Why didn't you tell me?" Now I know why he accompanied his parents to that ribbon cutting ceremony.

Gallant bows his head. "I felt too ashamed to admit that I needed some help. The pressure of the retrospective caused me much anxiety, and I loathed the way I was ignoring you and Calla." He tilts up my chin with his long, deft fingers. "Can you forgive me, my darling?"

"Of course, my love." Is he kidding? Just about everyone in Lalaland should be in therapy.

Gallant plants a warm kiss on my forehead. "Thank you, my darling. Now, what is *your* little secret?"

Eeks. I practically forgot about the baby. A little kick reminds me. Okay. Here goes.

"I'm having—"

Out of nowhere, a brouhaha cuts me off.

"I've got the proof!" shouts a scawny woman holding a large basket and running toward us. I don't believe my eyes. It's The Potato Sack Princess. Two armed guards are chasing after her along with Charming and Cinderella. And waddling behind them is Humpty Dumpty, scribbling notes in his notebook.

I leap out of Gallant's arms to my feet. Gallant jumps up too.

"Guards! Stop her!" screams Charming on the top of

his lungs.

With ease, the barefoot Potato Sack Princess outruns her assailants. She shoves the basket under my nose. "Here's all the proof you need. Gallant and Aurora's love child."

I look into the basket, and my eyes practically pop out of their sockets. It's Princess Swan! The baby recognizes me immediately and coos. Gallant gazes at me with bewilderment. Ooops. I never got to the love child part.

Charming and the guards catch up to The Potato Sack Princess. Cinderella is right behind them. A panting Humpty Dumpty continues to write down everything.

"Arrest her, guards!" commands Charming. "She's the one who's been stalking us and—"

"Kidnapped our baby!" cries Cinderella, snatching the basket with Swan out of the P.I.'s hand.

Oh my God. That shabby private eye tailed the wrong person. Gallant's identical twin brother Charming! And Miss Perfect Princess Cinderella does indeed fit the description of Aurora that I gave her.

The guards draw their spears and aim them at the scrawny P.I.

"Wait!" I shout at them.

While the perplexed guards hold their spears in midair, The Potato Sack Princess, still wearing my locket, yanks out a creased sheet of parchment from her grungy burlap dress. "Your invoice. This was an express job, and it reflects in my fee. I expect an immediate payment." She thrusts it at me.

As Gallant tries to make sense of the situation, Humpty is taking copious notes. I dread the headline story in tomorrow's *Fairytale Tattler*. "*Former Evil Queen Returns to Evil! Orchestrates Cinderella Baby Snatching!*" Seriously, can this night get any worse?

Yes... when I see how much the bill is. A potato sack full of gold! No way!

The scrawny P.I. smirks. With her filthy fingers, she toys with my locket.

"Give that back to me!" I yell at her. I snatch the locket off her neck and put it around mine. Where it belongs.

"Hey, lady!" snarls The Potato Sack Princess. "Give that back to me. You owe me!"

Gallant's eyes dart back and forth between us. "Jane, what is going on here?"

Full of shame, I explain how I hired The Potato Sack Princess to spy on him and Aurora. "I guess she confused you with your brother." Charming and Cinderella exchange a confounded look, but it's too long a story to get into.

The guards, caught up with the absurdity of the situation, finally handcuff The Potato Sack Princess.

"You don't know who you're messing with," she screams, struggling to free herself.

Gallant sighs. "Let her go. I shall explain everything later."

"Whatever," say Cinderella and Charming in perfect unison. With Swan in her basket, wailing from the commotion, they saunter off, hand in hand. The guards free The Potato Sack Princess. She rubs her wrists and scrunches her face in anger.

"Don't think I'm leaving so fast," she snorts. "I'm a highly cultured individual and happen to appreciate art." She fires me a scathing look. "You'd better pay up," she snivels as she moseys off to study a painting.

Humpty chases after her. "Mam, can you give me a statement?" he shouts out.

Gallant glowers at me. "Jane, I cannot believe you actually hired someone to spy on me!" Each word is sharper than the one before. He's angry. Very angry.

I feel as small as one of the peas on my plate. "I'm sorry," I say meekly.

"Don't pull that shit on me again!"

Eeeks! I've never heard him curse before. He must *really* be mad at me. I cower. And then, he breaks into a dazzling smile and sweeps me into his arms. "HA! Gotcha!"

Phew! He's over it. He still loves me!

"And what was that little secret you were about to tell me?" he whispers in my ear.

The baby! Why do I keep forgetting? But before I can get out a word, Winnie and Elz come racing up to me, each from a different direction.

"Jane, Aurora is about to exit the powder room!" Winnie says breathlessly.

Elz raises her brows. "But I just saw her at the buffet." Turning, she points at a woman wearing a black taffeta gown, standing at the end of the long table. "Look, there she is."

Sure enough, it's Aurora, the woman who threatened me earlier.

"That's odd," says Winnie. She scratches her head, perturbed.

Gallant beams. "Jane, let me introduce you to my cousin, Princess Aurora." He takes my hand and leads me to the banquet table.

"So lovely to finally meet you, Jane." She smiles warmly and embraces me. "My cousin has told me so much about you."

Weird! I swear she sounds and looks just like the Aurora I met earlier. Except she's so sweet. Gallant must be right. I was hallucinating. Hearing what I wanted to hear. That dragon chase must have messed with my head.

"What do you think of the painting?" She bends over the table and scoops some vegetable pâté onto her plate. "Gallant told me you're his best critic."

"It's wonderful," I stammer. "One of a kind." Except Aurora may not be. Coming our way is a woman who's identical to the woman who's standing next to me. She's even wearing the same black taffeta gown.

Gallant is bent over, helping himself to a truffle tart. I tap his shoulder. "Darling, when were you going to tell me that Aurora is a twin?"

Gallant straightens up; a puzzled look is scrawled across his face. And then he sees her and gapes.

This Aurora makes eye contact with him, smiles, and

heads our way. She has the same athletic gait as the Aurora I saw with Gallant at The Trove.

"Gallant, is this your lovely wife?" Her voice is identical to Aurora #1's.

"Yes, this is Jane." Gallant's brows furrow. "But who are you?"

"Your cousin Aurora." She looks taken aback.

"Then, who is she?" He points to the other Aurora who has made her way down the buffet.

Something's wrong. *Very* wrong.

Aurora #2 gasps. And then Aurora #1 gasps in the exact same manner when she discovers her identical other.

Gallant's eyes dart from Aurora to Aurora. His face grows stern. "Tell me now, which one of you is the *real* Aurora?"

"I am!" the two say simultaneously with the exact same voice and conviction.

There's only one way to find out.

I grab two handfuls of my peas, one in each hand. I fling one into the face of Aurora #1. The other into the face of Aurora #2.

"What are you doing?" screams Aurora #1.

Aurora #2 winces in pain. Tiny red welts erupt all over her face.

YES! The pea test—or at least my version of it—has worked! I know who is the real Aurora. The real *Princess* Aurora!

"She's the imposter!" I scream, pointing my finger at Aurora #1.

Gallant's eyes narrow; his lips curl, and a fury, like none other I've seen, falls over him. He utters only one word, syllable by syllable.

"MA-LEV-O-LENCE!"

Malevolence! The shape-shifting dark fairy who put the curse of death on Aurora! The deadly dragon that Gallant battled! The very she-dragon who stopped me from escaping Faraway. And likely attacked Armando and me earlier tonight.

Lalaland's most wanted villain. The one who's eluded my father, The Huntsman, for years.

A wicked smile curls on her face.

I turn to Elz and Winnie. "Find my father. Hurry!"

Winnie looks at me, worry written all over her face. And an expression that reads: "I can't leave you."

"Go, now," I command her.

She squeezes my hand and races off with Elz.

Still in pain, Aurora #2, the real deal, gazes at Malevolence. Terror flickers in her eyes.

"Where's my husband?" she cries out.

"Don't worry, he had a little horseback riding accident," snickers her evil imposter. "He'll live... unfortunately."

Teary-eyed, the real Aurora trembles "Why can't you just leave us alone?"

"It's no longer you—or your pathetic prince—I want," sneers her evil imposter. Her sinister voice is identical to that of the Aurora who told me to think about eating for one. *One*. The singular word reverberates in my head. *One*. Reality hits me like a spear. Oh my God! She's going to kill Gallant!

Without wasting a second, I grab a sharp knife off the buffet table and lunge at her. Her reflexes are swift, and she dodges me. The knife falls out of my shaking hand, but before she can retaliate, Gallant pulls me back into his arms.

"Nice try," she snorts. She glares at Gallant. Her face takes on an evil green glow, and her voice grows more sinister. "Always there to rescue the princess... and botch my curse of death."

"I should have killed you!" shouts Gallant, full of rage and regret.

Malevolence roars with laughter. "I've waited a long time to bring you down, Gallant-one."

Gallant's blue eyes turn into blades of steel. I clutch his hand. It's as cold as ice.

A fire flickers in the dark fairy's eyes. "Over the years, I've perfected my shape-shifting magic. It's been fun being

Aurora, but it's getting a little old. I could morph into you, pretty boy. Or your incompetent father. Or your self-absorbed wife." She eyes me contemptuously and cackles again. "But really, why bother, when I can still morph into something bigger and better."

"Oh, God!" says Gallant. "Aurora, run!" She dashes off. "Jane, hold on to me." Squeezing my hand, he takes off like the wind. I struggle to keep up with him, my baby weight threatening to make me fall behind.

Breathing heavily, I steal a glance behind me and gasp in horror. Malevolence has gone up in flames. Her skin is crisping, turning into charcoal black scales. Her nostrils flare, and razor-sharp fangs descend from her now monstrous jaw. Consumed by red-hot flames, her voluminous black taffeta dress morphs into a powerful reptilian torso. The long black train transforms into a serpentine tail; her hair ornament into hideous horns, and the gown's batwing bow expands into wings that span half the width of the museum.

In the blink of an eye, she grows so tall that her monstrous head appears tiny in comparison to her now massive body. She opens her jaw wide and roars. Flames shoot out. She's become a deadly, five-story, fire-breathing dragon.

The crowd screams.

"Hello, everyone," she thunders, her voice fierce. "Welcome to *my* show." She roars again and blasts her fiery breath across the museum, separating Gallant and me.

Oh my God! The museum is on fire! Flames are everywhere! With horror, I watch the blazing tongues consume Gallant's masterpieces. There is screaming all around me. "Run for your lives!" I hear The King and Queen yell. Panic-stricken guests trample over each other as they clamber to any exit they can find. Some even jump out the windows. Chaos. As Malevolence's wicked laughter fills my ears, my tearing eyes frantically search the museum, now a towering inferno. My heart is hammering. Where is Gallant?

"Darling, run!" Gallant's voice! But I cannot see him.

Flames and smoke are blinding me. He calls out to me again. "JAAAANE!" This time, it's a moan. Oh, my God. He's in pain. Terrible pain! He cries out my name again as I battle the mass exodus, heading toward his distressed voice as fast as I can. "JAAAANE!" *Oh, my darling, I'm getting closer. Please let him be okay. Please!*

Finally, by the ramp, I spot My Prince. He's sprawled on the marble floor, his clothes cinders. He writhes in agony. Panic rips through my body. Tears spring to my eyes. I crouch down beside him and run my fingers over his sooty yet so beautiful face. "My love, I'm here," I tell him, flames soaring all around me.

"Jane," he moans. "Hold my hand."

I take one look at his hands and almost vomit. They're horrifically burnt, some parts red-raw and others blistered white or charred black. Scalding tears rush down my face. Oh, God! My Prince will never paint again.

I brush a tumbled strand of hair out of his face. "Oh my darling, stay calm," My voice sounds soothing, but inside me, I'm bleeding tears. Malevolence has punished him in a way that, for him, is on par with death. I stifle the sobs that are piling up in my throat. "I'm here my darling," I say again, choking out the words.

"Where are you, Jane?" There is a panic in his voice. "I can't see you."

His glazed blue eyes gaze up blankly at the glass rotunda. Disbelief fights reality but loses. Oh my God. Oh my God. Malevolence has not only maimed his hands. She has also blinded him. I open my mouth wide and squeeze my eyes. A silent wail fills my head. *Stay calm, Jane. Stay, calm!* I cradle his head in my arms.

"My darling, I'm right here. Everything will be okay," I say as calmly as I can. But I can't stop my tears from falling into his vacant eyes. My poor darling Gallant has lost far more than his ability to paint. Beauty will never again be his to behold.

I stroke his singed golden hair and silently pray to God to spare his life, whatever that life will be. My Prince looks up at me, and I swear, his blinded eyes are filled with longing. "Oh, my darling, I will love you forever." The words, "until death do us part," stay on my tongue. His parched lips part. He wants a kiss! Yes, a magical kiss will make everything better. As I lean in to him, ready to press my lips against his, he loses consciousness.

"Wake up, my darling! Please wake up!" Desperate, I shake him.

He does not stir. His breathing is barely audible. Oh no! Oh no! He's dying.

In the near distance, Malevolence roars yet another fiery breath and cackles. "I should have barbecued your husband a long time ago. But better late than never. Right, Jane?"

Rage fills me. Rage like none I've ever known before. Malevolence needs to pay!

Before I can spring into action, someone, carrying a shield and spear, charges through the canvas of smoke and flames.

"Tisk. Tisk. Not you again." The she-dragon's sarcasm gives way to wicked laughter. She roars another fierce, fiery breath, blowing her brave assailant across the room, close to me. The assailant's hat flies into my lap. A helmet with a seared red feather, the color of blood. I'd recognize it anywhere. Oh my God! It's my father's. The Huntsman.

I run over to him, my blood pulsing through my veins. I fall to my knees and cradle his limp body in my arms. "Oh, Father!" I cry, the pain inside me the only thing keeping me conscious. The force of the blow has all but consumed him. His face is ashen, his eyes mere slits, and his breathing labored. With all that he's got left, he takes my hand in his. He struggles to lift up his head to tell me something. I lean in close to him.

"Jane," he says softly, "I loved your mother. She was a good woman."

"Father, don't leave me," I plead. Tears spill from my eyes.

"My name is really Humperdinck. Only she called me Beau." His voice is a whisper, almost inaudible. And then he takes a breath. A final breath. He smiles. And dies in my arms. Inside, I die with him.

Malevolence flaps her wings and laughs with contempt. "The Evil Queen is no match for me, is she?"

My father. My husband. "Take me!" I scream at the ruthless monster. Tears scorch my face. I've lost my will to live. There's no reason. The baby gives me a hard, painful kick. *"What about me? Don't I deserve to live?"*

A loud shatter startles me. I look up. It's Gothel. She's jumped through the glass rotunda and landed on the dragon's thick, scaly neck. Clad head to toe in silver leather and shiny metal armor, she's gripping a massive six-foot-long sword. Assorted daggers and knives are lodged in a wide leather utility belt around her narrow hips. She's a warrior.

Malevolence is taken aback. She flings her monstrous head.

"I'm going to finish you this time," says Gothel with a fierceness in her voice I've never heard before.

She grips the dragon's neck with one hand, and with her other, plows her sword into its thick scaly skin. As Gothel yanks out the blade, Malevolence winces in pain. Red blood pours from the wound and puddles around me.

"Fuck you!" The she-dragon's jaundiced eyes flicker with rage, and her scales stand up on edge, making her look bigger than she already is.

Whipping her long tail around, she swats Gothel, sending her flying. Gothel lands onto one of Malevolence's outstretched wings. The black she-dragon flaps her wings madly, trying to shake her off. Her sword lodged in her belt, Gothel manages to hold on with her strong, muscle-packed arms. She works her way on all fours to the dragon's powerful torso. *Go, Gothel, go!*

A sudden blast of water of water almost knocks me off my feet. Water is blasting out of valves all over the blazing museum. The Seven Dwarfs must have installed an automatic fire protection system. I run back to Gallant. He's still breathing! The water is quickly rising around us. I must get him to safety! I start to drag him by his forearms, trying hard not look at his charred hands. My lungs are burning. My eyes are stinging. Flames engulf me. *Don't panic, Jane. Focus.* Yes, I must save the man I love. My Prince. The father of my child. If only I could get him out of the museum or to a higher level. But his dead weight makes the going slow. I can barely see two feet ahead of me. And the waves of nausea that rise to my chest each time I glimpse my beloved's once beautiful hands hold me back. Flames threaten to consume us, and the water keeps rising. We're doomed!

"Babe, let me help you." A familiar voice startles me. I whirl around. It's Hook!

"Hook, take this and save Jane!" Gothel yells, still scaling the dragon's torso. She tosses the swashbuckler a large, shiny dagger. He intercepts it with his iron hook in midair.

"Nice catch if I must say so myself," says Hook as full of himself as ever. "But I've got this." He pulls out a sparkling sword from his belt and replaces it with the dagger. Gothel smirks.

"So, babe, how's it going?" Before I can respond to the swine, he hoists me over his shoulder with his good arm. Sloshing through the rising water, he lopes toward the museum's main entrance. He grips my ass tightly. The water splashes in my face.

"Put me down!" I scream. "It's Gallant you must save." I try to free myself. Furiously kicking, pounding his back, and yanking his glorious hair. I choke from the smoke. It's futile.

"Yo, babe. Just how much do you weigh?"

That's it. I snatch the dagger and press the tip into his backside. "Put me down if you want to live."

Hook comes to dead halt and shouts up to Gothel. "Yo, babe, I have a little problem down here." I twist my upside down head and glimpse her scaling Malevolence's back. She's oblivious to the swine. I press the blade deeper—I'm sure I've drawn blood—and at last, a wincing Hook releases me. He won't be sitting any time soon.

The water is now above my ankles. With Hook close behind me, I run back to Gallant. I gasp. His body is covered by the water. In no time, he'll be completely under. And floating like a dead man.

"Hook, please, I beg of you. Get him out of here!" My voice is a desperate, hoarse plea.

Wordlessly and effortlessly, Hook lifts my lifeless prince into his arms. Even in the thick, blinding smoke, I catch a tear roll down his sooty face.

"Stay with me friend," he says, his voice tearful. His soulful eyes meet mine. "I'll be back for you, Jane."

I hug my arms around him and gently kiss Gallant. The water is now knee-deep. "Just go!"

Hook throws Gallant over his broad shoulder and charges toward the front doors of the museum.

"You're not going anywhere, pirate-boy!" roars Malevolence. To my horror, she stomps toward him and seizes both Hook and Gallant in one of her enormous claws. Oh no! They're going to be dragon dung.

Hook snarls. "No one calls *me* a boy." He plunges his sword deep into the beast's groin. She groans.

"I've always wanted to do that," gloats Hook.

Contorting her face in pain, Malevolence lets go of Hook and Gallant. They land safely in the water, now almost hip-deep.

"Good one, babe," shouts Gothel from high up on Malevolence's back.

Hook gazes up at her and blows her a chivalrous kiss. Wasting no more time, he wades through the water, using the sword as an oar and his hook to secure Gallant, who's dangling lifelessly over his broad shoulder.

I take a deep breath and wipe sweat off my brow. My eyes stay fixed on Hook and Gallant as my heart thuds in my ear. *Go, Hook, Go!* Thank god! They've made it to safety! I pray for my Gallant to live. *Please, God, let him live!*

The water is rising faster and faster. My gown is completely drenched, and I'm shivering cold. I look up at Gothel. She's still scaling Malevolence's back, jabbing her with a dagger as she creeps along. Malevolence swats her powerful serpentine tail at her, but keeps missing. Frustrated, she roars another blinding breath of fire. Letting go of Hook's dagger, I shield my face with my hands and pray for my life. I'm spared.

Gallant's paintings continue to burn, all but the portrait of Aurora on the top level. It's been ironically spared from Malevolence's fiery rampage. Angry tears burn my eyes. Perhaps it's for the best that My Prince will never able to see this devastation. An afterthought stabs my heart. That is, *if* he lives!

The water is so deep now that it's covered the banquet table and washed everything on it—all of Winnie's exquisite hard work—into this sea of evil. Fruits, vegetables, and ornaments float by me while centerpieces, platters, and dinner plates quickly sink to the bottom. For the sake of the baby, I should just get out of here when I can. But I can't leave Gothel here alone with Malevolence. It's become personal. I want revenge for what Malevolence has done to Gallant! To my father! To me! To Calla! And to my child! She's destroyed our lives!

The icy water rapidly hits my shoulders. I can no longer just stand here; I must swim. But when I stroke my arms, I hardly move. The weight of the long lace train, floating across the surface of the water, is holding me back. I frantically struggle to rip it off, but it's sewn on too tightly. Damn Armando and his fairy godmother magic. And for being such a good tailor.

"Jane, hang in there!" screams Gothel.

The ground floor of the museum has become a violent ocean. I struggle to keep my head above the water as it rushes in from valves on the upper levels. I gasp for breath.

Exhausted, I don't know how much longer I can keep this up. And then one of Gallant's masterpieces floats by me. I reach out for it. It keeps me afloat. My Prince, in his own way, has once again saved my life. The baby kicks madly. HA! My little one is going to be a great swimmer.

I hold on to the canvas for dear life as the water swiftly rises. It now must be twenty-feet deep or more. It's up to the dragon's middle. Malevolence thrashes her wings around in it, creating violent waves, while Gothel continues to stab her in the back repeatedly.

"You bitches!" Malevolence roars hoarsely. She opens her jaw wide, exposing her super-sized, razor-sharp fangs. Terror fills every part of my being. She's about to shoot her fiery breath right at me. Holding on to Gallant's painting, I kick my legs as fast as I can. The bolt of fire hits the water, missing me by an inch, and creates a sizzling, steamy mist. Mad as hell, the she-dragon snaps at me with her deadly fangs. I hold up the painting like a shield, and her fangs rip into the canvas. The canvas is in shreds, but I am spared once again.

I gaze up. Gothel has reached the dragon's head. Malevolence flings it madly, trying to shake her assailant off. Gothel clings to the dragon's horns and stays put. My eyes stay riveted on her as she slithers forward on her tummy to the very front of the beast's head. She pulls out her sword, and with a powerful grunt, she plunges it right between the black dragon's wretched yellow eyes. Malevolence curls over and roars in pain.

"Suffer, you whore!" I scream out at the monster.

Gothel stands up victoriously on the monster's bowed head, brandishing her sword. Why is she stopping? She's supposed to be keeping her mind in the fight. That's what she taught me. Without warning, Malevolence straightens, and Gothel goes flying off her head. To my horror, Malevolence snatches her in midair with one of her monstrous claws. Gothel curses and struggles to free herself. But she can't.

"Let's see now who's going to finish whom." Laughing

wickedly, Malevolence squeezes the life out of her prey. Gothel gasps for air. Oh no! Gothel can't die now!

Her life slipping away, Gothel lets go of her sword. It plummets into the water, landing with a splash close to me. I grab for it and slash off my train. It sails away. I'm free! Clutching the sword, I call upon every muscle in my worn out body and sidestroke toward Malevolence. Gothel's desperate eyes make contact with mine.

"Gothel, hang in there!" I yell.

I'm going to finish it! I know what to do! I swim up to Malevolence until I can go no further. I'm right up against her torso. Smack in the middle. Her repulsive scales brush against my skin. *This is it!* With all my might, I plunge the sword deep into her heart.

Malevolence lets out a scream unlike any other I've ever heard. It's a siren. An endless, deafening siren. She loosens her grip around Gothel, who free-falls into the water.

Blood spurts out of the mutilated beast. I'm sickened by the sight of it; gumball-size droplets accumulate around me in the water. She slaps a clawed limb over her heart, but cannot stop the flow. I watch in horror as her jaundiced eyes roll back, and her hideous tongue falls out of her fang-filled mouth like a limp rag.

With the sword still lodged in her chest, she slowly collapses into the water. Vertebrae by vertebrae. Like a fortress that's been bombarded. I swim away, fearful she will crash on top of me. From the corner of my eye, I see that Gothel has swum to safety; she's by the entrance to the museum. Thank goodness, she's a strong swimmer like me. I steal a glance behind me. My eyes grow wide as Malevolence's limp head hits the water with a geyser-like splash. The water sizzles, and a steamy green mist rises.

Yes! I've slain my first dragon. The evil Malevolence who killed my father. And destroyed my beloved husband. The satisfaction of victory quickly succumbs to sadness. Unbearable, gut-wrenching sadness. It's time to get the hell out of here. But before I take a single stroke, two monstrous horns bolt through the water. Malevolence! She's still alive!

"You may be finished with me! But I'm not finished with you!" She bursts out of the water, creating a colossal tidal wave. I thrash around in the water, unable to move forward.

She opens her monstrous mouth wide. I can feel the heat of her breath on my face as I toss and turn.

"Get ready to be reunited with your mother and father," she sneers.

I gasp. How does she know about my mother? I'm not going to find out. A puff of smoke blasts out of her mouth. Red-hot flames can't be far behind. Oh God, she's going to poach me! But just as she roars, the rising water seeps into her mouth. She chokes. To my shock and relief, the water extinguishes the deadly flames. I'm saved.

Malevolence flounders. The water is almost over her head. I remember what Armando told me. That dragons cannot swim and are susceptible to drowning. Panicked, she thrashes her wide wings to help keep her afloat. I ride her mighty waves, trying desperately to keep my head above the water. Despite what a strong swimmer I am, I keep going under. After all this, am I going to drown? My worst nightmare becomes a reality when she grips me in one her powerful claws and holds me under. I'm going to die! And so is my baby! As my breath leaves me, questions swim in my head. Who will take care of my sweet Calla? And my beloved blinded Gallant? Will Winnie tell them about the baby?

She thrashes me around while I hold my breath praying for my life. Luck! Gothel's dagger gets caught in the deadly whirlpool. I grab for it and stab Malevolence's limb. She lets go of me, and I shoot up to the surface of the water. I suck in the smoky air and cough. I'm alive. Malevolence is flailing madly, her jaw frozen in panic. More luck! My long lace train has entangled her like a net! She's trapped! Battling the waves, I stroke furiously and manage to swim away.

"Help me!" she screams hoarsely. "Don't leave me here!"

I don't know what or why, but something makes me want

to swim back for her. Swimming against the swells of the waves is virtually impossible; each crash sends me backward, further away. She cries out again, her voice weak and desperate. To my shock, flames shoot out of her. Everywhere. She roars in pain and then suddenly she implodes. The sound is deafening. Smoke, water, and scaly remains shoot up to the rotunda. I thrash around in the tumultuous water like her once angry dragon's tail.

The water calms. The monster is gone. But *she* is not! A holographic image of Malevolence, The Mistress of Evil, floats by me on the surface of the water. Her body is emaciated, her skin a ghastly green, and her glazed eyes, the color of urine. And there are tiny horns growing out of her head. So, this is what she looked like in her human form. A freak. I wonder what her life was like. Did her fairy family hide her because they were ashamed of her? Was she lonely and misunderstood? Embarrassed and angry that fate had dealt her a rotten hand? An unexpected sadness fills me. Malevolence was *not* born evil; I'm sure of it. I gaze at her frozen smile. At last, this tormented soul has found peace. The holographic form floats away from me, and I swim toward the entrance of the museum without looking back at the devastation evil has caused.

"Are you okay?" asks Gothel, sprinting up to me outside.

I nod. Truthfully, I'm cold, soaked, and exhausted. And numbed by the night's events. Even my near-death battle with my monstrous mother Nelle did not prepare me for what I faced tonight.

Flames and smoke continue to shoot out from the museum. Sadness courses through me as parts of it collapse. Once the kingdom's crowning glory, The Midas Museum of Art is now in shambles. And my father's body is still inside. Oh, how I already miss my brave father! Tears leak out of my eyes.

"I fucked up in there," says Gothel, her head bowed low.

She must be referring to her premature victory stance. "No, you were great," I say, meaning it.

"You were too."

"I had a great teacher." I flash a smile.

Gothel smiles back and brushes off some soot on her face. "Shit! I lost my nose ring!"

Nervously, I fumble for Shrink's mirrored locket. Phew! It's miraculously still around my neck.

Gothel looks glum.

"Don't worry, I'll buy you a new one."

"Thanks, babe." Gothel smiles again. "I'll give you a free haircut."

I feel closer to Gothel than I ever have. Our ordeal has made us like sisters. I want to hug her. Before I can wrap my arms around her, an enormous explosion rocks us. Oh my God! It's the museum! A fireworks-like display of embers shoots into the sky. We run for cover behind a wide tree as sparks and debris fly everywhere. My eyes follow one spark, bigger and brighter than the rest, as it ascends into the universe, rising way above the cloud of smoke. A star magically appears. One like I've never seen before. It's green just like my eyes. As I gaze at it, it twinkles brightly. Warmth courses through my cold, soaked body. Of course. It's my father, The Huntsman. He's going to watch over me! Tears trickle down my face.

The sound of loud stomping footsteps steals my attention. I can make out the silhouette of a tall, well-built man coming toward us. He appears to be holding some kind of weapon. I tremble with fear. Now, what terror awaits us? Haven't we had enough for one night?

"Yo, Ho, Ho." Damn! I never thought I'd be happy to hear those words.

"I've come back to rescue you two damsels." It's unmistakably Hook, carrying his sword in his good hand and blankets over the other.

"What took you so long?" asks Gothel with obvious sarcasm. She grabs the two blankets, wrapping one around me and the other around her. The thick blanket warms my body but not my heart.

"How's Gallant?" I ask anxiously.

Hook presses his lips into a thin grim line. I fear the worst.

"I got him back to your palace." He shakes his head as sadness sweeps over him.

I know what he's going to say and hold on to Gothel's arm to steady myself. Tears are flooding my stinging eyes.

Hook takes a deep breath. "He's in critical condition, but he's alive."

Yes! He's alive! I feel a glimmer of hope.

"Please, Hook, take me to him." Silently, I pray for My Prince to live.

As I take a step forward, a sharp pain grips my stomach. A warm liquid immediately pours down between my cold, damp legs. I know what's happening. I've experienced this once before.

"Gothel." My voice trembles. "I'm having my baby."

She says only one word. Her favorite one. "FUCK!"

The contractions keep coming. Faster and sharper. I clutch my stomach.

"Lie down!" Gothel takes off her blanket and spreads it across the damp earth.

Reclining, I look up at my father's star and take deep breaths. Nothing can stop the stabbing pains, and I scream out in agony.

Gothel gets down on her knees beside me and rips open my dress. "What's in your flask?" she asks Hook.

"Water." Hook's voice waivers.

Gothel grabs it and takes a sniff. "Liar!" She takes a couple of swigs and makes me drink the rest. The rum runs through my veins and relaxes me.

"PUSH!" yells Gothel.

I try to push, but the result is another agonizing contraction. And then another and another. I scream out again in pain.

"Hook, she needs something calming to hold on to!" I hear Gothel mumble. The rum has made me light-headed.

"What about my hook?" He sounds freaked out.

"I don't think so." She sounds stressed. "But I may need it later."

"What about my good hand?" He perks up.

"Fuck you, Hook." She sneers at him. "But I may need it later too."

Gothel slides her cold hands up my legs and digs one of them deep inside the cavity between them. She makes a disturbing face.

"PUSH!" she shouts again.

With all my force, I push. Something is sliding out between my legs!

"I need your hook! NOW!" yells Gothel at her sometimes mate.

Hook gets to his knees. Gothel grabs his hooked hand and guides it between my legs. My heart thuds in my ear. Something's wrong. *Very* wrong. My mind flashes back to my first pregnancy. The excruciating, blood-bath birthing that almost took my life. Oh no! My baby is going to be stillborn, and this time I'm going to die!

Gothel pushes a horrified Hook aside. "FUCK! It's not going to work."

I watch in horror as she pulls out a shiny knife from her leather utility belt.

"Jane, your baby's breech. I'm going to have to cut the baby out like I did for Rapunzel."

I sob uncontrollably. Fear consumes me. Frightening images of my mother, my father, my little stillborn, and Gallant bombard me. What ever happened to happily ever after? Life has fucked me. Big time. It's just as well it ends now.

I reach for Shrink's locket. The smooth, cold metal feels good in my hand. As it rubs against my palm, a strange calmness washes over me. A euphoria like I've never felt before. I have no worries. I'm at peace with the universe and myself. Shrink's locket was magical after all. I'm ready.

"Hook, did Jane ever punch you?" I overhear Gothel ask.

Hood snickers. "It was one of her favorite things to do at Faraway."

"Well, babe it's payback time. Bring it on."

Hook's tightly curled fist comes at me—POW!—and everything fades to black. The last thing I see is my father's star.

CHAPTER 23

The Forbidden Forest. Flames engulf me. My eyes burn. I cannot breathe. A face appears in the flames. It's Gallant! His piercing blue eyes beg me for help. I call out his name, but it is a silent cry. My throat is too parched. I have no voice. He reaches his arms out to me. I rush to him. He needs me. But the monstrous trees won't let me save him, blocking me with their fiery limbs. Gallant evaporates in an explosion of flames. All that remains is a cloud of smoke. Scorching tears fall down my face as I sob silently. Gallant's life is over, and soon mine will be too. It wasn't so supposed to end this way. Not my story. It was supposed to be happily ever after. That's how I wrote it!

A wail pierces my ears. It's a baby! I must find it, rescue it! This time, I'm not going to let the burning trees stop me. Dodging them, I run toward the sound of the baby. I quickly spot it. It's naked on a blanket of ashes, flailing its tiny arms and legs. I quicken my pace. I'm almost there. Without warning, a monstrous black dragon swoops down and scoops up the child. The dragon roars. "You took what was mine. And now I will take what is yours." A breath of fire shoots out from its fanged mouth, and I meet my fiery demise.

"You belong with us now," says a familiar voice. The silhouette of a man appears in the smoldering flames. He moves closer to me and reaches out his hand. It's my father! A beautiful woman with long flowing hair and iridescent purple eyes magically appears next to him and holds his other hand. She looks strangely familiar to me, but I can't pinpoint how I know her. Faraway? "Come, Jane," she says, her voice melodic and haunting. "It's time to meet your son." My son? I have no son; my son is dead. A young boy steps out from behind them. He is the most angelic child I have ever seen. His hair is the color of ebony; his lips as red as roses, and his skin as white as snow.

"Mama, why didn't you give me a name?"

"I'm sorry, my baby," I cry out. "Take me with you." I reach out my hand. He stares at me as motionless as a statue.

My father and the woman join hands with the boy. They turn their backs on me.

"Please," I beg. "Don't leave me here."

They disappear into the flames. Fear and sweat soak my body. If only My Prince were still alive to rescue me.

A sharp, sudden pain jabs my abdomen. It's as if someone has stabbed me with a dagger. I slap my hand over the terrible pain, expecting warm blood to drench my hand. Instead, a thick layer of gauze covers the tender area. My hands wander down my torso. My hipbones. My jutting hipbones! I haven't felt those in months! I must be disintegrating. Turning to dust. I'm dying! "I don't want to die," I scream, squeezing my eyes shut.

"Darling, you are not going to die." I know that voice! It's Gallant's. It can't be! He's dead! Charred to death by that evil dragon!

I pry open my eyes. I'm not in the blazing forest! I'm in the luxurious bed I share with My Prince. He's sitting next to me, clasping my hands in his. I bolt up from my pillows and wrap my arms around him. It hurts like hell. But I don't care. I'm alive! He's alive! And we're together!

Everything comes back to me with the force of a rockslide. The museum gala... Gallant's story...The two Auroras... The fire... My father... My battle with Malevolence... The labor pains... Gothel's knife. And then no more. My eyes water.

"Darling, but your hands were burnt, and you were

blinded." I gaze at him in disbelief. Miraculously, he looks perfect, heart-stoppingly handsome as ever, except for a small scar above his right brow. I run my fingers over the surface of his face to make sure I'm not dreaming. I'm not. His lips curl into that dazzling smile that renders me breathless.

"Fairweather blessed me with the gift of healing when I was born, thinking that one day I would be a warrior leader."

"Fairweather?"

"Yes, the Good Fairies have worked for our family forever."

I can't wait any more. I fear the truth. But I need to know. "How is the baby?"

"There isn't *a* baby." Gallant's voice is solemn.

My heart falls off a cliff. My baby died! That dragon witch killed by baby! *Our* baby! I burst into tears.

Gallant brushes away my tears. "Darling, there are two babies! A boy and a girl!"

What! I had twins? I don't know whether to laugh or continue to cry. I cry. Tears of joy. Gothel did it!

"Mommy!" There's a word I thought I'd never hear again. It's Calla. She is beaming with happiness. With Secret trailing close behind her, she runs over to hug me. OW! I say nothing. Sometimes, love is pain.

"I love my new brother and sister!" she exclaims. "Why did you keep it a secret?"

I falter for an excuse. "I wanted to surprise you." Gallant rolls his eyes while Calla giggles.

"Guess what! Cinderella let me feed them and bathe them."

Cinderella? Gallant explains that while I was recovering she stayed at our palace and helped care for the twins. He couldn't have done it without her.

"Where is she?" I ask, wrought with emotion. "I must thank her."

"She went back to her palace a little while ago to take care of Princess Swan."

"Darling, where are the babies? I want to see them!"

Just at that moment, Winnie and Elz, my two best friends,

enter the room, each carrying a small bundle in their arms. One is wrapped in a pale blue blanket; the other in pink. Two babies. *My babies!*

"Jane, the babies are hungry. Are you ready to nurse them?" asks a smiling Winnie.

Gently, she and Elz place the tiny life forms in my arms. A jumble of emotions swarms me. Excitement. Joy. Nervousness. Fear. Disbelief. I take one look at them and fall in love with them instantly. How perfect they are! The little girl is a spitting image of me, with a tuft of thick black hair, and the little boy looks just like Gallant, with a glistening cap of golden hair and eyes the shade of the bluest blue.

"Hi," I say softly. Their bright eyes look up at me, and I swear they recognize me!

I play with their tiny fingers and then kiss them each on the forehead. How delicious their newborn skin feels against my lips. For a moment, they are all I can focus on. I am oblivious to the world.

Elz takes me out of my trance. "Jane, they're great little eaters. Dr. Grimm says he's never seen two healthier babies."

Slowly, I lower my dressing gown and place the boy on the right breast, the girl on the left. They take to my breasts like pros. They suck until they have fallen asleep. Burping will have to wait.

My gaze meets Gallant's. The look on his face is intense, loving, and all-encompassing. Oh, how I love My Prince. My husband, my lover, and the father of my children. He squeezes my hand. "We need to give them names."

Calla thoughtfully covers the babies with their blankets; she's going to be such a great big sister and help to me.

"Grandpa says my baby sister is *bellisima*. Just like me. It means beautiful."

Bellisima. What a lovely word to say. And she *is* so beautiful. I think I've got a name. We'll call her Bellie for short. I look down at my sweet little girl and kiss her soft, silky head.

And our son, he already looks so strong and brave. Like my father. Of course, I'll name him Beau. The spirit of my father will live both among the stars and here on earth.

I share my name choices with Gallant. He smiles and then kisses me. He lips are so warm and delicious. And they're mine.

Bellie, Beau, and Calla. We now have three beautiful children. An unexpected wave of sadness washes over me. The memory of my beautiful stillborn son fills my head, making me wish he could have been part of our family. And I wish my father could be with us too. How much he would have loved helping me raise these three children. His grandchildren. I miss him so much!

Gallant's voice brings me back to the moment. "My darling, the Good Fairies will be here any minute."

Fairweather, Flossie, and Fanta are coming? Outside my room, I hear a loud collective thud and what sounds like broken furniture. Yes, the three Badass Fairies are here.

"They've come to give our babies blessings," beams Gallant.

My Prince explains that he didn't think I wanted a big to-do. He was right. Right here in this room surrounded by the people I love the most is perfect.

The big butt fairies toddle into the room, one after another.

"Hello, dear. Have you decided on the three blessings you'd like to have?" asks Fairweather.

Huh! I get to pick out my own blessings? *Okay, Jane, think.* What three things would you like Bellie and Beau to have most in this world?

"You can't go wrong with Beauty," chimes Flossie.

I look down at the little darlings sleeping peacefully on my chest. They're breathtaking. Beauty is one blessing I can definitely eliminate.

"I'm big on Grace," pouts Fairweather, who could certainly use some of her own.

Interesting choice but I can always send the twins to

charm school or give them dancing lessons.

"Given the dangerous times we live in, I'm pushing Longevity," says Fanta.

I think about the cut-off life of my father, and sadness again sweeps over me. Longevity is a good one. But it's not how long you live your life; it's how you live it.

Think, Jane, think. A flurry of virtues spins around my head, each a moving target—patience, intelligence, humor, and so many more. This is hard. And then my brain lands on three, one right after another.

Creativity—let the world be their canvas.

Courage—let them never be afraid.

Compassion—let them feel and they will love and be loved.

Creativity. Courage. Compassion. Yes, those are qualities I want our children to have. They are the ones I most admire in the people I love the most. Gallant, Calla, Winnie, Elz —and Gothel, my new "sister." And of course, my father, The Huntsman.

Fairweather, Flossie, and Fanta bicker over who's handling each blessing. Gallant and I exchange a glance and suppress our laughter. Some things just never change. Finally, they work it out. Gallant takes my hand in his. As each fairy waves her magic wand over our beloved babies with her blessing—Fairweather, courage; Flossie, creativity; and Fanta, compassion—tears well up my eyes.

A gust of wind sweeps over me. Emperor Armando flies into our chamber, making a total fashion statement in an outlandish fairy godmother outfit I've never seen before. A pink tutu with matching wings! I suppose this was a perfect occasion for the Emperor to get some new clothes.

"Phew! I got here just in time to give the little dahlings my blessing," he says breathlessly.

Yes! A fourth blessing. "Do I get to pick it out?" I ask eagerly, already thinking of the endless possibilities.

"Sorry, dahling. There's only one blessing I give all my

fairy godchildren." Holding his magic wand over Bellie and Beau, he chants:

"Remember, clothes do not make the man;
I give you both the gift that can.
It'll help you go the extra mile;
I give you both a sense of style."

Style! I love it! Bellie and Beau will be individuals and bring their own special style to whatever they do in life. I love my fairy godmother! I really do!

It doesn't get better than this. I am surrounded by love—a wonderful husband, an adoring daughter, my best friends, and a gaggle of crazy fairy godmothers. The babies stir. And I am awed by these two tiny miracles. For the first time, I realize that life itself is a fairy tale.

EPILOGUE

Six Months Later

Dr. Grimm will soon have another fairy tale to bring into this world. Elz is pregnant again. She and Rump are still naming the child Bob—whether it's a boy or a girl.

King Midas and The Queen of Hearts decided to move from their castle and build a one-story compound because it was getting too difficult for them to navigate all the stairs. And besides, The Queen wanted more land for her new rescue animal sanctuary. Their former castle is now the new Midas Museum of Art. Gallant has been working on a new collection of paintings for a major retrospective in the future.

Gallant was able to restore the painting of Aurora—ironically, the only that survived Malevolence's rampage. It now hangs in the new Aurora's Secret store in Wonderland. We went to the opening night party. You wouldn't believe how many men were there! Aurora's hunch paid off. Best of all, Gallant's cut funds his career as a painter. And Aurora and I have become great friends.

Hook bought Gothel a new ring. No, not a nose ring. Rather, one for her fourth finger. They're engaged. Winnie is helping her plan her wedding. And Armando is designing her wedding gown—he's thinking white leather, studs, and a touch of lace. Oh yeah. I almost forgot. Gothel left My Fair Hair and opened up a Dragon Slaying Academy for Girls. Calla and Gretel go there regularly. Trust me, those girls can kick butt.

Calla loves her baby brother and sister. Now, she's begging for another pet. A baby dragon she saw at The Queen's animal rescue sanctuary. I don't think so. She's still wearing Hansel's bracelet.

Secret ended up being a good name for our dog. He had a big one—who would have thought that the little pup would grow overnight to the size of a small pony. He never leaves my side and watches over the babies.

The babies are doing great. You wouldn't believe how big they've gotten. We have regularly scheduled playdates with Princess Swan, but Cinderella never makes them because she's always late. By the way, I never did The Queen's princess pea test for Bellie. I decided that I didn't want to raise a princess. I just wanted to raise a little girl.

Talking about princesses, The Potato Sack Princess traded in her potato sack for a new uniform. And a new career. She's an around-the-clock security guard at the new Midas Museum of Art and happily gets to look at paintings 24-7. Her raven Amigo is perfectly content living there too.

The Badass Fairies wrote a book, *The Good Fairies' Yoga Guide for Pregnant Women*. Elz swears by it.

And Shrink decided to extend her vacation into an indefinite sabbatical. I'm handling it. Well, most of the time. For a baby present, she sent over that worn-out velvet chaise lounge in her office—yes, the one I've spilled my life on. Once a fixture in the Midas palace, it's where The Queen nursed Gallant. Shrink thought I might like to have it. As usual, she was right.

As for me, what a life I'm living, huh? It's frightening and beautiful and magical and absolutely inexplicable. I've learned that life has no outline. You've got to let the chapters unfold. And not skip ahead or jump to the conclusion. Sometimes, we will miss something that will change the whole ending and make your story make total sense. I did.

Not long after Bellie and Beau were born, I was

straightening Gallant's portrait of Calla and me that hangs in our dining room. Something from behind it fell to the floor. A folded up sheet of parchment. The love letter I wrote Gallant on the eve of his marriage to my mother. The one that was sealed with my tears and signed *"Forever~Jane."* He found it and read it! And saved it forever. If only I had found it in the first place! How different this story would have been!

The lesson learned… we need to battle the other dragons— the illusions we cling to, the false loves we perpetuate, the fantasies we dress up in pretty clothes, and the lies we tell ourselves. Only then will dreams come true.

Every night I look up at the sky and gaze at my father's star. I miss him terribly. Baby Beau is looking more and more like him every day. I also think about my mother a lot. It didn't take me long to figure out that Ellena, Gothel's birth mother, is Anelle spelled backwards. *A Nelle.* Like my mother's name. More than a coincidence, right? Gothel gave me the hope that my mother was born good person. We may even be sisters by blood. I still need a lot more proof. Unfortunately, between my family and my career and everything else in my crazy life, I haven't had the time to investigate my mother's past. That's just going to have to be another story.

Most importantly, I've learned that there's no such thing as a fairy-tale marriage. That's the stuff only books are made of. Actually, when I think about it, I've never read a fairy tale about a marriage. It's always a story about some unmarried princess who overcomes the impossible to get her prince. That "they lived happily ever after" ending is just a bunch of bull, if you ask me. Personally. I don't think the writers of fairy tales have any interest in reality—in the ups and downs of real-life marriage. Maybe they're just clueless. Or afraid of them. Or not talented enough to write about them.

Gallant and I celebrated our second anniversary. A miracle given all we've been through. When my beloved asked me what I wanted, I told him nothing. That I had everything in the world I needed. He surprised me with a bauble anyway.

One of Rump's bracelets with the names of our three children woven into the gold threads. It was the perfect present. I, in turn, gave him what I always intended to give him—my forever love letter, beautifully framed. We both shed tears and then made passionate love. To think I once imagined us *unhitched* is unthinkable.

We're working much harder at our relationship. Gallant is still seeing Dr. Grimm (the therapist) on a regular basis. It's paying off. My beloved is learning to balance his life and is spending so much more quality time with the children and me. Right now, he's working on a family portrait, so we get to be part of his life, and he gets to be part of ours. It's going to hang in our bedroom above our bed. Not in the museum.

Despite no Shrink, I'm doing well too. I'm loving motherhood more than I could have ever imagined. The twins are a handful, but I cherish every minute I spend with them. You should see how fast I can change a diaper.

Finally, after a long bout of writer's block, I'm writing a new children's book. I'm done with fairy tales, and to tell the truth, they're so overrated. Move over, Mother Goose. My new book, *Plain Jane's Big Book of Fun and Games,* is a collection of nursery rhymes. Gallant is doing the illustrations; they're exquisite. It starts off with a picture of a woman rocking her two babies and this verse:

> *Magic wands and wishing wells,*
> *Birthing stones and magic spells;*
> *Try them all, let yourself go wild,*
> *But only love can make a child.*

I'm not sure what will come next.

~THE END~

ACKNOWLEDGEMENTS

I am forever beholden to my family—my husband, Danny and my twin daughters, Lilly and Isabella—for putting up with me; they're beginning to accept the fact that I am permanently glued to my computer. I also want to thank my friend Dana for reading an early draft and giving me insightful comments and Kathie of Kat's Eye Editing whose amazing eyes found all the typos I didn't catch. A big place in my heart belongs to Glendon Haddix of Streetlight Graphics, who once again did the fabulous cover and interior formatting. I also want to give a special thanks to Greg and Rachelle of *Ereader News Today* for choosing *DEWITCHED: The Untold Story of the Evil Queen* to be "Book of the Day" and mentioning *UNHITCHED*. Finally, a big shout out to my readers. Without you, I would not be a writer. Thank you. Thank you.

Love~ els

ABOUT THE AUTHOR

Ellen Levy-Sarnoff, writing under the name E. L. Sarnoff, has enjoyed a prolific career in the entertainment industry, creating, writing, and producing television series, including the original *Power Rangers*. She lives in Los Angeles with her Prince Charming-ish husband, twin teenage princesses, and a bevy of pets. She's also a not-too-evil stepmother. When she's not writing in her PJ's, she likes to dress up and pretend she's Hollywood royalty.

She is also the author of *DEWITCHED: The Untold Story of the Evil Queen*, available both as an e-book and paperback at all major book retailers.

Ellen would love to hear from you. Connect to her at:

www.elsarnoff.com
www.facebook.com/ElSarnoff
www.facebook.com/Dewitched
www.twitter.com/elsarnoff
elsarnoff@gmail.com

PRAISE FOR DEWITCHED:
THE UNTOLD STORY OF THE EVIL QUEEN

*"The pages just flew by... funny... touching...
emotional... action-packed."*
—Storm Goddess Book Review

*"... a biting satire that puts a fresh, new spin on an
age-old villainess... hip, mature, and different."*
—John Ling, Amazon Reviewer and Author

"... one of the best books I've read all year."
—Samantha March, Chick Lit Plus Book Reviews

"Delicious and dishy."
—Shelley Miles, Amazon Reviewer

*"... real, magical, and beautiful. This novel
comes with one huge side effect—sleepless
nights. You wouldn't want to put it down."*
—Liz Grace Davis, Author

*"Nora Ephron meets the Brothers Grimm in this
whimsical twist of a classic fairy tale."*
—Barnes & Noble's Reviewer

*"...A fabulously told...cleverly written story that
gracefully probes ideas like Good, Evil, and Beauty.*
—Amazon Reviewer

COMING IN 2013

*Be*witched

Jane learns she should be careful for what she wishes when she finds herself magically transported to another Lalaland—present day Los Angeles. When she falls in love with Hollywood royalty, a dashing billionaire movie producer, she must confront her moral compass as she wonders—will she ever see her once-upon-a-time prince again?

15486510R10152

Made in the USA
Charleston, SC
06 November 2012